LADY IN BLACK

Christina Dodd

A KISMET® Romance

METEOR PUBLISHING CORPORATION
Bensalem, Pennsylvania

To Marilyn Black, Kate Duffy, Terri Register, Peggy Carpino and Dorothy Grow of Meteor Books, and especially to my editor, Catherine Carpenter.

Thank you for a delightful publishing experience. Congratulations on your many fabulous successes. Live long and prosper!

CHRISTINA DODD

Take a pinch of Texas fortune, a handful of real life adventure, and a large helping of happy endings, and you have Christina Dodd's recipe for a successful Kismet® romance. LADY IN BLACK won the Maggie award from Georgia Romance Writers, and Christina has also won a Golden Heart and a Rita Award from Romance Writers of America. She lives with her husband and her two daughters in Texas. (Is there any place else?)

CHRISTINA DODD

ONE

"Who the hell are you?" Reid Donovan shrugged his arms out of his suit coat.

"I'm the butler, sir."

Reid stared incredulously as the butler, acting with the pomp of a seasoned retainer, plucked the coat from his hands.

It was handed to a footman clad in simulated eighteenth-century splendor before the butler urged, "Your hat, sir?"

Reid caught the brim and sailed it across the wide entrance hall. It fell short of the painted parrot umbrella stand. "How long have you been employed here?"

"For eighteen months, sir."

"Has my grandfather cracked up at last? Or fallen into senility? It's the only explanation I can think of for hiring *you*. How old is he now?"

"Ninety-two, sir, but I believe your grandfather is in possession of all his faculties. You'll find him in the library, anxiously awaiting your arrival." Impassively the butler led the way, stopping only to pick up the hat. "This way, sir."

"I know the way to the library," Reid said between clenched teeth. "I grew up here."

"As you say, sir." The butler opened the library door and announced, "Your grandson, sir."

Reid strode into the book-lined room, around the desk piled high with papers and up to the withered man in the wheelchair. "Granddad, are you insane? Where did you collect that butler?" He leaned down and embraced the old man with obvious affection.

"Don't you like her?" Jim Donovan swung his gleaming chrome chair a quarter turn, and he and his grandson examined the still figure in the black silk suit. "She's a graduate of Ivor Spencer's London School for Butler Administrators. She's steady, reliable, quiet, anticipatory—"

"I'll bet." Reid Donovan swept her with the keen eye of a connoisseur.

"Will there be anything else, sirs?"

"Don't go yet, Margaret." Jim smiled at her wickedly. "A man my age has to have his pleasures, Reid. Look at her. She's a pleasure to the eye with those big blue eyes and icy white hair."

"Thank you, sir. Now may I . . . ?"

"What's her name?"

"Margaret Guarneri," Jim drawled, watching his grandson closely.

Reid stiffened. "A. M. Guarneri?"

Margaret stilled her desire to retreat. "Yes, sir. You've heard of me?"

"Yeah, but I hadn't connected the name with Granddad's new butler." Reid scrutinized her again, a different comprehension in his eyes. "This explains a lot. Been making changes again, Granddad?"

"Been snooping in my legal affairs again, Grandson?"

"I didn't have to snoop. Your own lawyer got worried enough to call me in."

"Did he now?"

The old man fairly purred, and Reid lifted his chin. "Yes. Don't worry, I fired him."

"Did you now?" The purr was louder.

"We can't have our legal help betraying our trust."
Confused by the satisfaction radiating from his grandfather, he said, "You'd have done the same thing."

"You don't even realize what I've done." Jim laughed.
"You're a stupid young fool."

"Young? Thanks, Granddad, but I'm thirty-eight; I've
been around."

"So you're only a stupid fool. Margaret, you may go."
Jim turned back to his grandson. "If it weren't for Margaret, I'd have no girlfriend at all."

Margaret quietly closed the library door behind her. She
didn't begrudge Jim his fun, but the misinformation he
had released to his grandson was bound to cause her trouble—more trouble than she had anticipated when she
swung wide the gigantic front doors to welcome Reid
James Donovan III.

She knew about him, of course. Had even seen him, in
the portraits his fond grandfather hung on the walls. And
on television, debating the government's effect on industry. She had prepared Jim to join him in Europe and in
Japan, had known a profound gratitude that Reid respected
his grandfather enough to ask his advice on business matters. But nothing had readied her to meet him.

He was gorgeous. He towered five inches above her—
no insignificant accomplishment. His hair was auburn, perhaps, or just brown with red highlights, and straight and
short. A longer style would have softened that jawline of
his, would have de-emphasized the cutting edge of his
cheekbones, but Margaret suspected he didn't want that.
This man had a reputation for ruthlessness. He had the
caustic wit and impatient energy of a barracuda. He was
rich and powerful and handsome—and he knew it.

But in a very human way, she had discounted much of
his mystique. Surely it was exaggerated? Surely she was
prepared? Surely to God when she first laid eyes on the
man and saw the whole package—the hair and the sherry
brown eyes and the vigor that motivated the body—surely

she should not have experienced, for the first time in three years, that restless stir of desire.

He was the kind of man who made her remember men had another use besides that of an annoyance factor. He was the kind of man who scared her half to death—not that she ever showed it. The lack of displayed emotion was only one of many reasons she had been attracted to the position of majordomo to the wealthy. The role of the phlegmatic butler suited her well, blessing her with a rigid set of rules covering every eventuality. Including this one, she supposed, but why did his eyes sharpen with determination at the mention of her name?

Reaching down, she turned off the persistent security beeper attached to her belt. The man guarding the front gate spewed his message, his voice lurching as the radio connection cut out. "Ms. Guarneri, Mr. Martin's coming up for the daily consultation."

Margaret raised the microphone to her mouth. "Thank you," she answered, and releasing the speak button, she added, "Goody." Opening the door, she stepped out onto the huge porch. Her legs immediately produced a film of sweat beneath her nylons, and the white silk shirt stuck to her sides beneath the waistband of her skirt. Her chignon weighed heavy on her neck. Her fingers itched to loosen the button under her black bow tie and release herself from her black vest.

Her only relief from the temperature was the sight of Cliff Martin riding up the curved drive on a bicycle. His paisley tie drooped across his chest, heavy with moisture; his white shirt had wet patches at the armpits. His suit coat hung over the handlebars, and his ample belly heaved as he panted. He glowed red with exertion, but Jim insisted the hired help not disturb his serenity, and so the head of their security firm rode a broken-down one-speed from his car to Donovan's Castle. Margaret's exterior remained impassive, never revealing her amusement.

"Mr. Martin, how good to see you," she intoned in a

stately tempo, and was delighted to see him roll his eyes with disgust.

"I suspect," he puffed, laying the bike over in the bower of crepe myrtles beside the front step, "that old man Donovan could give a damn about his quiet. It's just that the thought of us mere mortals peddling our rumps through this heat gives him his jollies."

Since Margaret suspected the same thing, she didn't acknowledge his comment.

Pulling a huge red bandanna out of his brown pin-striped coat, he mopped his dripping face and said what millions of people say every day of every summer in Houston, Texas: "It's not the heat, it's the humidity."

She puckered her mouth in insincere sympathy. "August is not the month for Yankees."

"I'm not a Yankee." He glared with ready ire. "I'm from Kentucky."

"Quite." To her inner amusement, Margaret found her British accent strengthened in reaction to his country twang. She opened the oak door and held it open, observing with bland interest as he grappled with the idea of a female holding the door for him. Did it make him less of a man, or an employee of superior position? She urged, "This way, Mr. Martin."

Shrugging, the hefty man shambled over and squeezed through the narrow, short entrance. "Is old man Donovan in a good mood?"

She stiffened. This oaf was trying to make her a comrade in his presumption. Shutting the door behind her with a precise click, she replied, "I'm not at liberty to say, sir," and walked to the house phone. "Mr. Donovan, Mr. Martin is here to report."

It was Reid, rather than Jim, who replied irritably, "Send him in, and bring in the food I ordered. It's way past dinnertime in London."

"Yes, sir." As she called the kitchen and spoke with Abigail, she watched Mr. Martin fan himself with his hands, then roll down his sleeves. He slipped into his coat and tightened his tie while she stared at his profile and wondered about the sharp look of intelligence on his usually bovine face.

He glanced at her, and his expression altered. "Guess I better get in there, hadn't I? Old man Donovan might yell at me." He grinned amiably as she turned away.

She hurried through the dining room and into the dim hall that led to the kitchen—and stopped. There in the shadows stood a man, posed with the stoic immobility of a statue. Pivoting on the ball of her foot, Margaret dropped into a fighting posture.

"That's not necessary." The statue spoke with the plain, flat tones of a computer. "I'm here with Mr. Reid Donovan."

"What are you doing back by the kitchen?" she asked suspiciously.

He moved with careful deliberation, switching on the lights and then staring her up and down as if she were the intruder. "I'm Reid's bodyguard," he said at last. "It's my job to come in the back door."

Relaxing, but still cautious, Margaret examined the square little piece of man before her. His shoulders were square, fitted with shoulder pads beneath his somber brown suit coat to seem squarer. His hands dangled at his sides, square palms and square fingertips absolutely motionless. Cut in a flat top, his black hair completed the square box of his jaw. He was so flat, front and back, and so unmoving, that Margaret half believed he had been popped in a toaster slot and shot out in his present form. The toaster that created him had been set on dark, for the man's skin matched his suit.

When she was done, the man slid his hand into the inside pocket of his jacket. He didn't seem to move quickly, but before she could react, a wallet rested open in his spatulate fingers and his identification appeared.

"Donovan Corporation," she said, nodding.

"Now," he said, in that flat monotone. "Who are you?"

"I'm the butler."

"Yes." He agreed as if she had answered a difficult question. "You are A. M. Guarneri."

Astounded, she asked, "Why does everyone know my name?"

"It's my job to know about the people in any household Reid enters."

"He knew my name, too, but he didn't know I was the butler." Her eyes narrowed with suspicion. "Or was he testing me?"

"Perhaps as A. M. Guarneri, you are of significance. As butler, you are not." The man bowed impassively and left, his square feet carrying him silently away.

Margaret stared after him. If she was of no importance to him as butler, why had her name attained celebrity status? And where, oh where, had Reid dredged up that bodyguard? Amazed, she continued to the kitchen. Dynamic Reid Donovan and that unemotional automaton. What an odd couple they must be.

The kitchen was a chrome and white room, the kitchen of the future—thirty years ago. The predictions of the designer hadn't come to pass, and now it was a charming anachronism, livened with blooming plants and a black cook dressed in pink and green and orange ruffles.

"Oh, Abigail." Margaret covered her mouth in mock horror. "Where did you get that outfit?"

"Can't all of us dress like a penguin," Abigail assured her, lifting pieces of chicken out of a box and arranging them on a Sevres china platter. The meaty aroma infiltrated Margaret's nostrils, and her stomach growled about its neglect. "I copied it from *M*A*S*H*. Klinger wore it."

"Oh, please." Margaret collapsed onto a bar stool and surveyed her friend from head to toe. "That turban and the feather earrings . . ."

"The perfect finishing touches, aren't they?" Abigail grinned at her, white teeth flashing in her dimpled face. Raising her arms, she whirled in a circle, showing off a trim figure.

"Perfect. I always think you can't top yourself, and then you prance in wearing another bizarre concoction." Puzzled, Margaret watched as she scooped red beans and rice out of an insulated container into a serving bowl and pulled biscuits out of a paper bag and placed them in a basket. "What *are* you doing?"

"Reid called down to me as soon as he got here and had me order him southern fried chicken from N'Awlens Chicken Ranch Take-out." Abigail glanced up at Margaret and laughed at the dumbfounded expression on her face. "Spicy variety."

She licked her fingers with flair, and Margaret sighed. "I didn't even know I was hungry until I smelled it. It's your night off, then."

"That's why I wore my newest creation to work. Whenever Reid comes into town, all I have to do the first night is pick up the phone and dial the Chicken Ranch—they deliver. Second and third night, too, until Mr. Jim complains."

"Mr. Donovan's so stuffy, I never thought he'd eat takeout chicken."

"Mr. Donovan? You don't mean—are you talking about Reid?" Abigail's mouth dropped open when Margaret nodded. "Stuffy? He hasn't got a stuffy bone in his body."

"Chauvinist, then."

"Chauvinist! Why, girl, that man doesn't care about sex or social station or age. Not as long as you do your job. You know what he did? Mr. Jim wanted to hire me, and Reid wanted to hire this Frenchman. Reid suggested a cook-off, with the guy cooking the first night, and me the second. After Reid tasted my shrimp étouffée, he called me to the dining room and went down on one knee and begged my pardon for doubting me and begged me to work for his grandfather." Abigail threw back her head and roared with laughter. "I was twenty-two and embarrassed, but he was so kind. Been here eight years now." She nodded at Margaret. "For the salary he pays, who am I to find fault if he wants chicken takeout on his first night home?''

"He seemed less pleased to see me," Margaret informed her. "Perhaps in eight years he's become a snob.''

"No," Abigail flatly denied. "Any man who comes down during a dinner party last year to dance me around the kitchen is not a snob. It must have been you.''

"Marvelous. He looked me over and decided in an instant—''

"Looked you over?''

"Yeah, like a man-to-woman overview? It's been a long time since any man dared.''

Abigail stepped back and looked her over, too. "Mm. Interesting. That man will dare anything.''

"Don't start on it, Abigail." Margaret stood up and straightened her lapels. "I'm not on the market.''

"Not every man's gonna die, you know.'' She centered the platter on the serving cart. "How long has it been?''

"Two years and seven months. The look Mr. Donovan gave me was not a polite summing up of attraction. It was a leer. After he heard my name, it was more like . . . shrewdness.'' Pulling a handful of silverware from the drawer, she lined them up next to the platter.

"Let me do it." Abigail snatched up the silver Margaret had arranged and laid them in a geometric design. "Maybe he's just perturbed about the threats to his granddaddy. That's enough to throw anyone out of sorts.''

"I'm a mite out of sorts about it myself." Margaret grinned with sudden wry amusement. "But dear old Mr. Jim did me no favors. You know what he said? He said, 'If it weren't for Margaret, I'd have no girlfriend at all.' ''

"Why, that cranky old fraud." She chuckled with warm mirth.

"Abigail, who was that man in the hall?''

"Who—oh, you mean Nagumbi?''

"That was the name on the ID,'' Margaret agreed. "Who is he?''

A smile played on Abigail's lips. "Mr. Reid's body-guard. Didn't he tell you?"

"Yes, of course he told me that. Has he been with him long?"

"For years and years." Abigail put her hands on her hips and eyed the cart as she explained, "See, when Mr. Reid was just out of high school, he wanted adventure, and Mr. Jim didn't see anything wrong with that. So he hired him a man who'd been around the world a bit to make sure no one interfered with Mr. Reid's adventures, and also make sure Mr. Reid didn't plan adventures so brainless, he'd never come home again. That's Nagumbi."

Margaret squinted at the beaming cook. "Is he always so vivacious and quick-witted?"

"He's a challenge, that one is." Abigail hummed a measure of "Some Enchanted Evening" as she arranged the plates on the cart.

"A challenge? He's too old to challenge you."

"That's what he says, too. But all that means is, he can't run fast enough to hide from me."

"You ought to be spanked."

"I've been telling him that, too."

Laughing, Margaret patted Abigail's shoulder. "I'll see if I can arrange a fake—"

The intercom roared with blunt impatience. "Where the hell's my chicken?"

Abigail flung a handful of linen napkins on the cart as Margaret grasped the handles and wheeled it past. "On its way, Reid," the cook called. "She had to fix the wheel on the cart."

"Who?"

"The butler did it," Abigail said with satisfaction, and winked at the groaning Margaret as she fled the room.

Slipping into her sober persona as she pushed the cart into the library, she heard Reid say sharply, "Where do the police stand on all this?"

"Kidnapping is a serious charge." Cliff sat on the edge of his seat, his hands clasped between his knees. He was looking earnestly at Reid and Jim on either side of him. "The police are concerned, of course, but they can't keep up the constant surveillance necessary for complete confidence in his safety." He stared as Margaret rolled the mahogany cart into the center of the male triangle.

Stepping back, she leaned over Jim Donovan's shoulder and murmured, "May I serve you, sir?"

"Yes," he said testily, leaning back and allowing her to snap his tray onto the handles of the chair. "If this spicy chicken doesn't burn my mouth off before I can swallow it."

Reid lifted his head from his avid contemplation of the dinner. "That'll be the day, Jalapeño Jim." He pronounced both *J*s with an *H* sound, causing Margaret to clear her throat of sudden threatening mirth. "Didn't Abigail order me any corn on the cob?" His gaze compelled her attention.

"I couldn't say, sir. Would you like me to call down?" Placing the silverware by Jim's left hand, she laid a plate filled with beans, biscuit, and a chicken wing on his tray, and prepared to do her duty.

"Aren't you the butler, Margaret?" Reid asked caustically. "Don't you plan the meals?"

"Normally, yes, sir. But—"

"No 'buts.' This is your responsibility."

"Don't be a blockhead, Reid," Jim interrupted. "Margaret's got nothing to do with this dinner, and you know it. You can have corn on the cob tomorrow night—with your damn spicy chicken."

The old man and his grandson went eyeball to eyeball, and neither seemed willing to back down until Cliff chuckled. In a fake Texas accent, he said, "These women! Always switching roles to suit themselves. Firstly, they want us to open the doors for them, and secondly, they covet our jobs. They just want to make life difficult for us men."

Reid and Jim broke apart and glared at the intruder in

unison. Jim said, "I imagine I'm not so old I can't keep track of male and female without a schedule."

Reid snarled, "Life's difficult enough without drawing battle lines between the sexes. I've got no patience for that."

Cliff, you jerk, Margaret thought as she stripped the skin from Jim's chicken wing. Outside you try to line up the employees against the employers; in here you try to line up the men against the women. Divide and conquer.

"What I want to know"—Reid poked around the chicken parts and captured a breast—"is how that second extortion note arrived on my grandfather's desk."

"Easy. The extortionists have an inside accomplice." Cliff fumbled with his inner suit pocket and drew out a short, battered cigar.

"I thought you were giving those up." With bright eyes, Jim watched as the man flicked his lighter and ignited the wide tip.

"I am." Cliff puffed until the fire crept up the well-wrapped stogie and fumes billowed from the sides of his mouth. "Sometimes the craving's just too strong."

"You must be nervous," Jim suggested. "You don't have to be nervous with us." He smirked as the annoyed security man chewed the end of his cigar and brown flecks of tobacco escaped onto his lips. "Margaret, get the file on my little problem."

"Little problem!" Reid exploded.

Jim grinned into Reid's irritated glare. "What's the matter, boy? I've been in worse situations."

"You've never been ninety-two before, though, and Granddad"—he shook a finger at Jim—"I'd like to see you make ninety-three."

"You weren't worried about me at eighty-two, and I was damn old then. Why, there are actually men who give up and die at eighty. But the women don't." He leaned back and winked at Margaret as she pulled the file marked KIDNAPPING from the cabinet. "That's why I stick around.

The women positively fawn on an old man like me." He corrected himself. "A rich old man like me."

"Yes, don't forget the rich part." Reid glanced meaningfully at Margaret.

"Admit it, it's the stroke that put me in this wheelchair that scares you."

"Oh, I'll admit it. You're all the family I have; you raised me and trained me, and no criminal is going to end your life."

"No, boy, no criminal's going to end my life."

"You say that like a vow, yet you're helpless in a way you've never been before. What are you going to do if someone grabs you? Roll over their feet?"

Handing Margaret his plate, Jim took the file in his unimpaired left hand and thumbed through it. "I found the first note on August twenty-first, but it could have arrived on my desk any time the week before—"

"That's precise," Reid observed.

"My desk is a hell of a mess."

"Any fingerprints?"

"Yeah, Margaret's. Margaret was helping me tidy up—she found the note."

"Margaret found it?" Reid subjected her to a long, cool stare as she picked up an ashtray, her eyes fixed on the cigar clasped between Cliff's fingers like a chubby, brown extension of his hand. "Has Martin Security investigated Margaret?"

"Born and raised in California, graduate of Berkeley School of English Literature." Cliff spoke of Margaret's life in a singsong monotone, and Reid turned to him attentively. "Married at age twenty-three to Dr. Luke Guarneri, moved to Houston, where she worked at a now defunct oil company. Dr. Guarneri worked for M. D. Anderson Cancer Research—"

Jim glanced up at the rigid face of the butler and slapped his table with the flat of his hand. "That's enough—get down to facts. Did you find anything suspicious?"

"No, only that she speaks with a British accent after

having lived in England for only one year.'' Cliff's petty triumph shone in his voice, and Margaret dove to catch the ash dangling off the end of the noxious cigar. ''Thanks, honey.''

''An English accent is part of the job description,'' Reid said dryly. ''If I need any information before tomorrow, I'm sure I'll be able to reach you?''

''Oh. Of course, anytime.'' Cliff remained seated, not realizing for one long moment he had been dismissed.

At the none too subtle hint, Margaret moved to the door and opened it. A painful flush lit Cliff's nose and ears and turned into a rash on his cheeks, and he abruptly stood and crushed his cigar in the ashtray. He nodded at Reid and then Jim. ''I'll keep checking on everything for you. In terms of reliability, my firm is fine for several reasons. Firstly, I keep close tabs on everyone who works for me.'' He stuck his hands into his pockets and rocked back on his heels. ''Yes, sirree, acts of a hostile nature like this one are my personal domain.''

''I appreciate that.'' Reid smiled politely.

''Secondly, at Martin Security every individual matter receives my personal attention. I'm a man who follows through on my responsibilities.''

Rising, Reid moved toward the door. ''That's a reassuring thought, Mr. Martin.''

Cliff followed with the ungainly lurch of a football linebacker. ''Thirdly''—he stepped into the hallway—''I handpick every man who works under me.''

Margaret prepared to follow him, but Reid laid a restraining hand on her shoulder. ''That's great, Mr. Martin.'' Leaning close to her ear, he hissed, ''Have the footman show him out. We need you here.''

''As you wish, sir.'' Relieved when he released her and returned to his seat, she signaled Simon and watched as he urged Cliff Martin under the crossed lances and out onto the porch. He returned to his post beside the knight's armor and gave her a thumbs up. She nodded to him and turned back to the two gentlemen waiting in judgment.

"Are you sure *he's* not our villain?" Reid asked testily.

Jim raised one eyebrow and stared at his grandson as if he were inspecting him. "You mean Martin? Naw, it's not Martin. He's too stupid."

"He is that," Reid muttered, then raised his voice. "But is he really? If he's smart enough to run a successful security firm—"

"Well, his daddy paid to set him up in business."

"So? My granddaddy set me up in business, and I've done all right."

Jim grinned. "Yeah, I never thought you'd do so well with those electronic gadgets, but you sure saved my ass when the oil market crashed."

"Thanks, but I doubt you would have been in a soup line regardless of your losses." Reid glared at his grandfather. "You're not going to distract me. I want to know about Cliff Martin. Who recommended him? What are his previous jobs? How—"

"Manuel recommended him," Jim interrupted.

"Uncle Manuel?" Reid visibly wavered, unwilling to abandon such a lead. "Are Manuel's contacts in the Houston Police as good as ever?"

"He'll be around; why don't you ask him?" Jim said.

"And force the old guy into a Hispanic hissy fit?" Reid asked. "No, no—if Uncle Manuel says Martin Security is fine, I'll believe him until I learn different. But I don't know how I'll put up with Cliff Martin. Is he always so wordy?"

"Martin?" Jim cackled. "Only when he's nervous—or you try to get him to leave. Aggravating, isn't it?"

"Ghastly. Nothing annoys me more. I'll avoid both his nerves and his leave-takings from now on. And his cigars. Where does he buy those suckers? Woolworth's?"

"Turn on the fan, Margaret," Jim ordered. "The stench does hang in the air, doesn't it?"

Margaret scanned their faces. Jim was amused. Everything amused Jim now. He had been a giant man, and a man among giants, moving the world according to his business acumen. He had enjoyed life, savored love, laughed at danger, but now all he could do was watch. It didn't bother him; he didn't mourn his lost freedom. He observed the comedy of existence with a rascally twinkle in his faded blue eyes, and she loved him for it.

"Come here."

The abrupt command shifted her attention to Reid—to those wine-dark eyes that glowed with virility—and from there she immediately shifted it to the set of elk antlers over his head. In her slow, stately stride, she walked toward the two men, but he barked, "Knock off the butler nonsense and sit right there." He pointed to the hot seat vacated by Cliff.

"Sir, it isn't proper—"

"If you're afraid he sweated in the chair, sit over here." He pointed to the chair set at right angles to his, separated only by an end table. "That's better, anyway. You can put your plate down if you need to."

Margaret stopped. "Plate?"

"Yeah, I could hear your stomach growling clear over here. Don't you schedule yourself dinner hours? Sit down and have some chicken."

"Sir, butler protocol prohibits eating with one's employer."

"Sit!" Reid's roar blasted her off her feet and into the designated easy chair. He surveyed her outraged form with satisfaction. "So that's how to handle you." She stiffened, but he paid no attention, picking up a dish and hovering over the platter. "White or dark?"

She thought frantically, wondering which would be easier to eat.

"A leg," he said. "Biscuit?"

It would make crumbs on her black skirt.

"I'll slather it with butter, too." He observed her chagrin and placed a big scoop of red beans and rice beside the leg. "There." He handed her the loaded plate.

"Spoon?" she asked weakly. "Fork?"

"You can't eat this stuff with a spoon and fork. It takes

one of these." He held up a combination plastic spoon/ fork, with rounded bowl and short tines. "It takes a spork."

"A foon," she corrected.

He held it out to her, but she indicated the spot by her elbow, and he laid it on the table. With a sensitivity she would never have suspected, he faced his grandfather and gave her the privacy she needed to eat.

"Let me see the note." He scanned the copy. "Who's got the original? The police? What kind of printing is this?"

"Dot matrix." Jim's eyes snapped. "*My* dot matrix. I haven't used the damned thing since I got my laser printer. I only keep it for emergencies."

"You only keep it because you never throw anything away," Reid corrected. He stared at his grandfather and then at Margaret. "What are you going to do about it?"

The kind old man whom Margaret knew disappeared, replaced by a cold, determined autocrat with iron in his soul. "I'm going to get the bastards. When have I ever let anyone take me like that?"

His grandson nodded. "Yeah, I figured. What happened after you received the first note?"

The autocrat faded. "First, I had to calm Margaret down. She was running around here squawking like an outraged chicken over a three-egg omelet."

Grinning a predator's appreciation, Reid leaned over and wiped a smear of oil from the side of her mouth with his napkin. "Whoops, that didn't do much good," he murmured. "My napkin's almost as greasy as the chicken. Here." He picked up a clean napkin and swiped it across his tongue, then scrubbed at her face.

She sat perfectly still, trying to remember what had been said in the London School of Butler Administrators that could apply to this occasion.

Her mind was blank.

"There." Reid examined the white linen. "No makeup.

Where did you get that gorgeous skin? You must be Scandinavian.''

"No, sir. American.'' She had the satisfaction of seeing his audacity take a check—but he recovered promptly.

"Except for the British accent.''

"As you said, sir, it's part of the job.''

"What do you think of our esteemed security man?''

He shot the question at her like a bullet, and she perceived his deadly flair for interrogation. Relax the victim and go for the throat. She put her plate down and wiped her hands, gathering her wits. "Martin Security was recommended to us by Mr. Manuel over six months ago, and my—and the police concurred. They've been operating in Houston over four years. Cliff Martin is the son of Frank Martin, owner of the largest chain of security firms in the world. When I found the first note—''

"What did it say?''

"I'll never forget,'' she sighed. She closed her eyes, and it popped into her mind, springing up on untorn, perforated computer paper.

To Whom it May Concern,

Good health for the elderly carries a big price tag, and it's easy for a man in a wheelchair to develop a flat tire.

All you have to do is slip once, and I'll have the old man and you'll have heartbreak. Wouldn't it be easier to pay for life insurance ahead of time? I'll give you a call when you're not busy.

I do know when you're busy and when you're not.

"He knows when you are sleeping,'' Reid sang. "He knows when you're awake. He knows if you've been bad or good . . .'' He gave the nonsense a sexy intonation, and she laughed, the white receding from her face. "What do *you* think of Cliff Martin?'' he queried.

Picking up her place once more, she answered, "He

seems to be very capable," and tore a big chunk of dark meat off with her teeth.

"When she hasn't got her mouth full," Jim advised Reid, "she says just because Cliff Martin smokes a smelly cigar doesn't mean he can't rely on his personality to drive people away."

Reid smiled at her—the sweetest, sexiest smile she'd ever seen outside of the movies—and she forgot to chew. Good Lord. She'd put him in a little slot under Barracuda, but perhaps she needed to change that.

A slot labeled Trickster, perhaps? Deceiver?

Enchanter?

She brought her teeth together in a hard collision. She was nothing more than a widow-woman looking for the hottest stud in pants.

He knew it, too. Look at that knowing grin, look at the way he watched her legs swing nervously and studied the hand twitching down the already lowered hem of her skirt.

But she could divert him, she could knock that smirk right off his face.

Taking a deep breath, she stared into his eyes and said, "I'm the one who found the second extortion note, too."

TWO

Margaret's arms flexed and extended, flexed and extended, the weights held steady in her hand. The early morning sunlight, tinted green by the dense foliage, crept through the windows of the daylight basement and dimly illuminated the shiny chrome exercise equipment. Pausing, she turned off the overhead fluorescent lights. Her arms ached with the repetition, and she shook the kinks out with the flick of her wrist. She had done her sit-ups on the inclined board, worked her neck and back, twisted from the waist, and struggled with her calves and big thigh muscles. Her shorts and T-shirt stuck in patches to her body, and wisps of straight hair stuck out from the braid at the back of her neck.

Unable to stall any longer, she moved to the stainless steel machine that was Hollywood's answer to the rack. Sitting on the padded bench, resting her spine against the back, she hooked her knees around the stainless steel rest and pushed in with all her might. A spring resisted her efforts, and when she reached the innermost point, the spring urged her thighs apart again. But she controlled it, compressed and released her muscles in a slow, steady rhythm until her breath caught in her throat and her teeth were clenched in agony.

"Why are you exercising in the dark?"

Margaret jumped and her knees snapped out. "Damn."

Reid strode out of the darkened stairwell. "Sorry," he apologized. "I thought you heard me."

"No, sir, I didn't." She sat with her legs lax for a moment, panting, and then began again.

"How could you?" He stepped in front of her and grinned. "That contraption destroys your senses—all you can hear is the pounding of blood in your ears."

Margaret reached for her proper butler demeanor and discovered it had oozed out her pores. "Demolishes the entire nervous system," she agreed.

"But it develops marvelous inner thighs."

His voice deepened and turned velvet, and she cast a quick glance at him. A mistake. He was still as gorgeous as he had been the night before—but now he didn't have on any clothes. He studied her legs as they opened and closed with the most rapacious—she turned her head away. Unable to resist, she glanced again. Shorts. He wore a pair of shorts. Sinfully brief, gloriously tight, toasty brown shorts. She would have sighed with relief, but all her breath was engaged.

His mouth twisted with amusement as she caught his gaze, and she wondered if he knew what she thought. That made her close her eyes, in physical and mental discomfort, and when she looked up again, he was gone. Rummaging in the supply closet, he hefted weights and grunted, "These should do it." He came back and stood right in front of her, and she cursed with unspoken conviction. Stretching his arms over her head, he bent his elbows until the weights touched his back, and straightened his elbows, and bent his elbows, and straightened his elbows . . .

Like a wave coming in to shore, the muscles in his chest and stomach rippled in unison as he lifted and strained. The thin arrow of auburn hair pointed along his breastbone and down his stomach, disappearing beneath the partition of his waistband. Her eyes ached with the exertion of watching, and Margaret found herself mesmerized, unable to break free.

"You never told me," his voice lulled her, "why you work in the dark."

"It's not dark." She nodded toward the brightening windows. "Besides, I hate fluorescent light."

"All the effort my granddad put into constructing the perfect gym, and you don't like the lighting?"

"Fluorescent lights remind me of a hospital." She snapped her mouth shut. Damn, how had he conned her into admitting that?

"We need to talk," he said, and she silently disagreed. "About the kidnapping threats."

Her exhale was less a pant than a gasp of relief. Paranoia dogged her; obviously he couldn't care less about her experience with hospitals. "What do you want to know?"

"You diverted me last night with your little admission—"

"Admission?"

"Discovering those notes," he reminded her impatiently. "By the time I stopped yelling, you had disappeared with my grandfather. A clever maneuver, and I salute you, but I still don't know the whole story. How did you find that note?"

"I was watching for it."

"Did they put it on his desk again?"

"No. They connected it to the front door in the classic method. With a knife."

"Dammit," he said reasonably. "Any fingerprints?"

"No."

"Where was the outside security?"

"Unconscious in the library—laid out on Mr. Jim's desk, for Lord's sake, bleeding from a head wound."

"*In* the library?" He lowered his arms and shifted into a tricep curl. "Whoever it was, was inside."

"Oh, yes. The guard is still in the hospital in satisfactory condition, and he swears he glimpsed a tall, fat woman in a plaid skirt."

"Plaid?"

"One of the kilts is missing." With a grin, she wiped her brow on her arm. "Mr. Jim had a fit because 'someone was mucking around with his collection.' "

"The contents of the note?"

"Were considerably more menacing. The note rambled, seemed bitter and personal."

"The same type as the first?"

"Printed on Mr. Jim's dot matrix." Margaret sat straight with outraged honesty. "I swear to you, that printer was guarded every moment."

"Couldn't it have been the same kind of dot matrix, but a different machine?"

"No. The police analyzed both notes. Some of the pins on Mr. Jim's printer stick, and it leaves a jagged text."

"Why isn't it clean?"

Margaret tucked the straggling bits of straight hair behind her ears and pushed her bangs off her forehead. "Because he's too cheap to let me call a serviceman."

"That's Granddad," Reid agreed. "So it's someone you left guarding the library—"

"Impossible. I stand by my people."

"—or the villain printed up several notes all at once. I read the police report, of course. The note seemed to be addressed to me this time, and it asked for one million—"

"Two," she corrected. He smiled sardonically, and she realized he'd been testing her.

"Two million. But the police reports don't mention a lot of things. Like why the hell haven't we changed security firms?"

"You heard your grandfather last night. Mr. Jim's dear old buddy in the Houston Police maintains Martin Security is above suspicion."

His arms bulged with a casual rhythm, deceptively effortless. "Isn't Uncle Manuel retired yet? He and my granddad used to get in trouble together. A lot of trouble together."

"Oh, he's retired, but he keeps a finger in the pie.

When he suggested Martin Security, Mr. Jim hired them sight unseen." Margaret wondered in torment how many times she had pressed her knees together. Her muscles quivered with strain. "Mr. Jim and Mr. Manuel gather in the library and chortle about the old times. They're two wicked old men." Remembering who she was and who she was talking to, she hastily tacked on, "Sir."

He ignored her courtesy. "Maybe, just maybe, Uncle Manuel's slipping."

"That occurred to me, too, so I checked it out. *My* contacts with the Houston Police Department insist Martin Security is the best."

"The police report seems vague, but there's a pattern. Have there been other kidnappings in Houston?"

"Like this? No kidnappings, just extortion. Whoever this is, he picks his victims well. Aged or disabled members of wealthy, doting families."

"So, how long have you been trying to seduce my grandfather?"

Distracted, she relaxed and her legs sprang apart. One of the abused muscles protested in a mighty spasm. "Oh, my God." She leaned, clutching her leg in anguish.

He dropped his weights onto the bench. "Let me." He loomed over her and pushed her hands aside. With long fingers, he captured her inner thigh and began to rock it back and forth. "That's quite a charley horse you have here. Can you bend your foot? Straighten your leg?"

She groaned with heartrending pain as she lifted her leg and bent her foot toward her calf.

"That's good." Dropping to his knees, he pressed his palm hard against the cramp, smoothing and massaging. She tried to wiggle away from the renewed agony. "I dreamed of having you writhing beneath my hands, but not like this."

Margaret glared right into his close, knowing eyes, and croaked, "I'm not seducing your grandfather. He's ninety-two! He's partially paralyzed."

"I know. But it got your attention."

Indignant beyond a reasonable point, she said, "How childish."

"Whatever it takes. I wanted to see how you'd react." He grinned when her mouth dropped open. "I learned quite a lot."

She wondered how he'd managed to live so long. "I'll just bet you did."

"But it still leaves the question—why did he change his will and leave you such a large bequest?"

Her spine melted onto the cushioned back. "Is that why you've been acting like a complete . . ." The serious set of his mouth stopped her. "It's not what you think."

"Are you not A. M. Guarneri? Did you not realize my grandfather left you a sizable sum in his will?"

"Not exactly." Now she knew why he'd prejudged her so harshly, and she wasn't sure she wanted to clarify the situation. She understood his concern, but she was irked to have been measured on the basis of her looks and her name.

"Not exactly A. M. Guarneri? Or not exactly a sizable sum?"

"Oh, I'm A. M. Guarneri, all right. While I'm appreciative of every penny, ten thousand dollars is hardly going to keep me in furs and caviar for the rest of my life."

He snorted. "Ten thousand. Very funny. I'm willing to listen to any logical explanation, so tell me—why did Granddad leave you such a large amount of money?"

"It's quite normal, sir, for an employer to leave a sum of money for the butler."

He stared at her. "Fine. Look me in the eye and tell me the facts."

Her gaze faltered.

Her mind worked furiously, trying to come up with an explanation that would pacify him without telling the whole truth, but time was a luxury he didn't grant her.

"I don't appreciate you sitting there trying to think up those little lies." His eyes sparked with frustration.

"You're obviously an amateur at the parasite game. Don't you know you're supposed to have your story ready ahead of time?"

"I'll remember," she snapped, too annoyed to ease his impatience.

"Normally I'd have approached you slowly, with a little tact, but all these lies about Granddad's money have freed me from that baloney. I want you, lady, and you gotta know I'm a better deal than my grandfather."

"My leg's fine." She tried to push his hands away from the inside of her leg, but his grip changed on the now slack muscle, changed to a sweep of callused fingertips.

"I've got just as much money, I'm a hell of a lot younger, and, darlin', I'll give you a ride you'll never forget."

Shivers slid down to her toes and up her spine to the roots of her hair. That light caress of his hand possessed more power than a bottle of Mr. Jim's best vintage. And that voice. Vibrant and appealing, saying words that shocked and excited her. She didn't know what to reply, so she took his wrist and pushed it away. His efficient fingers tangled with hers, and he stared at their entwined hands and then into her confused gaze.

"Or maybe you don't care about my money or my looks or how good I am in bed, because I haven't got one foot in the grave and the other on a banana peel?"

Without volition, her other hand flew to his face—and stopped an inch from his cheek. He hadn't moved, hadn't ducked, simply waited for the blow. It was frightening to see him measure her reaction to his words, her reaction to her own violence. Frozen with dismay, her palm trembled from the heat of his skin, too close to an irreparable mistake.

"Go ahead," he urged in a whisper. "I'll know what you're capable of. You'll find out what I'm capable of."

The tears filled her eyes as she held her palm so close to his chin. She dropped her head, then her hand. "I'm done with the machines." Her voice sounded husky, and she cleared her throat to continue. "I have to finish my routine." Still he watched her, kneeling against her calf, and she jiggled their clasped hands until they parted. "Please? Move?"

He inched back, giving her enough room to get up off the machine—but only just enough. With the wobbly legs of a colt, she sidled one step away, and then another. It was a test, an experiment doomed to failure; but an experiment she had to try.

He let her almost get out the door. "What do you do for the rest of your workout? Swim?"

"Um. Yeah."

He said the thing she feared. "I'll go with you."

"No, you can't," she said quickly. "I swim laps."

"You really should use the pool as a cool-down after working with weights," he advised.

"Aerobic exercise is just what I need." And she thought, You can't go, because I'll work too hard trying to show off. If you'd just go away, I could strip to my suit and take a leisurely swim. "You'll get in my way."

He raised one eloquent eyebrow. "It's an Olympic-sized pool."

They entered the house through the kitchen, and the air-conditioning felt like the blessing of a god. Margaret's face was crimson, she knew, and chlorinated water trickled into her eyes and down her back. Her plain racer's swimsuit heaved on her ribs, and her cover-up stuck in wet patches.

"I'd slow down on those laps if I were you, Margaret," Reid suggested. "Don't you know that swimming so hard after a workout isn't good for you?"

Panting, she glared at the odious man at her side. He wasn't wheezing; he wasn't broken by their half-hour traverse back and forth across the pool.

Why had she done such a foolish thing? She'd always been so scornful of otherwise intelligent women who became blithering idiots when faced with a man. Reid was just a man.

An attractive man.

Citing the already blazing Houston sun, he'd pulled on a plain white T-shirt before he leaped into the pool. What nonsense to stare at him while he stood on the checkered linoleum with the wet material etching every muscle and highlighting the suntanned skin beneath. He'd swum in his gym trunks, and they didn't cling like a second skin just because they were wet. She was relieved; she'd thought they would. And angry; she'd wanted to see.

He touched her shoulder. "Staring at my body won't answer the question. Don't you realize you could injure yourself exercising too much?"

When she thought what a fool she'd made of herself trying to keep up with him, her temper rose, drying her with a flush. She opened her mouth to blast him, to knock him off his high horse—

"What in heaven's name are you doing trying to race Mr. Reid in the water?" Abigail's voice burst into Margaret's daze.

Margaret swung on her. Dressed in a pink silk wrap, Abigail held a plate of toast in one hand and orange juice in the other, and she stared from one to the other with incredulous eyes.

"I saw you out there, churning up the water." Abigail nodded to the window with its view of the pool. "Are you mad?"

"What are you doing up at this hour?" Margaret badly wanted to distract her friend.

"I'm hungry. Why didn't you just swim like you always do?"

Desperate, Margaret protested, "You never eat so early."

"I do if I just got in, nosy." Abigail set the food on the counter and stepped over to pluck at Margaret's cover-up. "Girl, didn't you know Mr. Reid was a swimming champion in college?"

"No." Margaret stared stonily at Abigail. "I didn't."

"I bet this wretch didn't tell you." She crowed and dug her elbow into Reid's ribs.

Margaret snatched the hem out of Abigail's hand and wrung it out.

Abigail turned on Reid. "Are you the one that made her swim so hard this morning?"

"No." He stared right at Margaret. "I suggested that she take it easy."

If it was possible, her face turned redder.

Abigail said, "Hmm."

Margaret turned on her heel and fled.

Reid flipped his tie through its knot and studied the copy of the second note as it lay on his grandfather's desk. He paid special attention to the wording:

To Whom it Concerns Most Dreadfully,

Keep the knife. It's a little memento of my esteem. Old man Donovan isn't nearly as worried as he should be. Probably because he has no one who cares for him. Or does he? I know there's a man who treasures his grandfather very much and who should be more than willing to cough up just a little of his cash to ensure his safety. After all, it would be sad to see such a crippled gentleman become more crippled.

I know I can thank you in advance for the sum of two million dollars. Remember, if you wait until he's taken, the amount goes up. All you have to do to get the cash to me is say that you want to. I've got ears everywhere, and I'll tell you where to put it.

"I'll tell *you* where to put it, you simpleton," Reid muttered. This note reflected the extortionist's personality, unlike the first, more formal demand. It wasn't concise, as if the criminal had been in a hurry when he typed it. Jim Donovan wouldn't have missed this clue, Reid knew, and he bounded across the hall toward the suite of rooms at the back of the house.

He knocked at his grandfather's door and pushed it open. Stepping into the sitting room, he stopped short. From the bedroom, he heard the light laughter of a woman interspersed with Jim's gravelly voice, and he shook his head in disbelief. No, it wasn't possible. The woman whom he had just grilled in the gym, had just swum two miles with, the woman who had almost slapped him—she could not possibly be rolling around on Jim's bed.

Reid had questioned her, harassed her, embarrassed her, and she'd responded with such poise and sincerity, he'd believed every word. He'd been considering motivations—other than money—she could have for inveigling herself into Jim's affections. He'd wondered if she could possibly be as ingenuous as she appeared, and wondered more what he would do if she proved herself.

Ask for a date? Bring her flowers? Send her love letters? Hell, he'd been considering every one of those wistful courtship gestures. But now . . . His curiosity embarrassed him, but that didn't stop him from tiptoeing to the bedroom door and peeking around the corner.

"Dammit," he swore, disgusted with his own gullibility. "What the hell is going on here?"

Two faces, one wrinkled and overwhelmed with age, one firm and fresh and loving, turned toward him. Two different faces, one identical amazement.

"Oh, brother," Margaret said. She slid off the bed. Her feet were bare. Tossed across the bedside chair, her black suit coat and vest gave testimony to her shame. The two ends of her black bow tie hung from her collar, and her shirt was unbuttoned: only the top two buttons, but enough to condemn her in Reid's eyes.

Jim's surprise melted beneath the blistering stare of his grandson, and he cackled with outrageous joy. "You interrupted us, boy."

"So I see." He weighted each word with outraged significance.

"I was dressing him." Margaret held up Jim's pants as evidence, and then stuffed them behind her.

"Why?" Reid asked aggressively.

"Why?" she repeated. "So he can be dressed. So he'll be able to leave his room." She shrugged. "That's why."

"How altruistic of you." Striding forward, he braced his hand against the bedpost. His eyes swept his grandfather, clad only in a pair of boxer shorts. "And here I thought you wanted to cover your tracks."

She sucked in a gigantic breath of air and prepared to release it as dragon's fire, but Jim smacked the side of her arm. "Stop your jabbering and get back up here. It's already ten o'clock in the morning, and I'm not at my desk yet."

Swiveling on her heel, she stared at her employer until cold reason returned. "Of course, sir." She located the crumpled pants, climbed onto the foot of the mattress, and held one leg of the trousers up. He slipped his left leg in, and she grasped his right ankle—the ankle incapacitated by the stroke—and shoved it into the other leg. Grasping the waistband, she tugged it up over his knees.

Jim grunted with exertion as he tried to help her by raising his hips, but he only rolled to one side.

"I can get it, Jim," she soothed in a whisper, lifting his rear and scooting the pants up.

"I'm too big for you to handle." He chortled at his own joke, embarrassed to have his grandson observe the extent of his inabilities.

"Yeah, yeah." She settled the waistband. "I've handled you before."

"I can hear every word you're saying," Reid boomed from behind her, and she jumped and rolled her eyes.

"What can I tell you, boy?" Jim said in a normal voice. "I'm a man, she's woman. I'm divorced and she's a widow. I'm rich and she likes it."

"Your ass is grass and I'm the lawn mower," Margaret said in an identical tone of voice as she buttoned his waistband. "I have to zip you up, and I hold your life in my hands."

"You mean . . ." Jim mocked himself.

"Yes." She smiled with all her teeth. "If you don't shut up, I'm going to castrate you with the zipper."

He sighed. "I tremble. Why don't you threaten to remove something useful?"

"You could bleed to death," she assured him, "long before I call an ambulance."

"Is that how a proper English butler speaks to her employer?" Reid mocked. "Or have you progressed beyond the stage of offering respect?"

"*Simon* and I help Mr. Jim get dressed every morning." She glared at grandfather and grandson impartially. "Simon does the intimate stuff—"

"My underwear," Jim interrupted.

"And I do the rest."

"Why doesn't Simon do it all?" Reid interrogated.

Looking as innocent as a wolf picking wool from his teeth, Jim said, "Because he takes all the pleasure out of it."

"Because he's young, healthy, and efficient," she said through her teeth. "He's so efficient, Mr. Jim is exhausted by the time Simon finishes shoving him around. Clean up your dirty mind; there's nothing else to it."

Jim sighed with gusty chagrin. "Ah, darlin', if I were eighty again, you'd not be able to make that statement."

She laughed: she couldn't help it. "You're incorrigible."

Jim grinned and lapsed into silence.

She finished dressing him, aware that Reid scrutinized every move. "There," she said, sitting back on her heels. "You're done. You want to rest before I ring for Simon to get you in your chair?"

"Let my censorious grandson help me," he decided. "He ought to be good for more than glaring at us."

Reid stepped around to the bedside and asked, "What do you want me to do?"

Margaret examined Reid bitterly. Here she sat, in compromising circumstances, without the protective armor of her butler outfit, and he . . . he was perfectly clad from the shoulders of his designer suit to the tips of his Italian shoes. She wondered with aggravation whether he owned casual clothes. Clothes not worn to intimidate, but clothes just to slop around in. Was she destined to see him only in suits with the correctly knotted ties?

"Bring the wheelchair and set the brake," she told him.

Of course, he also pranced about half-naked in those brief and terrific gym shorts. Either way, he was formidable, and she acknowledged the disadvantage. Clothed, he portrayed a handsome, impressive tycoon. Unclothed, he was just a man. Just a handsome, impressive man who oozed sex appeal.

Hoisting Jim up by his shoulders, she steadied him as they maneuvered him into the chair. Reid took the full weight of his grandfather as he lowered him the last few inches.

"Whew, Granddad, it's a good thing you're not fat." He wiped imaginary drops of sweat from his brow.

Jim, who had done no more than be lifted, panted and groaned and shifted. "So they tell me." Groping, he extracted a handkerchief from his shirt pocket. "I hate this uselessness. Having to be carried like a . . . like an old man." He smiled weakly. "If I didn't have something to think about, I'd be insane."

"I'll get your pills," Margaret said, swinging into the bathroom. She returned with a glass of water and four pills in her outstretched hand.

Jim took the water and one capsule, and shook it admonishingly at his grandson. "Don't get old."

"What's the alternative, Granddad?"

"Bound to a chair, bound to a schedule of medication—"

Margaret grasped the handles of the chair and pushed him toward the hall and away from Reid. "Feeling sorry for yourself?"

"Being realistic. You know what happens if I don't take these pills? You know what happens?"

"What happens?" She humored him.

With outstretched finger, he pantomimed a knife slicing his throat. "I'm going to die soon anyway; might as well improve the world while I'm here."

"Finish your pills, or you won't have the chance to improve the world," she ordered affectionately, wheeling him into the library. "Now, do you need anything else?"

"A great-grandchild. Think you can handle that?"

Margaret laughed with unthinking glee, and then glanced toward his bedroom, where her latest encounter with his grandson had taken place. She blushed from the tips of her toes, up. "Lord, no," she choked. "Not if that's my choice for the father."

The old man reared back, offended. "I don't see what your problem is. Reid is handsome, virile, rich—"

"I know." She squatted beside the wheelchair and stared with meaning at Jim. "I already heard that once this morning—from him. This list of his finer qualities never seems to mention humility or modesty."

Relaxing, he waved a dismissing hand and snorted, "Pff! A modest man would have no effect on you. Admit it, you've noticed him, haven't you?"

"Like a snake notices a mongoose." She rose and buttoned her shirt tight against her collar. "Did you remember I've got a luncheon date today?"

Jim nodded. "I remember, I remember. I'm not senile yet. Just you remember I don't want another man horning in on my territory."

"Oh, the date's not with a man." She smiled at him affectionately. "It's with *two* men."

"Modern women." He sighed. "Don't even know how to make a proper assignation. Why don't you take Reid so he can size up the competition?"

"No," she said precisely.

He didn't seem surprised. "How many more days until you make me a happy man?"

She chuckled. "Three more days."

"What time?" he asked.

"Ohh"—she tapped her lips with her finger—"late afternoon, if everything goes well."

"I can't wait."

"Me, either." They exchanged conspiratorial grins, then she asked, "Can I get you anything before I straighten your bedroom?"

"Nah." He rolled himself to his desk. "I can keep myself out of trouble right here."

"That'll be the day," Margaret muttered as she slipped out the door.

Stopping at the hall mirror, she tied her bow tie before entering Jim's suite of rooms. As she feared, Reid waited for her, one hip perched on the mattress. Stern, humorless, he exuded dignified concern for his grandfather.

"I want to know what's been going on here."

Margaret slid her feet into her correct black shoes and considered how to reply. She buttoned her vest and pushed her arms into the black coat. Unable to ignore the training of a lifetime, Reid caught the collar and helped her.

"Thank you," she murmured. Reaching into the bed, she fished out the old man's pajamas and straightened the sheets.

"Are you trying to impress me with your efficiency?" he drawled. "The maids make the beds in this house."

"Not this bed, sir." Cool competence, she decided. "I make this bed. Your grandfather is uncomfortable with his occasional loss of control over his bodily functions."

"Ah." He thought about that and watched her tuck the blanket in tight. "I hired a nurse."

"He doesn't need a nurse—and he hated her. Not long after I obtained this position, she quit." She stared him right in the eye in cool challenge.

"You take a lot on yourself," he snapped, irate with guilt and dismay.

"I'm the butler, sir. A trained butler hires and directs the staff, lays out the master's clothes, selects the wines, takes care of the dogs, packs for trips, approves the menu, pays the bills, does the marketing. In return, a trained butler gets a good salary, a two-bedroom apartment in the main house, a personal computer, and insurance benefits." She paused delicately. "Mr. Jim has been, er, subtly inquiring about my preference in cars. For Christmas, I assume."

Reid nodded. "That sounds like him."

"Now, Mr. Jim doesn't have dogs, he doesn't take many trips, he doesn't eat much, can't drink wine, and his staff is so devoted to him, supervision is minimal. An accounting firm takes care of the bills. But my job is still to keep the master happy, and if caring for Mr. Jim with my own hands is what it takes, I'll do it." She turned away as if that settled the subject, and finished the bed. He no longer seemed hostile, she decided; reflective and calm, as if he weighed her words and intentions against her actions and awaited the results of his computations.

"What if he gets seriously ill?"

"I'm approved by the Red Cross in first aid and CPR, and at the first sign of trouble, I'll call an ambulance. I can dial a telephone as efficiently as a nurse."

"What makes you so much more desirable than . . . What was her name?"

"Mrs. Adams." She wondered if his choice of words was deliberate, and concluded it was.

"That's it. What makes you a more desirable companion?"

"Mr. Donovan." Crossing her arms across her chest, Margaret looked stern. "Your grandfather is ninety-two years old, but he is a sharp old devil: sharper than most men of thirty-eight."

His barracuda's grin told her he'd comprehended the jibe.

"He's moved mountains in his time, been a potentate of the business world—and he resents being told, 'It's time to take our bath, now.' "

Her imitation of the nurse was deadly, complete with a singsong voice that rose an octave. Reid winced.

"And 'We must go to bed for our nap, now.' Mr. Jim can be led and cajoled, but he cannot be forced. Mrs. Adams almost brought on another stroke with her heavy-handed administration."

"So you fired her."

"Certainly not." She placed her hand on her chest and drew back with sarcastic insult. "When the grandson of the master hires an attendant, the butler hasn't the power to fire her."

"You made it so uncomfortable, she didn't want to stay."

In Margaret's heart, the first stirrings of apprehension changed the tenor of her breathing. Reid seemed so nonchalant, one hand in his pocket, the other grasping the bedpost, and he examined the carpet beneath his shoe intently. His pose reminded her of a movie she had seen when she was young and impressionable; a movie that still haunted her nightmares. In the scene that terrified her, the villain stood with his head bowed before the cocky heroine until that moment when he raised his eyes—and they glowed red.

But when Reid raised his eyes, they were not dyed with hell's fires. They were cold as the moon afloat in the bleak night sky. He said, "Think about it. If the butler can make life so distasteful a nurse flees, how can the grandson of the master influence the butler's decision to seek a new position?"

Chilled to the bone, she rubbed her hands up and down her arms. "Are you threatening me?"

"I don't make threats. If I choose to make *you* uncomfortable, you'll go."

A spurt of anger warmed her temporarily. "Mr. Jim—"

"Would you involve my grandfather in our quarrel?"

"I . . . no." Her anger faded. "No, if we can't work together, I'll not involve Mr. Jim. But if you force me to leave, it will hurt him."

His smile was a mere curl of his mouth. "Why do you think I'm going to let you remain?"

THREE

"You're right, Jim, the boy *is* looking a little poorly." Manuel puffed on his pipe and stared at Reid from mellow brown eyes. "Do you suppose it's our weather?"

"Nah." Jim jerked a sheet of continuous-feed computer paper out of the box and crumpled it up. "He was born here. He's tough."

"Spent too much time away from Houston. Look closely at him. His neck's hardly red at all." Manuel blew a stream of smoke toward the library desk, where Reid worked on a plethora of paperwork that dogged him.

"It's not the weather." Jim lobbed the paper ball toward the trash can and missed, and pulled another paper out of the box.

"Maybe he hasn't kept up with his southern fried chicken."

"Believe me, he has," Jim said with heartfelt sincerity.

Manuel puffed until the smoke circled his chin like a Santa Claus beard. "Only one other thing could make a big, strong man like Reid look so feeble, but I don't rightly believe it."

"Believe it."

"You can't tell me it's women."

"I can, too."

"Women have Reid on the run?"

"Woman," Jim corrected. "One woman. You know what he's doing now?"

Reid raised his head at last. "Perhaps my green expression results from that tobacco you insist on smoking." He adjusted a miniature desk fan around so it blew toward Manuel.

The old men ignored him as if he were an insignificant gnat.

"What's he doing now?" Manuel asked in deep fascination.

Reid leaned down and scooped paper projectiles into the trash. "Or maybe it's the mess around my desk that's destroying my serenity."

Jim tossed another ball toward the can. "He has dressed me every morning for the past three days."

"Oh, my." Manuel's eyes sharpened as he examined his godson. "Well, the family that dresses together—"

"Confesses together." Reid glared at his grandfather.

"The boy doesn't do nearly the job Simon and Margaret did. They were a hell of a lot more fun. *She* was a hell of a lot more fun."

"I can imagine." Manuel nodded sagely. "What else is he doing?"

"Brooding."

"Brooding?" Manuel's eyebrows shot up, almost onto his shiny pate. "You mean like sighing and languishing?"

"Nah. Women sigh and languish. Men ponder and endure."

"Fascinating case study. What's Miz Margaret up to these days?"

"Sighing and—"

Irritated, Reid interrupted. "Since when is the butler called 'Miz'? All the butlers I've ever met are called by their last names."

"Ha!" Manuel snorted, replying to Reid at last. "You wanna call the butler 'Guarneri'? It sounds like what you say when somebody sneezes."

"Ah-choo!" Jim said.

"Guarneri," Manuel replied.

Reid stood and stretched. "If you want to spend you time babbling about the sexy blond sweetheart who just happens to be our butler—"

Jim smirked. "She's a widow, a respectable one, and she'd make you a fine wife."

"Wife?"

"You two would make beautiful babies for me to hold. I'm not getting any younger; you need to get with it pretty soon. Come to think of it"—Jim stroked his chin—"*you're* not getting any younger, either."

"What is this, some little plan you and she cooked up to trap me?" The thought of the butler plotting his downfall made him furious, and his hands curled with disgust.

"No, no, Margaret hates the idea. I suggested it after she'd had a chance to look you over, and she just laughed and refused."

"She laughed?" For some reason, that thought made him angrier, and he paced toward the window and stared into the garden, rife with afternoon shadows.

"I believe she compared you to a snake," Jim offered.

"That little—" Reid observed the gleeful smile on his grandfather's face and sighed with exaggerated patience. "All right, you old codgers. You win. I needed a break, anyway. I'm going to the kitchen to con a snack out of Abigail. *She* still likes me."

"The boy got an inferiority complex?" Manuel wondered. "Nobody likes him?"

"Oh, I like him." Jim gave up his basketball game and started shredding the perforations down the sides of the paper. "And you like him."

Manuel nodded.

"But now, Margaret . . . I don't know if Margaret likes him."

Reid strode to the door, but he didn't bolt fast enough.

"No, sirree," Jim drawled. "Like isn't nearly strong enough a word for what Margaret feels for him, or he for her. Why, when they're in the room together, the attraction gathers so thick, I get aroused purely from the emanations.''

Manuel choked on a puff of cigar, and Reid halted in the hall, waiting to see if the old man recovered. In a rasping voice, Manuel gasped, ''I better stick around, then. I can use all the help I can get.''

''Woo-ee,'' Abigail whistled. ''Don't you look nice!''

Margaret whirled in a circle, her ice green jacket hooked over her shoulder by one finger, a la Frank Sinatra. Her matching skirt clung close to her thighs, and her kelly green shirt accented the suit with a touch of wild color. ''Will I do?''

''You sure will. You think those shoes are high enough?''

Margaret stuck out one three-inch heel and examined it. ''I'm only five ten. I have to take care, or I'll be overlooked.''

''I'll remember that.'' The diminutive cook grinned.

Margaret moved to Abigail's side and rubbed up and down against her arm, like a cat scratching its back. ''What do you think of this?''

''Silk?''

''All the way.''

''Well, that shade sure looks pretty with that white hair of yours loose all over your shoulders. You want to borrow my nail polish?'' She lifted one hand out of a ceramic bowl. Drops of some ominous clear liquid dribbled off the frosted green fingernails and onto the eating bar.

''Where did you get that ghastly color?''

''Neiman-Marcus.''

''It's putrid.''

''Does that mean you don't want to borrow it?'' Abigail dipped her nails back into the bowl.

''What's in there?'' Margaret peered into the depths. ''Ice cubes?''

"Sure. If you really want to set your polish, you dip your nails in cold water."

Snapping her fingers, Margaret said, "I remember. I did that once, and all I got was ripple marks on the polish."

"You have a lot of class, Guarneri," Abigail snorted. Drying her hands on a towel, she leaned back in her bar stool and grinned. "So today's the big day. Excited?"

"Excited? Me?" Margaret assumed a debutante slouch, then threw her arms in the air and whooped. Pulling Abigail up, she whirled around the floor with her, humming the "Tennessee Waltz."

Abigail laughed until her breath caught, complaining, "Why don't I ever get to lead?"

A rough male voice invited, "You can, if you dance with me."

The ladies spun around.

Reid stood propped against the doorjamb, an insolent grin on his face and a smoldering passion in his eyes as he examined Margaret's outfit. He noticed it was silk, he noticed the green flattered her coloring: More than that, he noticed the split up the back of the tight skirt and the above-the-knee cut that looked so devastating with her long, slender legs. He noticed—and resented—the catch in his breath at the sight of her Slavic cheekbones and blue, blue eyes.

He resented the touch of caution underlying her swiftly smothered desire.

"Very pretty," he sneered. "Going somewhere?"

She slipped into her jacket, looking down at her hands as she buttoned each button.

It hid the thrust of her breasts against the fine silk of the blouse, and he resented that, too. "Well?"

"I have to go out for a few hours," she said softly. "Sir."

She didn't want to tell him where, he noted. She had the nerve to believe it was none of his business. "It's not possible. I need you in the study."

"I cleared it with Mr. Donovan weeks ago."

"Will you be back in time to direct the serving of the evening meal?"

"No, but the staff is well trained."

"This must be very important."

"Yes."

He paused, giving her a chance to expand, but the lady had formed ice over her features. He directed the blowtorch of his personality toward her. "Did you forget that little matter we discussed last week?"

Margaret's eyes frosted until they were cold blue. "About the nurse?"

"Exactly," he purred.

"Oh, I remember." She sauntered over to the shoulder bag flung on the floor. "It's simply of no concern to me."

The blowtorch heated to a mild red. "No concern? Is unemployment of concern to you?"

"As a social issue, yes. Regarding myself, I don't foresee unemployment in my future. May I go now, sir?" She turned on her heel and walked away from him, heading for the back door of the kitchen.

With a bound, Reid stood beside her, jerking her around to face him. "Don't turn your back on me," he ordered.

"Let go of my arm."

With slow deliberation, he grasped her other elbow and turned her to face him. "If you leave now, don't come back."

"Mr. Donovan hired me," she hissed. "Mr. Donovan will fire me."

"Yes." He released her. "He will."

They stared at each other intensely, one cold as the Arctic seas, one hot as the volcanoes beneath them. In simultaneous motion, they nodded curtly and strode in different directions: Margaret to the car that would drive her to the airport, Reid to the library.

Abigail stood in the middle of the kitchen floor where they left her, rubbing her arms and smiling. To the assembled pots hanging above the stove, she said, "This woman gets in a room with those two, and it fairly warms my female parts. I wonder what that big hunk of a bodyguard is doing tonight?"

"Did you bring her?" Jim called. "Did you bring my girlfriend home?"

An ebullient child of nine years danced through the doors of the library. "I'm here, Sir Gramps." She headed right for Jim's open arms. "I missed you."

Standing against the fireplace, Reid stared at the swarthy girl wrapped around his grandfather. Her short black hair curled with wild abandon, her black eyes snapped with vitality. She hopped on one foot as she squeezed him, too excited to stand still.

His grandfather trembled from pleasure, and his faded eyes teared as he held her. Then he pushed her away. "Go on and kiss your Uncle Manuel before he busts a gut."

"That's right, what am I, chopped liver?" Manuel braced himself for her titanic hug while Jim dabbed his eyes.

"Chopped enchiladas," the girl said, and they laughed, comfortable with the banter.

"Stand up now," Jim instructed. "Let me introduce you."

The child straightened, clasped her hands in front of her, and observed Reid with composure. Taken aback by the forthright stare of such an animated lass, Reid held out his hand.

"Reid, this is Amy Guarneri. Amy, my grandson, Reid Donovan."

Amy grasped the offered palm and shook it firmly. "How do you do, Mr. Donovan?"

From Amy, it was more than a polite phrase. It was a sincere inquiry of concern backed by a solid guaranty of curiosity.

"Later, Amy." Margaret's gentle voice broke the child's intense concentration. "You can cross-examine Mr. Donovan later."

For the first time, Reid's gaze was drawn to Margaret as she stood framed by the doorway. The three hours since she stormed out of the kitchen had changed her. No longer the proper butler or the hostile woman, she seemed strangely softened. The ice green jacket had vanished, the tie on her blouse dangled. Her skirt was shifted a quarter turn so a side seam ran right down the front, and the slit opened at the side. She held her shoes in her hand and smoothed the loose hair off her forehead.

She was, for the first time since he met her, totally unselfconscious in his presence.

Reid's brain began to perk with intuition. "Amy Guarneri," he mused aloud. "Amy *Margaret* Guarneri?"

"Not Margaret," Amy corrected. "Margot. My mother's name is Amelia Margaret—see? They sound alike, but we each have our very own name."

"Doesn't anyone ever get mixed up?"

"Oh, no. Only a dummy would mix those two names up," she assured him.

He nodded slowly in agreement. "Only a dummy." He looked up at Margaret, but she wasn't smirking—which spoke volumes for her control. If anything, her eyes held the sympathy of a fellow diner on hasty words.

Their gaze lingered until Jim chuckled and said, "You look done in, Margaret. Was the plane late?"

"I wouldn't look done in if it had been late," Margaret said wryly. She nodded at Amy. "It's chasing after *that* monkey that did it."

"Mah-om!" Amy clarified their relationship—the relationship Reid could hardly comprehend. "I'm not a monkey."

"No, but you certainly have more energy than I've ever had." Margaret limped into the library and sank into an easy chair on one side of the fireplace. Dropping her heels on the floor, she declared, "I should have worn running shoes."

"Ah, Mom!" Amy launched herself into her mother's lap. "Aren't you glad I'm back?"

In an excess of silliness, Margaret leaned her back and smooched her neck. "Yes, I'm glad you're back," she said, grinning at her squealing daughter. "Yes, I missed you. Yes, I can hardly wait for you to go back to school."

Amy made a face and kissed her, hugged her, and hopped up.

The two buttons at Margaret's bosom dangled loose, and a run started down her nylons.

"What did you do in California?" Jim asked.

"Heather and I—"

"Heather's her cousin, eight years old," Margaret informed them.

"Yeah, my cousin. She's my"—Amy screwed up her face in concentration—"my father's sister's daughter. She and I played a lot. The best thing we did was play a trick on Grandpa." She giggled, dancing a little jig as she spoke. "You know that green shaving gel? You know how really slick it is? We put some on the doorknob of the shed, and Grandpa grabbed it and thought it was—"

"Oh, Amy," Margaret said with horror.

"But that's not the good part." Amy charged on. "The good part came the next day when we flipped Grandpa for the last two Twinkies. You know what he did? You know what he *did*?"

"Tell us what he did," Jim invited, his wrinkled mouth twitching at the corners.

"He had a two-headed coin so he knew we'd win, and when we bit into the Twinkies they were filled with shaving cream."

The adults burst into laughter at the grimace of remembrance on her face.

"Mine was aloe vera." The grimace twisted tighter. "Heather's was *Old Spice*."

The adults laughed harder, and Amy began to giggle again. "Isn't that funny?"

Reid leaned over Margaret's shoulder. "How does she giggle and talk at the same time?"

She turned her festive, shiny face to his. "It's a preadolescent trait," she assured him. "She's priming herself for puberty."

"How do you keep up with her?" he asked.

"I don't. Look at her." Margaret stared at her daughter with a mushy smile. "If she were a puppy, her tail would be wagging."

Reid stepped back and considered the butler.

Things had changed now. Margaret had changed, he had changed, the situation had changed. His suspicion of her part in the kidnapping scheme was largely unfounded. Her relationship to his grandfather was obviously a myth, developed by Jim Donovan for the pleasure of watching his grandson jump to conclusions. The mixture of skepticism and anger had added to his desire, and no qualm had undermined his plan to ravish this villainess.

If the relationship between the butler and the master's grandson was to ripen to something more, he would have to think, and think hard, about the ramifications of consorting with a working widow with a child. A working widow with a child and his matchmaking grandfather's goodwill.

A working widow with a child who could very easily command his heart with her combination of fire and ice, duty and spirit.

Was he willing to take the chance of being trapped? Or was the shoe on the other foot? Would he have to trap her?

He wasn't a fool; there might be an attraction humming between the two of them, but Margaret wouldn't have him on a silver platter. He'd have to work and scheme and cajole to get her. A smile lifted one side of his mouth, but it disappeared at his next thought.

He'd have to put his whole life into keeping her.

"Excuse me." Reid straightened from his slouch beside her chair. "I have work to do."

He smiled on them impartially and strode out the door, leaving three adults and one child staring after him, and a huge pile of papers on the desk.

"In the dark again?"

Reid's voice should have surprised her, but it didn't. He lingered in her mind like a bubbling yeast, sometimes overpowering and sometimes barely noticed: but always there.

Margaret kicked and recovered, kicked and recovered. The loose-fitting white pants and wrap shirt of the martial arts, the *gi*, were damp from her efforts. Her hair was once again plaited into a single braid. "Is there hidden meaning in that comment?"

"Not at all." Reid stepped into her peripheral vision, off to the side of the mat where she practiced her repetitious exercises. "But August has turned to September, the sun rises at a later hour, and it's almost dark here in the gym."

"I don't need the lights for this kind of workout," she puffed, her bare feet lashing in the cutting kick.

He stepped in front of her, an indistinct shadow of male essence silhouetted against the dim windows. "I came to apologize."

Margaret planted both feet firmly on the mat. "Sir?"

"For my assumptions."

"I wish you wouldn't."

"Why?"

"Because it's easier to dislike you when you're an unjust boor," she said frankly.

He chuckled, a low chuckle of amusement and relief. "All the more reason to apologize. I don't want you to dislike me. That's too paltry an emotion for us."

"Paltry emotions are fine. They're safe and clean and uncomplicated."

"Ah," he said. Pacing away from her and then back, he offered, "My apologies, nevertheless. For making assumptions about you, and for ignoring your protestations—weak though they were. I had no reason to believe my grandfather's bequest was anything but his own doing.''

"He loves Amy, and she loves him. He fills a void in her life, that need she has for an ever-present male." She shrugged with sheepish embarrassment. "So he wanted to leave her something. I told him no, and he said half a million, and I said no, and he said one hundred thousand, and I said no, and he said ten thousand, and I said fine. I really should have told you who the bequest was for as soon as you accused me, but I thought you'd be suspicious until you met Amy."

"Amy *does* vanquish suspicion. You held him to ten thousand, huh? Ten thousand?" She nodded, and he laughed and shook his head. "So that's what he told you. Ten thousand. That old coot. Hardly enough money to have him kidnapped for." Holding up his hand, he stopped her comment. "I don't normally blunder into situations without formulating the facts in a logical manner. The only excuse I need to present you is the obvious one: that I was worried about my grandfather. But there is more to it than that. I wanted you."

Margaret sank into an unrehearsed knee bend.

"I wanted you, and a cold-blooded seduction seemed less despicable if you were a wanton bitch pushing Grand-dad toward a stroke."

She straightened up hopefully, "Does this mean the seduction is out?"

He chuckled again, another low, warm chuckle. "No, it means the 'cold-blooded' is out."

Resigned to weakened joints, she began a series of knee bends.

"I'm not proud of persecuting a woman for no more good reason than unfounded suspicion and well-founded desire. Excuses are unacceptable, in my employees and certainly in myself. You can calculate your effect on me by the lies I was willing to tell myself." The brightening morning ignited behind him, and she could discern the shape of his body clad in slacks and a shirt. "Do you accept my apologies?"

His cool gambler's features were hidden in the shadow, and she couldn't help presuming a deliberate maneuver on his part. He frightened her more now than he ever had. Any man who could examine his own motivations with such cool clarity required careful handling.

"I have to apologize, too, sir." She paused in her workout. "I lost my temper yesterday in the kitchen—something I haven't done in years. I deliberately provoked you."

"Why do you suppose you did that?" His voice echoed smooth and comforting, like a psychiatrist guiding a patient.

"I don't know," she said sharply, her trepidation gone in a blast of temper. "You're the brains here, you tell me."

But he didn't. "Are those karate exercises?" he inquired, his tone indicating only a slight interest.

She wasn't fooled. "A little judo, a little aikido, a little karate. My martial arts master teaches me whatever he thinks I can handle."

"What do you do it for?"

"Sir, I'm a butler for a very wealthy man. It behooves me to be able to protect your grandfather—and myself—should the situation arise. For chauffeurs and body servants of every type, there are special schools that teach methods of defending the master against trouble."

"Wouldn't it be easier just to run and leave the 'master,' as you call him, in trouble?" he asked.

She didn't blame him for his cynicism, but she'd learned the lessons at that special school very well, and responded, "To most kidnappers and extortionists, the servants are just an unimportant encumbrance to be disposed of without thought. If I fail to properly care for Mr. Jim, it's likely I'll be the first victim."

He frowned. "Granddad wouldn't ask you to give your life for him."

"That's why I do my best to stay alive. I assess everyone who comes on the grounds. I personally check in any deliveries, and if the delivery is made by someone new, I use a portable metal detector on them."

"For firearms, I suppose." He shrugged out of his shirt and hung it on the stationary bicycle. "What would you do if you found a greedy anarchist prowling around?"

"I'd call in reinforcements. All of the staff are at least slightly trained in fighting, and they're strictly trained in how to call the police."

"What if he comes on you while you're alone?"

The thought made her tense. "He'd better be a better fighter than I am."

"Isn't that likely?" His belt swooshed out of his belt loops.

Soberly she said, "Only too likely. That's why I practice."

"When do you take lessons?"

"During the school year. I simply work to remain in shape during the summer months."

"Do you fight in your classes?" He clenched one fist, watching as the cords of his wrist tightened. "Bouts with your classmates? Your teacher?"

"Of course." The rasp of his zipper echoed loudly in the room, and Margaret suddenly remembered her training. One fist against her chest, one fist outstretched, she switched hands in a lunging punch. Left, right, left, right: ignore, the man, without, the clothes.

"I have a little martial arts training." He flung his pants after his other apparel and stood in his shorts and socks. "I wouldn't mind a bout." Before Margaret could refuse, he quickly added, "If you don't mind dealing with amateurs."

"Of course not, but—"

"Think of the chance to beat up the boss's kid," he suggested.

"Very tempting, but—"

"Or are you afraid I would flatten you?"

No, she wasn't afraid he would flatten her. She was damned good, and she knew it. For a woman who hadn't begun training until her thirties, she was remarkable. But she didn't trust this sneaky, conniving bastard.

"I bet I can beat you," he teased. "Bet you fifty bucks."

"Fifty? You must think well of your fighting," she answered, wrestling with her conscience.

He rummaged in the supply closet and pulled out a *gi*. Shaking out the crumpled white pants, he slipped them on and flung the jacket back onto a shelf. "I left these last time I had a lesson here. Must be two years. So what do you say?"

"All right." She drawled it reluctantly, almost sure she could beat him and almost sure she could afford the fifty dollars if she didn't. "Am I being hustled?"

He spread his hands in appeal. "There's only one way to find out." With cool determination, he strode over and turned on the fluorescent lights.

By the end of the second bout, she believed he had *wanted* to hustle her. He worked so hard, feigning and kicking, but he didn't have enough varied fighting techniques. He was good, she gave him that. He had almost beaten her the last time, until a brilliant defense on her part had opened the way to an equally brilliant offense, and she flattened him with a right reverse punch. It was just as satisfying as he had promised.

Extending her hand, she pulled him to his feet. "Good job. I thought you had me that time." She could afford to be gracious in victory.

"Yeah." He put his hands on his knees and puffed. "The agony of defeat. The ashes of embarrassment. But I still think I could have you, now that I know your technique."

"I know yours, too," she pointed out.

"Yeah, but you have one big hole in your defense."

His palms touched flat on the floor as he bobbed down and then placed his hands on his knees again.

"Oh, come on. You're just a sore loser. Fifty dollars for the first bout, one hundred for the second." She stretched her fingertips up high.

His shoulders slumped as he stared at the mat. "One more bout."

"I've already beaten you twice."

"Just one more."

"No!"

"One more, and we'll make it interesting." His head was still bent, not looking at her.

"How?" she asked, in spite of the good sense that urged her to quit.

"We could bet something we both really want this time."

Warning bells chimed in her brain, but her surging adrenaline ignored them. "Like what?"

"What do you want more than anything in the world?"

"Stability." He glanced up, measuring her sincerity against her answer. He was interested—more than interested, fascinated—and she shifted and wished she had considered before she replied.

To her relief, he only said, "You have it. You'll run this house as long as it stands. That's what you *need*. But what do you *want*? Summers off? A sailboat? A guaranteed college education at Harvard for your daughter?"

Her quick inhalation of air told him what he wanted to know.

"That's it? The college education? Okay, you fight for the education. I'll pay for four years and make sure she gets in. You know you can trust me to do it."

That was true, she realized. She could trust him: she *did* trust him, but . . . "What do you get if you win?" she asked suspiciously.

His eyes were on the mat again. "You."

"Oh, no." She laughed and stepped back. "We're not going to play that game."

He glanced around with every appearance of shock. "You don't mean you think . . . ? Oh, no. I need someone to go with me to look at houses."

"At houses?" She vacillated between embarrassment and disbelief. "Why are you looking at houses?"

"Why does a grown man look at houses?" he asked reasonably.

"To buy?"

"Yes." He drew it out as if he couldn't comprehend her disbelief.

"To live in? For investment?"

"That's it," he agreed.

"The Houston market's down right now," she said, still doubtful about his motives.

He rubbed his eyes with elaborate weariness. "Buy low, sell high. Some free real estate advice for you."

"Thanks." She watched him closely as she spelled out, "The terms are these. If I win, Amy gets a Harvard education. If you win, I help you find a house—or houses? Is this a trick to make me spend time with you?"

"Suspicious, aren't you?" he chided. "No, it's no *trick*. Let's just forget another match, shall we? My wallet can bear a hundred-and-fifty-dollar loss."

So it *had* been a clumsy male contrivance, an attempt to keep her close by his side. It embarrassed him, and she couldn't help teasing, "I thought it was your ego you were concerned about."

He winced, and said quickly, "Never mind. Forget the match. I'm tired, and so are you."

Her audacity flared to life. "You were so sure you could win."

"I could."

He didn't sound as if he meant it, and she taunted, "Remember the hole in my defense? Remember how you know my techniques? Just one more match. To see who's the champion of the world."

"Well," he said grudgingly. "Okay." He lifted his hand from his knee and grasped hers to shake it. From his downcast position rose the phoenix. He shed exhaustion like a snake's skin. He stood straight up, his body sparkling with vitality. His sherry brown eyes shone alert and satisfied. His bright, even teeth flashed in a smile that sent chills up her spine.

FOUR

"Match refused."

"No." Reid stepped back and bent in the standing bow. Automatically Margaret returned the *rei*. "I'm not letting you chicken out now."

"I'm not chickening out," she said tensely. "I'm getting smart."

He dropped into the right back stance. "Fight or don't fight. The bet stands."

She barely ducked his high blow, defending herself with a return punch. She had no more breath with which to protest. The bout developed rapidly, moved smoothly, pushed her to the limit. She still attacked with finesse, she still parried spontaneously, but Reid dealt with her with heated efficiency. This was no longer sparring, it was fighting.

The end arrived in only moments. Reid dropped to the floor and knocked her leg out from under her. In a series of moves she had never seen before, he had her pinned. Helpless beneath the male body that swarmed over her, surrounded her, settled on her, she tugged at her wrists held above her head and demanded, "What was that?"

"Break-dancing." His mouth creased in smug satisfaction. "My master in New York advises putting an element of surprise in the arts."

"Sandbagger," she panted.

"Not at all." He grinned at her, nose to nose. "I simply saved myself for the championship bout. Every strategist knows that."

"You didn't know we'd have a championship bout," she objected.

"Oh, yes, I knew. Sooner or later, I knew we'd have one."

"Who's your master in New York?" she asked suspiciously.

He named a well-known champion, adding, "Not only do the servants of rich men take special training. If possible, the men themselves take the training. It's so much better than having to rely on others for defense."

"Naturally," she said in disgust. "You wouldn't like having to depend on someone else."

"I wouldn't want someone else to give up their life for me." Leaning closer, he whispered, "Especially not someone as attractive as you."

His breath fanned her face; he overwhelmed her with himself, and she didn't like that. "Let me go."

"Of course."

He immediately released his grip, and she brought her hands up to his chest. The shock of his flesh against her hands made her sputter like a Victorian maiden. "Get off of me."

"Of course," he agreed again, but this time his obedience wasn't so prompt. Showing off with the sizzle of an adolescent, he let her feel his weight; feel, too, the excitement she engendered in him.

Furious, dismayed, and unwillingly exhilarated, she made her second stupid mistake of the day. Stiffening her body, wiping all expression from her face, calling on every ounce of her butler-stuffiness, she said, "Please get off of me, sir. This isn't proper."

She saw his flare of anger, heard his leonine growl. His

fingers snagged her chin. "Don't turn away from me. Not with your body, not with your mind. Don't play games with me."

Clenching her jaw in anticipation of some dreadful punishment, she muttered, "Don't threaten me."

His gaze softened, and she swiveled her head away from his tenderness. Laying his head into the curve of her neck, he rasped his night beard against her skin, and she turned back to him at once. He commanded, "Don't try to ignore me, either. I have ways to make you notice that aren't as pleasant as this."

His sibilance warned her only moments before their lips met; firmly he pressed them together. Their noses met, tip to tip, and his eloquent eyes stared into hers, communicating his amusement at her tightly closed mouth.

Lifting his head, he ordered, "Breathe," and she sucked in the air the rigidity of her muscles had denied her. "Good, now open." And he pushed his head down to hers once more. His lips fed velvet coercion to her mouth, brushing and urging until he passed the threshold of her teeth and submerged his tongue. It tasted delicious. The kiss was melted hot fudge, rich and smooth and delicious.

Margaret wanted more, but he chuckled at her awkward eagerness. Raising himself, he untied the belt and the ties of the jacket and spread it apart, baring her chest to the chill of the air conditioner. He watched with fascination as a trickle of sweat dribbled between her breasts, as her nipples puckered with cold. The fluorescent lights blared and she lay perfectly still, like an animal caught in a trap and hoping to escape detection. When he raised his eyes, they had melted into pools of heated sherry. His lashes were a mixture of auburn and brown, his brows thick and almost meeting in the middle of his brow.

The odor of a healthy man assailed her nostrils, the cool mat warmed beneath her, the firm padding laid her before him like a feast. "You can't mean to do—*this*," she whispered hoarsely.

"This?" he teased. "What do you mean—*this*?"

She ignored his nonsense. "You'd be forcing me."

"True, for your mind isn't ready. Although your body has been ready since we met." He smiled with all his teeth. "Hasn't it?"

She tore her gaze away and thumped her head back. How did he know? How did he know about the damp that wet her thighs, about the frustrated longing to climax with the mere application of his tongue?

"You have bruises on your ribs," he muttered, his open mouth wetting them. "I apologize. I thought my control was better than that."

Husky with regret, his voice wakened a polite response. "You have bruises, too. I'm sorry."

A faint surprise overcame him. Had she meant it?

His eyes were bold as lions, speaking in silence of his delight. Nourished by the sight of her, they lingered on her face and traced her mouth. Her flush extended from the tips of her rosy breasts to the top of her ears. Her eyelids drooped, her nostrils quivered with every breath. That fine body had lost the stiffness of dignity and the vigor of combat, and it was soft, pliant, feminine. She looked similar to the way she had when Amy ran her through the wringer and transformed her into a mother.

He'd done the same thing, seeking different results; he'd transformed her into a lover. No longer the proper butler, no longer the aggressive fighter, she looked like a woman.

His lips curved with devilish pleasure. He liked this feeling of power. Margaret was so self-contained, so marvelously reserved, and now she trembled in his hands like a tender leaf in the wind. Pulled by the lips parted so sweetly, he kissed her lightly, then stood and pulled her to her feet.

She floundered, unbalanced by passion, missing her social graces and her suitable role, and deliberately he cracked her facade wider. "I've watched you, Margaret. Without even trying, you've manipulated me, and that means only one thing. You and I are tuned to each other's thoughts, to each other's motivations and ambitions. My grandfather and I are like that: always on the same wavelength, speaking without words. Some of my top men are like that. But you're the first woman."

Pulling her jacket together, she fumbled for her belt—the belt still lying on the mat. "I don't want to be on your wavelength."

"No, I know you don't."

Shoes clattered down the stairs outside the room.

Reid ignored them. "I don't like having you inside my mind, either, but sometimes fate—"

A body hit the door and tried the knob. "Reid?" It was Nagumbi, sounding stern and almost urgent.

With immediate reflex, Reid turned her to face him and brushed her hands aside.

"The door's locked!" she said. "How did it get locked?"

Leaning down to pick up her belt, he wrapped it around her waist and knotted it. "I locked it, but Nagumbi picks locks."

"Get the door," she hissed, struggling to take control of her clothing, but he shook his head.

"He wouldn't interrupt us if it weren't—"

"Reid?" Nagumbi's voice sounded again.

"—important. And I'll not have anyone looking at you." Raising his voice, Reid called, "Coming." He twitched at her top until it was arranged to his satisfaction, and raised his rapier gaze to her face. He saw it all—distress, embarrassment, worry—and he touched her cheek for a moment and promised with his eyes.

Turning, he sprinted to the door and reached it just as the knob began to turn. Taking command of the door, he shoved his head out and demanded, "What the hell do you want?"

Nagumbi's bland voice sounded a knell of doom. "Your grandfather has been kidnapped."

Reid snapped the door wide, slamming it against the

wall. In contrast to his display of temper, his voice was firm and quiet. "How did that happen?"

Margaret moved to the door, and he glanced at her. The feminine lover was gone, vanquished as if it had never been. But mixed with her dignity was a new element of determination, of resolve and of fury.

Reid was glad to have her standing at his side.

"How long," she asked, "has he been gone?"

"I just got a call from the police." Nagumbi answered her as if she had the right to know. "He was taken thirty-two minutes ago, at the Romania Bakery."

"It's one of his favorite's." She nodded for him to continue.

Nagumbi nodded back. "The police are hot on Mr. Donovan's trail. They expect a break right away." Having given the essentials, he turned and started back up the stairs.

Reid and Margaret followed on his heels.

"Who nabbed him?" Reid asked.

"Two men, their faces concealed by ski masks."

"Where was the chauffeur?"

They stepped into the kitchen, and Nagumbi said, "I wasn't given a complete answer to that question."

"What do you mean?" Margaret tugged at his sleeve, and Nagumbi stopped and faced her. Her hand fell away under his intense stare, but she asked again. "Do you mean the chauffeur didn't resist the kidnappers?"

"The officer didn't mention any struggle." Nagumbi turned around and swept past Abigail, who stood worried and wide-eyed.

"Was the chauffeur wounded?" Margaret insisted.

"No."

Margaret frowned and fell back. She watched the play of muscles on Reid's back and listened as he shot questions at Nagumbi. She'd hired the chauffeur, and she could have sworn he was reliable. He'd protected a former employer from an attack by revolutionaries in the streets of

Rome. He'd had a toughness she associated with fearless youth.

Just wait until he got back here. The interrogation the police gave him would be nothing compared to the grilling he'd get from *her*.

They swept into the study in a purposeful triangle. Nagumbi and Margaret stopped, flanking the door, and Reid rounded his desk. He lifted the phone and slapped it on top of a pile of papers. He picked up the receiver and punched a button on the automatic dialer. His lips were tucked tight in anger, and his gaze roamed the room with restless energy. His eyes lit on Margaret and paused, neither warming nor frosting.

She was no longer the enemy and no longer the sweetheart, but an entity trapped in the weights and balances of events. The driving passion was gone, as was the positive animosity. Until she earned his trust, he'd wait for the truth.

And right now, she didn't even blame him.

"Manuel!" he barked into the phone. "They've got Granddad, and I want you to find out what the police are doing about it."

He listened and nodded. "About a half hour ago. Yeah, let me know right—" He lifted his head and listened to the pounding at the front door.

Nagumbi stepped out into the hall; Margaret strode past him. Simon, the footman, moved with stately splendor to the door, never hurrying his pace as the pounding got louder and louder. Margaret cursed the training she'd force-fed him; one never hurried, no matter how frantically one was summoned.

Simon swung the double doors open, and like water spilling over the dam, humanity surged in. In the midst of the tide of blue uniforms, one motorized chrome wheelchair rolled, and a furious voice roared its frustration. "Damn you all, you had the perfect setup and you let them get away. Too afraid to wait to close in, now we have to—"

Jim caught sight of Margaret and snapped his mouth shut. Color mounted his forehead and he seemed almost choleric, forcing himself to cease his harangue, and unhappy about it. "Where's my grandson?" he snapped at her.

"In the study, sir." She stepped aside and gestured him in.

He rolled toward the entrance, and when he came even with her, she put her hand on his shoulder. Without looking at her, he patted her fingers. "No need to worry, dear. I was never in danger."

She stepped back and he went into the room, officers trailing behind. She looked helplessly at Nagumbi, but he was staring after Jim, a frown on his brow. Spinning on his heel, Nagumbi marched away, as if he wanted to find answers and didn't expect they'd be in the study.

Everything was out of kilter, everyone was reacting oddly. She shook her head to clear it and stepped back into the study.

A pale Reid was holding his grandfather's hand and demanding a report. Jim was still spitting invective at the officers for rescuing him too soon. The police were milling about, mostly staring at the assortment of medieval weapons lining the walls. One very harried spokesman, a Mr. Morris, was trying to explain to Reid why it had happened in the first place, and Jim kept interrupting him with snorts and insults.

In Margaret's opinion, if this was the way the HPD always handled their cases, it was a wonder the insanity rate wasn't higher among the victims.

Two things were very, very clear. Reid was furious that Jim had been taken; Jim was furious for being released. Reid demanded to know where the cops had been during the kidnapping; Jim wanted to know why they'd arrived before there could be identification of the mastermind behind the threats.

In exasperation, Reid demanded, "Where was the

chauffeur we hired to protect Granddad when he went out?''

For an instant, a silence fell, and then Jim and the spokesman stated together:

"He was shot."

"He was chicken."

Reid's eyebrows shot up, and his suspicion dropped the temperature in the room perceptibly.

Jim and Mr. Morris looked at each other in dismay. Jim gestured in defeat. "You may as well tell him the truth."

Mr. Morris barely paused. "Yes, I suppose." He looked square in Reid's face. "He ran when it happened, and one of the police mistook him for a suspect. He refused to halt, and the officer fired on him."

Reid wasn't buying. "I'll want to interview him in the hospital."

"Unfortunately"—the spokesman took a deep breath—"he was killed."

Margaret made a soft sound of consternation—appalled at the loss and confused by this performance, so contrary to the chauffeur's character.

Reid glanced at her. "Killed?" He shook his head. "Come, now—the officer shot to kill?"

"No, but the victim tripped and fell into the trajectory of the bullet."

Reid rolled his eyes. "Who hired this clumsy coward?"

"I did." Margaret stepped forward at once. "I replaced the chauffeur we had when we got the first note. I wanted someone specially trained—at the same school that trained me—to defend his employer."

"You did a fine job," Reid lashed.

"Well, I can't figure it out." Jim rubbed his chin with his arthritic fingers. "I count myself a good judge of character, and I didn't read him as a coward. I wonder if they'd bought him off."

Mr. Morris flipped out his notebook and scribbled officiously. "We'll check his bank account, but I suspect that's something we'll never know for sure."

Reid refrained from saying the obvious, but Margaret was afraid she could hear him thinking it. If she hadn't hired a coward, she'd hired a thief instead. "Have his parents been notified?" she asked.

"Not yet, ma'am."

"I'll have to call them," she decided, but an officer took her arm.

"No. The police prefer to notify the next of kin in these instances. If you would please refrain from making contact until we've taken care of the formalities."

Margaret nodded her agreement.

Reid rubbed the bridge of his nose between his two fingers as if a headache were in the offing. "You'll send me the report of your interrogation as soon as you're done, of course."

"Interrogation?" Mr. Morris stepped back. "Of whom?"

Reid raised his head and fixed him with a cold gaze. "Of the kidnappers."

"They weren't apprehended."

"What?" Reid put all his considerable lung power behind the shout.

"They weren't—"

"How the hell could you let them get away?" He was still yelling.

"They, er, abandoned your grandfather and escaped on foot through the arboretum in Memorial Park." The spokesman spread his fingers with apologetic humility.

"Bunch of incompetents," Jim growled.

"I've been raised to respect the police," Reid said coldly, "but I'm inclined to agree."

Jim wrestled his hand from his grandson. "I was talking about the kidnappers."

At a signal from Mr. Morris, the officers began to back from the room. "I'm sorry this has been handled so badly," the spokesman apologized. "I believe that Mr. Donovan is well protected by the security firm you have here, and we'll recommend another chauffeur. One that's been cleared through our department.''

Margaret said, ''I checked with your department when I hired the chauffeur we have now.'' She corrected herself. ''The chauffeur we *had*.''

Mr. Morris hesitated. ''It would seem our information was wrong.''

''And all his references checked out. All his former employers adored him.''

''Then, I would say, someone offered him enough money.'' He smiled nervously at her. ''Everyone has their price.''

''It's too bad he won't have the time to spend it,'' Margaret sniped.

Mr. Morris looked pained, the officers looked angry. She said nothing else, and the exodus out the door continued.

As the room emptied, Reid turned to her. ''You defend your friend well.''

''He didn't deserve death on the assumption of guilt.'' Her eyes lit on Jim's damaged clothing. ''You look like you've had a little rough handling yourself, sir. What happened to the buttons on your shirt?''

Jim glanced down. ''The kidnappers tore it.''

''And you've got cords hanging off your wheelchair.'' She leaned down and picked up the yellow and blue wires. ''Did they tear that up, too?''

He looked as distinctly uncomfortable as she'd ever imagined the old reprobate could look. ''I can't imagine how that happened.''

''Something must be broken on the chair. Can you go forward, backward, side to side?''

''Everything seems to be working fine,'' he assured her.

Kneeling beside him, she followed the wires to nothing. ''It looks like they tore something off completely.''

''I can't imagine what it was.'' Mr. Jim sounded angelic.

Reid stepped over and knelt beside Margaret. ''What

do you suppose it was?" he marveled. "I didn't realize Granddad had controls there."

"Nor I," she agreed. "I'll have it checked in the morning." She stood and brushed her knees, and looked into his eyes.

He looked back. The events of the past moments faded, and the memory of what came before washed over them. Suddenly she saw his chest, bare and carved with muscle, and the low-riding pants of the *gi* that concealed and teased. Suddenly she remembered how his hair had become mussed. She raised a nervous hand to her own and found wisps of it evading her braid and hanging about her face. Afraid she looked like an abandoned hussy, she popped the band off the end and finger-combed her hair.

From the expression in Reid's eyes, that didn't help. If anything, the sweep of moonlight blond against her shoulders seemed to guide his gaze down, to linger against the dips and rises of her figure.

"Well, would you look at you two." Relaxing back into his chair, Jim subjected them both to the X-ray of his vision. His voice was clear and thoughtful. "Did you two reach an understanding while I was gone?"

Margaret gawked at him dumbly.

Reid warned, "Granddad."

"No," Jim decided. "If you'd reached an understanding, Margaret would have that soft, blurred look that women get, and Reid's temper would be a bit better."

She wanted to halt Mr. Jim's ramblings, and she was willing to lie to do it. "Sir, you know what I think about employees becoming involved with their employers, and you know what I told you about Mr. Donovan." Her tone was firm, her gaze unwavering, right until she spoke Reid's name. Then her voice cracked and her eyes dropped.

"By God, Margaret." Jim struck the arm of his chair with his palm. "You look like you discovered *something* about my grandson you like."

Her gaze jerked back to his, and he was grinning—

grinning just as Reid had when he'd won the bout. Grinning as if he'd just carried off the biggest canary and wanted to gloat over it. His blue eyes zipped back and forth between his butler and his grandson in lively amusement, and he pursed his wrinkled lips. "You two been fighting like a couple of men?"

Margaret stared at Jim. If she kept her attention fixed on the elder Donovan, she could refuse to meet Reid's eyes, refuse his demand for her attention.

Jim cackled. "And who won, Margaret? Did you wrestle him into submission and put those nail marks on his shoulders, or did he toss you and beat you to the floor?"

That made her look at Reid. She saw the red crescents on his skin and the way he reminded her, using his eyes and his body and the tilt of his head, that she still owed him his forfeit.

"Strip him of his clothes, and he's not such a bad fellow," Jim advised her.

"Damn you, Jim." She groaned with mortification. Wheeling around, she left for her quarters. Her knees felt too shaky to run, but she abandoned her butler's dignity and accelerated to a rapid pace.

Reid transferred his attention to Jim in disgust. "Thanks, Granddad. I always know I can count on you to throw a ringer into the works."

He strode out, heading for his room, and left the old man alone slapping his knee and gasping with delighted laughter.

"But it's his birthday, Mom."

"I don't care, Amy. I'm not *his* mother."

"He hasn't got a mother. He's an orphan."

"My heart bleeds."

"Mah-om!" Amy sighed. "That's mean."

Margaret blended the blusher over her cheekbone. "*I'm* mean."

"No, you're not. You're the best mother in the whole world. You take care of me all the time." Amy tucked one knee into her elbow, and let the other foot dangle. She sat on the toilet lid, watching her mother make up her face, and she nagged.

Sometimes, it seemed to Margaret, Amy was the best nagger in the world. Especially when someone's well-being was involved. Especially when it was an act of kindness. Especially when she knew she was right.

With the earnest goodwill of a child, Amy said, "Sometimes you don't like what I do, but you love me no matter how awful I am. You teach me all kinds of things about relationships and to be self-confident and do what I know is right in my heart. You tell me if I can't say something nice, don't say anything at all and—"

Margaret put her cosmetic brush down beside the sink and turned to face her daughter. "Amy, why are you regurgitating everything I've ever told you?"

Her little blackmailer smiled with all of her considerable charm. "Because we need to give Reid a birthday party. Mr. Jim's not planning anything. He hardly even remembered it was his birthday. He says he never gives Reid a party. He says he never ever even gave Reid a party when he was little. He says Reid hardly remembers it's his birthday. You'd never let me go without celebrating my birthday, and I'd never let you go without celebrating your birthday. It's a shame to let anyone go without—"

"Amy." Margaret interrupted the unceasing flow of rhetoric. "Don't you think you should call him Mr. Donovan?"

"Who, Reid?"

Margaret nodded.

"Okay." Amy nodded back. "It's a deal. I'll call him Mr. Donovan and we'll give him a party."

"Oh, no, my dear." Margaret leaned into the mirror and wiped color across her lids with her fingertip. "I'm not making deals with anyone else. I learned my lesson on that." There was a crushed little silence, and she glanced sideways at her daughter. Amy's shoulders sagged and she was studying the tip of her swinging shoe. Margaret knew it was foolish, but she tried to reason with her. "Look, honey, what kind of a party could we give someone like Mr. Donovan? He's rich and he's old enough to be your father." *That* was a stupid thought to implant in her daughter's mind, and she rushed on. "A thirty-eight-year-old man doesn't want balloons and paper hats and treat bags with Mickey Mouse on them. He'd want a naked woman jumping out of a cake."

"Bet he wouldn't," Amy muttered.

"Even if he liked Mickey Mouse, he'd probably be chagrined if we made him sit at a table with a paper tablecloth. He'd be annoyed if we invited his friends to come and watch him blow out thirty-eight—"

"Thirty-nine."

"Okay, thirty-nine candles. And when we spilled red punch on his"—Margaret's lips pursed in thought—"carpet, he'd probably be very angry. Hmm." And maybe, just maybe, he'd stop looking at me like he can't decide whether to drag me off to jail or drag me off to bed. Maybe he'd talk to me, instead of gloating over me. Maybe he'd remember his position and stop giving the household ideas by the way he watches me. "You know, Amy, you might just have an idea there. Who do you suppose he'd want? Batman or Waldo?"

"Zorro?"

FIVE

Simon flung open the dining room doors, and Reid wheeled Jim in. Jim set the brake; Reid skidded to a stop. Both Jim and Reid looked absolutely flabbergasted. The guests savored the expressions of total amazement for a split second and then they yelled, "Surprise!"

Everyone took a breath and laughed, yelled, "Surprise!" again, and broke into little groups, streaming over to greet the birthday boy.

Margaret watched as Reid looked around at the assemblage. His closest friends were here, some with their families and some alone. There were babies chewing their feet, adults leaning on canes, and every age in between. She'd culled the names of twenty-five of Reid's buddies, consulting Nagumbi and Abigail and Manuel, and subtly sounding out Mr. Jim. She'd stood by the phone, ever vigilant of RSVPs. Twenty of the twenty-five had come. The other five had sent greetings and presents and disappointed excuses.

"This is wonderful," Reid gasped, when he realized what was happening. "This is for me?" He looked around the room with the wide eyes of an eight-year-old who has just had his greatest desire fulfilled. "This is *wonderful*."

Margaret surveyed the dining room with self-righteous pleasure. Plastic balloons crept along the vaulted ceiling, their brilliant colors inching toward the return air vents. Mylar balloons bobbed, tied to the back of every chair and marked with a guest's name. The paper tablecloths were weighted down by plates of cupcakes and bags of treats and whistles and hats. The center table held a sheet cake. A gigantic wall hanging showed the birthday boy and his best friend in a smiling fantasy drawing. The friend had round black ears and a black bow tie and wore a cheerful grin.

Everything—*everything*—shouted M-I-C . . . K-E-Y . . . M-O-U-S-E. Every available space held a picture of Mickey. The balloons were shaped like Mickey, the cake was a miracle of Mickey frosting, the cupcakes were stuck with tiny Mickey toothpicks. The hats had ears, the whistles squeaked when blown, the treat bags held Mickey gum and Mickey candy and Mickey cards.

She turned back to Reid and found his eyes lingering on the one guest he didn't know; the one present she'd brought for him. She'd met Chantal at one of Mr. Jim's functions during the past year. Chantal was young—in her middle twenties—and charming. She was tall, but not as tall as Margaret, and lush—her puberty had obviously been a resounding success. Her clothes hugged her every curve and shouted good taste. Her auburn hair curled in a mad riot down her back, and one teeny wisp teased her brow. One look from her blue eyes caused previously sane men to abandon their talk of finance and follow her like begging puppy dogs. They found, to their horror, that Chantal could talk finance with the best of them. And politics, and the current state of the Houston economy. The woman was a freelance reporter, selling her investigative articles to the largest local newspapers, and sometimes to the news services.

The woman was not only beautiful, she was smart. Worst of all, in Margaret's view—she was nice.

Genuinely nice. Other women liked her. Ruefully, but

they liked her. The first words she'd spoken to Margaret were a compliment on her black uniform and how well it accented her blond hair. Margaret had taken that with a grain of salt, but when Chantal had sought her out to ask if she could go down and applaud the cook, Margaret had surrendered. She'd become a member in good standing of the Chantal Fan Club, and now she was her biggest supporter. How could she not be? Beautiful, smart, and nice; three of the biggest clichés in the English language as redefined by Chantal.

They were friends, and when Margaret had invited her to lunch and begged her to come and vamp Reid, Chantal had agreed. Without vanity, she'd been sure she could lure Reid into her coils, and from what she'd heard, he'd be a pleasure to keep. "But, Margaret," Chantal had warned, "as worried as you are about this—are you sure you want me to take him?"

"Take him and welcome," Margaret had replied, and now she watched as Chantal shook Jim's hand and obtained an introduction to his grandson. What a triumph. She'd embarrassed him with a party and tossed him a distraction, all in one smooth maneuver. Boy, was she glad.

Reid met Chantal, and Margaret could see the gleam in his eye from here. He raised her hand to his mouth and stared at her with such open appreciation, Margaret wanted to . . . arrange some party activities.

Reid found Amy in the crowd surrounding him, and he lifted her into his arms. Big girl that she was, she didn't complain. She laughed and chatted and pointed about the room, and Margaret knew just what she was saying. I sent the invitations, Amy was confessing. Nagumbi arranged the Mickey-o-gram. Manuel and his wife had insisted on providing the Hispanic delicacies. Abigail decorated the Mickey Mouse cake herself.

Mommy—Amy's accusatory little finger shot her way— Mommy coordinated everything just for you.

Reid's eyes met hers across the room, and she wanted

to gasp and sigh. He didn't look angry. Perhaps he was a marvelous actor, but he looked happy. Amused, astonished, and pleased, and warmly endorsing her kindness.

Uh-oh.

She kept staring at Reid, and he kept staring at her until the rasping voice of Mr. Jim demanded, "Why the hell wasn't I told?"

Margaret looked down at him, surprised he'd reached her side without her noticing. She looked up at Manuel, who stood beside his friend and grinned and twisted the end of his mustache. Hands outspread, she shrugged at both of them.

"Were you afraid an old man of ninety-two would slip?"

"Oh, no, not you." She shook a finger at Jim. "You'd never slip *accidentally*; you're too sharp for that. You'd do it on purpose, out of loyalty to your grandson, and no one was going to spoil this surprise."

"I'd have never thought it, but you may be right. He seems to like this childishness." He raised his head and stared at the Reid-and-Mickey banner. "Who'd you get to paint that?"

"Norma Van. She couldn't come. She has a showing in New York this weekend, but she insisted she wanted to do something, and now Reid has a Mickey Mouse painting worth thousands." Margaret chuckled.

"She's a lady," he answered, bestowing his highest compliment.

"Most of these people are just great," she agreed.

Jim turned his wheelchair to face her. "You don't have to sound so shocked. What kind of friends did you think Reid would have?"

She didn't answer—for what could she say that wouldn't sound rude? Looking across at Reid as he worked his way through the crowd, greeting them all with a special smile or a smack on the back or a tender hug, she wondered what she *had* expected Reid's friends to be like.

Not what she had gotten. She'd found their lack of arrogance surprising—surely Reid's good friends should be snooty? Shouldn't the head of the largest oil corporation in the world be a bit stuck-up? Shouldn't an exiled prince of Bulgaria be too good to chat with a butler? Shouldn't a Japanese magnate shake her hand with less enthusiasm? Shouldn't the French chief of a big city police department complain about her security? But no—all of them displayed an unselfconscious delight, exclaiming how glad they were that Reid was at last having the party he deserved.

They'd taken the rooms she assigned them, and when the mansion had run out of bedrooms, they'd agreed to stay at a hotel without a grumble. They'd lavishly praised her great idea and exclaimed about her innovation. They just weren't like any rich people she'd ever met—and she'd met quite a few. Why, some of these friends weren't even rich. None of them were even haughty.

It seemed that Reid's business associates could be as rude as they liked, but his intimates had to be real folk. She ignored the doubts that circled her brain. She ignored Mr. Jim and Manuel, too, who sat there watching her with their bright eyes analyzing her every expression.

Stepping forward, she clapped her hands and called, "All right! It's time for birthday games. Amy, get the birthday boy his ears and his whistle."

"That's not fair," the corporation president called. "Reid gets real Mickey Mouse ears with his name sewn on."

"Reid is the birthday boy—"

"Yeah," Reid interjected.

"—and you haven't got your treats yet, so behave yourself or you won't get a surprise. Now, everyone put on your hats."

Every one of them pulled the elastic bands under their chins and settled the pointed paper hats on their heads.

"You'll have to take the whistles out of your mouths

to play this game. We can't have you running with a whistle in your mouth—you'll fall and shove it down your throat.''

"Thank you for caring," one voice called from amid the laughter, and they all grinned at Margaret as if she were the head cheerleader and they were the school pep team.

"We're going to play musical chairs."

"I must complain about your unprofessional attire."

Margaret looked down at herself, her smile fading. "What? Why?" she stammered. Her black skirt sported a spot or two of frosting, and her white shirt looked a little wilted, and her jacket had been discarded in the excitement of the piñata, but other than that, she thought her appearance was conventional.

Reid reached up and touched the maroon scarf she'd knotted around her neck. "Rather radical, isn't it?"

"Oh," she faltered. She'd forgotten about the bow Amy teased her into wearing. "I thought that at a party—"

He studied her with a lazy pleasure. "It's too much. That black and white suit is severe enough to scare many a mighty man, but the color throws out a hint of temptation. It might give the braver fellows I call my friends ideas, and I want to keep them as friends."

She didn't say anything—well, what could she say? She didn't want to pursue that comment. His sherry brown eyes were just too pleased, too contented, too possessive.

"Pierre has already commented on the frosty lady in the black suit, and her hint of passion beneath."

"Pierre? Ah, the French policeman. He's charming."

"All the women say that about Pierre." He sighed with mock dismay and leaned close. "Beware, he's a wolf in sheep's clothing."

"Thank you for the warning," she said ironically.

He contrived to look hurt. "Are you insinuating *I'm* a wolf in sheep's clothing?"

"Not at all. You don't even own a set of sheep's clothing."

He chuckled. "How well you know me. What do you think of the rest of my friends?"

A warm smile lit her face. "They're marvelous. Pleasant and witty and interesting."

"All of them?"

"All of your friends are at least one of the above," she assured him.

"They like you, too." A deep contentment colored his speech. "They seem to be under the impression you're a dear pal first and a punctilious butler second."

"Well." She studied her nails. "I can't imagine what made them think that."

"Maybe it's all the work you did organizing this party."

The warm note of pleasure made her squirm with guilt, and she avoided his eyes. "Don't make more of this than you should. It was Amy's idea."

"She says you did all the labor."

"No, no. I'm great at delegating responsibility. Everyone did their part, and besides, I've organized a lot of these parties." She darted a look at him, but her disclaimer seemed to be making no impression. "For Amy, you know. I can do it with my eyes closed."

"Good." He sounded eager and pleased. "You'll do me another one next year."

"I will?" She pivoted her head around and glared.

"Please?" Butter wouldn't melt in his mouth. His eyes gleamed with soulful pleading, his mobile mouth pouted.

"You remind me of Amy."

"Does that mean you'll do it?"

"Call me sucker," she admitted wryly.

Instead he bent his knees until he was eye level and gave her a big, smacking kiss. Heads turned at the sound, and Margaret felt the heat of a blush climb from her toes to the roots of her hair.

"Pushing, pushing," she murmured. "You act like a child, I'll treat you like a child."

Straightening up, he smirked with accomplishment. "I am not a child. I thought I'd proved that to you."

She turned to march away, but a strong arm at her waist stopped her. "Stay here," he commanded. "I won't tease anymore."

Glancing around, she saw too many faces observing them with intense goodwill. "Fine," she said tersely, and she leaned her elbows against the antique oak buffet behind her—and upset the glasses stacked there.

Reid rescued them while Margaret wished she were far, far away, and then a silence fell between them.

"I don't want to be that young anymore." Reid sounded reflective, and Margaret followed his gaze. He stared at Chantal, chatting vivaciously to Mr. Kioto.

"Why do you say that?"

"Look at her, hustling for a story. Her greatest happiness is standing on a pier in the Gulf of Mexico during a hurricane. Or interviewing some politician's ex-girlfriend. Or getting the goods on a financial scandal." He cocked an eyebrow at Margaret.

"She promised to keep everything she heard tonight confidential," she assured him. "In return, I told her she could make as many contacts as possible."

"I know I can depend on you." He blessed her with a slow rub on the back, then looked back at Chantal and grimaced. "She lives a miserable existence."

Margaret snorted.

"Yes, she does. I know, because I've been there."

"It made you very successful," Margaret observed.

"Yeah, that's why God gives you driving ambition when you're twenty. When you're forty, you don't want to contend with it."

She laughed; she couldn't help it. He sounded so doleful, so wise.

"Okay, Miss Smart Aleck, didn't you have a driving ambition when you were young?"

"Of course. I wanted to travel, to see the world. I was going to be a teacher of English in far-off Pakistan. Or Kuwait, or France, or Hong Kong. I wasn't fussy."

He leaned up against the buffet and crossed his arms across his chest. "What derailed that ambition?"

"My husband. He came along, and my sights narrowed considerably." She grinned, entertained by the memory of her younger self. "I just wanted to get him through medical school so he could discover the cure for cancer and we'd be on easy street and save the world at the same time."

"And then?"

Her smile faded, and she didn't answer for a long time. She wandered, lost in her memories and her ancient pain. "Then I found out what really counts in life." She rubbed her arms with her hands and realized she was staring at Chantal. "So," she said brightly. "What do you think of her? Isn't she gorgeous?"

"Gorgeous," he agreed. "She looks like she went to the Golden Globe Awards and won twice."

Stupidly, Margaret almost told him Chantal wasn't in show business, when his meaning came clear. She choked, coughed, and wished he hadn't tapped into her sense of humor so precisely. Gaining control, she queried, "Isn't she irresistible?"

"Oh, no doubt irresistible. Especially for men who are jaded and older and look for the cure in the adoration of a much younger woman."

She turned to him, detected the bite of sarcasm.

He took her chin between his fingers and pinched it hard. "Unfortunately for you, my darling, this method of distraction won't work."

She had the depressing feeling she knew just what he implied, but still she asked, "What do you mean?"

He smiled that five-hundred-watt smile straight in her face. "I've got my mind set on one woman who is, I admit, younger than me. But not too much younger. Not obscenely younger. She's warm and kind and gives great surprise parties. I think I'll leave little Chantal to a man who's more her age.'' He pointed to Jim. ''Like Granddad.''

''That's horrible.''

''Did that destroy your little plot? Did you ask Chantal to tempt me? She tried. She tried valiantly. But she's no fool—unlike some people I could name—and she knows a lost cause when she sees one. So let's have no more tossing of fair maidens at my head, and I won't toss myself at you.'' He released her chin and patted her cheek. ''At least, not for the moment.''

Margaret remained silent, stubbornly refusing to agree to his pact.

''Perhaps I misread the situation. Did you want me to toss myself at you?'' He moved closer to her side, sliding his arm behind her on the buffet.

''No!'' She jumped away and upset the glasses again, and this time they hit the floor—hundreds of dollars worth of shards and splinters flying into corners and seeking the fringe of the rug to hide in. She stared at the glittering catastrophe and groaned, ''Oh, no.''

Reid shook his head. ''Drunk on red punch.''

Margaret didn't signify she'd heard him. In the blink of an eye, she switched from being a woman to being a butler—or mother. ''We've got to get the kids out of here.'' She pushed the button on the intercom and spoke to the answering Simon. ''We've had an accident. Get a cleanup crew in here, and have the caterers set up the buffet in the ballroom.'' Releasing the button, she snapped her fingers and pointed. ''Amy, you put your shoes back on and herd the other children into the entry.''

Her daughter pulled a pitiful face. ''But we haven't opened the presents yet.''

''I'll have them moved; now, do as you're told, please.''

To her relief, Reid stepped forward and announced, ''Due to this ghastly mess, we're moving the party so we can eat and open presents . . . and dance.''

''Wh . . . ?'' Margaret whipped her head around, but

it was too late. Reid was ushering the smiling, chattering group out into the hall, and he turned and winked at her with sly humor.

Reid stripped off his suit coat and white shirt, flinging them on the floor amid cheers and laughter. Reaching into the box lined with tissue paper, he reverently raised his new Mickey Mouse T-shirt and slipped it over his head. It went well with the new red Mickey Mouse tie, knotted around his neck, and the new Mickey Mouse watch on his wrist.

Margaret leaned across to Mr. Jim. "If he doesn't stop blowing that Donald Duck whistle, I'm going to scream."

"Scream all you want, my dear." Jim patted her fanny and laughed when she jumped. "After what you've done for my grandson, you could answer the door in a Mickey Mouse *costume* and I wouldn't care."

"It's not such a big thing." Margaret shrugged.

"Oh, but it is. Look at him. He looks like he did when he was a boy, before his parents died."

"They died?"

"Of course; did you think he was hatched?"

"I didn't know when he came to live with you," she answered patiently.

"When he was eight. His parents were both scientists. Mad scientists, I believe, and teachers both."

"Where did they teach?"

"At a high school in Seattle."

"A high school?" Margaret was surprised and amused. "I would have thought you'd have bought them a college."

"James and Brenda were idealists, believing the future of the world lay in the youth of today." Mr. Jim's mouth quirked. "Couple of fools in love."

"Car wreck?"

"Hiking accident."

"Was Reid with them?"

"Oh, yes." He shook his head sadly. "They had the school science club out identifying plants in the mountains, and some youngster decided to dance beside the cliff. James lunged for him, Brenda caught at James, and they both flew off the precipice."

Nudged by the sardonic twist of his mouth, she queried, "The boy didn't fall?"

"Of course not. But James was killed instantly. It damaged Brenda enough to keep her in the hospital for a month."

"Then what happened?"

"Then she died, too."

Margaret had known what he was going to say, but even so, she was shocked. "Good God."

"So an eight-year-old boy came to live with a sixty-one-year-old man." He raised one withered hand and rubbed his eyes tiredly. "I did the best I could."

She checked him with a suspicious gaze. Mr. Jim had been known to use his age and his infirmity to deliberately touch the heart, but she acquitted him of manipulation now. He wasn't watching her for her reactions; just sat with pursed lips, remembering.

"I wasn't retired then. I had a hell of a big corporation to run. I hadn't had a boy around for years; I'd forgotten how rambunctious they got. But one thing I did remember." He raised one crooked finger. "I remembered James at that age. I remembered how he'd wanted to be with me and how I'd never had the time, and I resolved not to make that mistake again. I took Reid everywhere with me."

"That must have been something to see."

"The boy could discuss municipal bonds with the best of them at the tender age of ten, and predicted his first oil well strike at eleven."

"And you?"

"I played G.I. Joe."

She sputtered with laughter. "Good for you."

He tilted his head and looked at her sideways. "I never could decide if it kept me young or aged me fast."

"Well, you're still here at ninety-two," she pointed out.

"He brought one thing to me, for sure. It had been so long since I'd had it, I'd even forgotten to miss it." He smiled mistily. "That snot-nose brat brought me love."

Margaret sought Amy with her eyes. Her daughter had found a friend from among the other girls, and those two girls had attracted a following of younger children. The little ones paddled after them like a hatching of ducks after their mothers. "That's all kids are good for," she scoffed, her heart in her eyes.

"Amy's having a good time, isn't she?"

"She never meets a stranger," Margaret admitted.

"Nor Reid. If he has any fault, it's that he recognizes people through his intuition and makes his decisions about them immediately. It used to drive me mad. I warned him he'd get hurt."

"Did he?"

"No, not him. He warned me about a business associate, and I ignored him. You see, I based my perception on previous actions and known factors. I got taken for a bundle. That's when I realized that the little bugger might have a disturbing tendency to be right."

Margaret laughed.

Taking her hand, he stroked it. "But I never even thought to give the boy a birthday party. He never said he wanted one. But when he walked in this afternoon and saw this nonsense—I guess maybe he missed a normal life."

"Perhaps he missed some of the aspects of a normal life," she corrected. "He loves you, and the way you raised him made him the man he is."

"You think I did a good job?"

She reassured him, her voice too warm and her expression too kind. "I think you did a marvelous job."

"Good." His mouth curled with satisfaction. "I took care of him for the first half of his life." He turned his wheelchair and headed for the door. "You take care of him for the second half. Come and help me get ready for bed. I'm tired."

Like a prickling on the back of his neck, Reid knew when Margaret reentered the ballroom. Shifting so he could see the door, he viewed her and sighed with pleasure. She was so beautiful.

He shook his head and laughed at himself. She wasn't actually stunning, he supposed. Tall and thin and well formed—so what? The women he'd escorted all fell into that category. What caught a man's attention was the way she moved; fluid grace bred into every bone. It made him think of long summer nights filled with slow, careful lovemaking. The light stroke of a hand, the gentle use of teeth and tongue. Fires lit and tended with care until they flared out of control.

Shifting uncomfortably, Reid returned from his erotic dreams and focused on Margaret again. Her skin shone unfashionably pale, like the base of his grandfather's china lamp. She wore little makeup—some blusher, he guessed, and mascara to cover her white lashes—and it told on her when she was weary. Like now.

He checked the ballroom with his eyes. When she had disappeared and he'd discovered she'd gone to care for his grandfather, he'd taken over the job of butler. Under his command, the buffet had been removed and was now nothing but a comfortable memory. Most of the children had been put to bed or worn to the point of silence. The candelabra had been dimmed, and compact disks played a pleasant combination of jazzy tunes and old-fashioned melodies. Abigail had snared Nagumbi; Uncle Manuel had caught up with his little dynamo of a wife, and they danced. Couples swayed, wrapped in music and communicating heated, leisurely ideas.

This was the end of one very successful party, and Margaret had done it all: all for him.

Cruising the edges of the floor, he coasted up to her and murmured, "Dance with me."

SIX

She jumped and brushed at her ear, tired enough to be cranky when he breathed on her neck, tired enough to have missed his approach. "Sir, I have to start the cleanup."

"Will you call my name when we make love?"

She glared at him.

"Or will you moan, 'More, sir, please, sir'?" He laughed at her frustrated fury.

"I have to organize the cleanup," she enunciated clearly.

"It's done. I delegated some of that authority you bragged about." He put his arm around her waist, but she resisted.

"Everyone's coming for breakfast."

"Let 'em eat frozen waffles."

"That is not what the Donovan guests expect."

She sounded so fussy, so unbearably stuffy, that he abandoned his plans of subtle seduction and did what he did best. His hands reached out for her hips, and he pulled her into his body, saying, "To hell with the Donovan guests."

The touch of their bodies jolted her from her fatigue and her orneriness. Her eyes widened as she looked up at him, and he rubbed the dark patches beneath. "Your mascara has smudged."

"Sir." He rubbed himself against her. "Reid!"

He could see her awareness grow, and it reaffirmed his first impression. Margaret needed to be swept from her feet before she could be handled.

She looked down at their joined bodies. "I don't dance like that—or at least, I haven't since I learned better."

"It doesn't *get* any better than this. Or at least . . . not while you're dancing," he mocked.

She tried a bargain. "I'll dance with you if you'll be good."

He smiled a wicked smile, and dancing wasn't all that was on his mind. "I'll be good if you'll dance with me."

He stepped out to the blatantly romantic tune, crooned by Linda Ronstadt and backed by Nelson Riddle and his orchestra. The sound system surrounded them in the romantic rhythm; the other dancers were silent. The room was large; there was no danger of collision and no reason to speak. Clearly unwilling, she slid her arms around his shoulders. It gave him a chauvinistic thrill to know he could take that initial reluctance and turn it to tapioca. It gave him an even greater thrill—a pure masculine thrill— to know why she was reluctant. She wanted to stay away from his fire. It was too warm, too enveloping. She feared the burn, yet needed the warmth.

God, he *was* warm. With a buffer of time, he could account for the true reason he'd been antagonistic when he'd first seen her.

She was the one.

Like any man, he hadn't been ready to admit defeat. Especially to a woman who failed to realize what a prince she'd snagged. He much preferred his previous philosophy—it was so much more flattering for his own ego. Before, he'd thought women had invented marriage. Women did the chasing, women captured unwilling victims and tangled them in their snares.

When he'd thought about it, that's how he suspected

he'd go: strung up by some devious woman. Hell, here he was, madly pursuing a woman who didn't like him, didn't admire him—she only wanted him. And she didn't like doing that at all.

She wanted to remain phlegmatic, caught in the workaday world. In pursuit of that unattainable goal, she was keeping her head up, away from his shoulder. She was keeping her upper body curved back; if his fingers hadn't been flexed on her hips, their bodies would have met nowhere in the dance.

But when they were together, the world changed.

Like a wizard, he snared her in a bubble. The air around them glistened and quivered, and she breathed deeply of his cologne, dipping toward his neck in unconscious betrayal. He pressed his hand against her cheek until she laid it on his chest. He rubbed his chin on the top of her head, and her perfume came up in clear, seductive waves. Unable to resist, he hummed a deep and mellow accompaniment to Linda and the band.

He rubbed one of his hands up and down her spine, sliding too far down her buttocks, then, before she could react, sliding back up to fondle her ear. Either extreme made her uncomfortable; she'd stiffen a bit. But the part in the middle felt divine, if her boneless lassitude was anything to judge by.

Like a psychic in a grocery store newspaper, he read her thoughts. She wanted to forbid him; she *would* forbid him, just as soon as the music stopped. He nodded to Pierre over her shoulder, and like an endless enticement, the disks drifted from one song to the other with nary a break between.

"You know what I've been thinking?" Reid used a rumbly voice, new to Margaret and meant to soothe.

It worked.

Cuddling her close, he repeated, "You know what I've been thinking? I've been thinking how well we fit together."

"Sure," she breathed.

"When we make love—"

She rose up, but he pushed her head back down. "When we make love, we'll fit just as well."

"No." But it was just a whisper.

Reaching between them, he released her tie and let it float way. "I've always wanted to be part of a family. Like Dick and Jane, Spot and Puff, Mother and Father. That's the American ideal, isn't it?"

"Um? Oh, yes."

"There's you and me—that's Mother and Father." He felt the tension invade her limbs. "And Jane—that's Amy. Spot and Puff, we can get at the pound—and Dick. Well," he chuckled softly, laying tender lips on her forehead, "Dick would be *our* project."

She jerked back, and he let her go. "Are you crazy? That's one sick proposition. What would happen to Amy and me when you got tired of playing house?"

His eyebrow quirked, and he smiled with sultry intent, "How long do you plan to live?"

"Forever. The question is: How long do you plan to live?"

He'd touched a nerve; that he could see. Her nostrils flared, her chin squared defiantly, but her lips quivered. With firm hands, he gathered her back against his chest, and he led her in the dance until he felt the iron subside in her spine. "The ghost of the husband raises his head," he guessed.

"He's not a ghost."

"He's not alive, either."

"I mean," she said, sounding provoked, "I'm not haunted by him."

"Has someone suggested you were?"

It was a trap, and he felt sorry to have set it, but if this was an explanation of her skittish behavior, he needed to know. But she didn't reply, and she kept her face turned away from him, and he said, "That's an answer all its own."

He saw the way she set her jaw. Nothing more would

be forthcoming from her. Intent on bringing her back to him, he whispered, "You certainly know how to freeze a proposal."

Her face skewed around to his, and she leaped back, her expression incredulous. "What do you mean by that?"

"Think about it," he ordered.

With trembling hands, she pushed her hair out of her eyes and glanced up at the ceiling, then at the other dancers. Her eyes lingered on Nagumbi, trapped in a glittering Abigail's arms and showing an unwilling enjoyment. She felt a kinship for him, and in a quavery voice, she said, "You do a mean fox-trot."

"Um." He touched her lower lip with one fingernail. "The music's still playing."

She ignored that. "I guess you had a lot of lessons when you were young, huh?"

"Not too many." He'd not push anymore tonight. He tucked the silky strands of hair behind her ears, lingering to stroke the outer shell and the curve of her cheek.

"Well, thanks for the dance." Swinging her arms, she rolled her eyes. "I . . . enjoyed it."

With a finger on her chin, he turned her face to his. "I . . . enjoyed it, too." His eyes were smoky, his face was kind, and his mouth was very, very amused. "See you around," he whispered, and he turned without another word and found himself in Chantal's arms, weaving romance in a dance.

Margaret stared after them. She was glad he danced with Chantal. Maybe Chantal's looks and sexuality would knock some of that nonsense out of his head. Some of that scary nonsense. Yes, she was glad that Reid had gone and found himself another partner with no fuss.

Then she turned up the lights, went to the compact disk player, and put on some good ol' rock and roll, and livened up the party enough to keep it going until two in the morning.

When at last the guests drifted away, some out the door,

some up the stairs, Margaret nodded good night with acute satisfaction.

Beside her, Reid said, "You missed one party game."

Margaret pressed her palm to the small of her back. "Believe it or not, I missed several. It only *seemed* like we played every game in existence."

"See ya, Margaret." Abigail headed down the hallway, her sequins sagging with exhaustion. Nagumbi stood looking after her, and then moved with his natural majesty in quite the opposite direction.

Moving behind Margaret, Reid pushed her hand aside and began a slow, rotating massage. All the muscles along her spine contracted, vying for attention, and she groaned pitifully.

"What are you so tense for?"

"Hostessing a party for forty rowdy and happy adults—not to mention a pack of wild kids—is not an easy job."

"It's over now," he soothed.

"Worrying about security has been no picnic, either."

"Granddad's fine."

"I know." She broke away from his hands and turned to face him. "But do you know the trouble I had convincing Cliff Martin he couldn't come in and mingle with the guests?"

"God forbid."

"I heard a million dire warnings, including a threat to go to you with the plans—"

Reid's face tightened in anger.

"—but good sense—and police advice—prevailed at last." She rubbed the side of her face with careworn concentration. "If you don't mind, sir . . . um, Reid, I'd like to go to bed."

"Are you going to start calling me Sir Reid now? Don't you think that's a little formal?"

She laughed uneasily and backed up.

His hand shot out and caught her elbow. "You never asked which game we didn't play."

"Huh?" Befuddled, she shook her head to clear it.

"Look, if we didn't get to a game you liked, write me a list. I've already contracted to do your party next year." She glared, trying to pile a little guilt on his unrepentant head, and noticed the diabolical smile that parted his lips.

"But I can't *wait* for next year to play spin the bottle."

He took one Giant Step forward, and she audibly said, "Uh-oh."

He leaned down to her mouth.

Putting her finger on his chest, she warned, "You didn't say, 'Mother, may I?' "

He just kept coming. "Yes, I may."

The kiss branded her. It blurred the already fuzzy edges of reality. It tasted like chocolate cake and cherry punch and bubble gum. The innocence of the flavors and the experience of the kisser confused her. It made her reply more than she should, give more than she wanted. It wasn't until he began to unbutton her vest, with a touch here and a touch there for emphasis, that Margaret dragged herself away from his seduction. When Reid leaned back, he was holding her against him—to keep her upright. He waited until her knees stopped wobbling, then he set her back and ran up the stairs two at a time.

When she recovered enough to walk, she turned and ran smack into Chantal.

"Who are you trying to kid?" Chantal's eyes were big and round, and her feet seemed grown to the floor.

It took Margaret two tries to get her mouth set to articulate. "What do you mean?"

"Any man who kisses a woman like that is worth hand-to-hand combat. You don't just pass him on to me without a qualm." Chantal was indignant on Reid's behalf, and then said sensibly, "Besides, he doesn't want me."

"What?" Margaret shook her head as if she'd been hit. "What?"

"He doesn't want me," Chantal enunciated.

"Did he say that?"

"Dear girl, he didn't have to. He was very pleasant,

very nice, and handed me to his friend from France with no hesitation.''

''Damn.'' Margaret's sense of imbalance, so typical when Reid was around, had disappeared, and she imagined and discarded options with lightning speed. She snapped her fingers and suggested, ''Maybe we could—''

''No.''

''You haven't even heard—''

''I don't need to. Margaret''—Chantal wrapped her hands around Margaret's jaw—''listen to me. The man is nuts about you. He gives off an aura of desire so strong, I breathe it in when I stand close to him.''

''Maybe he should bathe,'' Margaret mumbled.

Chantal ignored her and continued with her litany. ''He watches you across the room. He admires you with his eyes. He listens for your voice. He threatens other men verbally when they get too close to you.''

''It's only unrequited lust,'' Margaret said in despair.

''If I could find a man who'd lust after me like that, he'd never escape my clutches. He's not going to let you go.'' Chantal released Margaret's jaw and took her by the shoulders. Punctuating each word with a shake, she said, ''So you might as well enjoy the ride.''

''She's a fine-looking woman.''

Reid looked up from his plate of scrambled eggs to see Margaret coming through the door of the dining room, two plates of Abigail's fluffy biscuits steaming in her hands. The conversationalist sat beside him, waggling his eyebrows in exaggerated continental flare, and Reid commanded, ''Shut up and eat your waffles, Pierre.''

Pierre, of course, paid no attention. Reid had been issuing orders and Pierre had been ignoring them from their fraternity days, and Reid would have been surprised to see the handsome Frenchman listen for once. Instead Pierre rambled, ''I've always been a sucker for women in uniform. Those prim outfits make a man wonder how she looks beneath.''

Reid glared at his friend—who was rapidly becoming his former friend. "She's not as good-looking as you think."

"Ah?"

"Yes, there's a reason you never see her with her collar unbuttoned." He leaned toward Pierre and bared his teeth. "She's hairy all over, like a bear."

"But only during the full moon, right?" Pierre laughed aloud, and the other guests turned from their conversations and stared at the two men huddled at the head of the table. Lowering his voice, he suggested, "Maybe she'll eat me up."

"Only if all her taste is in her mouth." Pierre opened his lips to speak, and Reid said, "Which it isn't, so don't even try."

Pierre grinned and stuffed in another bite of waffles and groaned with pleasure. "You Americans eat the most wonderful things."

"Homemade biscuits, bacon, sausage, scrambled eggs, grapefruit halves, all from Abigail's loving hands—and you eat frozen waffles. How did Frenchmen ever get the reputation for being gourmets?"

Waving his fork in a dripping syrup circle over his place mat, Pierre proclaimed, "It is our lovemaking that addles a woman's brain and makes her susceptible to suggestion."

"So?"

"We make love to them, then we tell them we're gourmets." He shrugged.

"What a plan," Reid said. "Maybe I should make love to her and then tell her she loves me."

"You *are* glum this morning. Didn't you get the birthday present she was promising last night when she danced with you?"

"*Non.*" With that one word, Reid exhausted half of his repertoire of French. "She wants me, but she doesn't want to want me."

"Maybe she needs another man to open the blossom of

her womanhood." Pierre kissed his fingers with Gallic
fervor.

"Maybe you'd leave in a body bag if you tried."

"Oh, ho! *Mon ami* sees the green monster of jeal-
ously." Pierre lifted one of Reid's eyelids and peered beneath. "Oh, ho! *Mon ami* has been stricken with ze
amour."

"Knock it off with the Maurice Chevalier imitations,"
Reid growled. "Never mind about my love life. Tell me
what you think of Martin Security."

Pierre dropped the accent, and his English sounded almost pure American. With the accent, he dropped the
guise of French rake, and became what he was—an *agent
de police*. "My professional opinion, you mean?"

"Yeah."

"I can only tell you what I was told." He held up a
fist and lifted one finger. "One. The Houston Police are
almost fanatically certain that this firm is stable." Another
finger. "Two. Your dear uncle Manuel insists Martin Security is solid." Another finger. "Three. Cliff Martin
checks out with every source I could find in the States."

"Damn."

Pierre folded his fingers into a fist. "Why are you
worried?"

"I have this niggling feeling—"

"That something's not right?"

Reid nodded. "With Martin."

Examining his friend thoughtfully, Pierre said, "As a
colleague, I have great respect for your instincts. As a
policeman . . . pfft. Instincts are nothing but the uneasy
feeling you get when you're in a situation and tension is
building."

"That's what I'm afraid of."

"Nevertheless . . ." Pierre visibly debated with himself, then made the decision to speak. "Corruption is a
European problem. A Latin American problem. In Europe
and Latin America, it's well known that the police can be

bribed. Here in America, that's not a problem." He lifted his eyebrows. "Is it?"

"Not usually." Thinking hard, Reid fiddled with his napkin. "Of course, any time you put people in a position of power, there are those few who abuse it."

"But it's not just a few. It seems as if, well . . . Usually, you understand, as a foreign *agent de police,* I am shown almost anything I ask to see. You Americans, you are so proud of your computers, your organization. You think that we in France are probably in the Stone Age of police enforcement, so you brag. This time, when I made a few casual inquiries about this case, the police shut me down as if I were a common nosy citizen. And from what you've told me, they've been criminally reluctant to give even you information."

"That's true, but I've never been involved with the police before. I thought they were always so—"

"*Non,* not to the family involved. I tell you, I've been trained to observe, to tell if a man is lying by the way he stands, by the way he moves his hands, and *mon ami*"—Pierre placed his hand on Reid's shoulder—"I think the whole Houston Police Department is lying through their teeth."

"The Houston Police"—Pierre hushed him, and Reid lowered his voice—"have been lying to you?"

"And you."

"My God. Why?"

"If this were Europe or Latin America, I would know why. It's not, so I'm lost."

Still incredulous, Reid insisted, "The Houston Police are corrupt?"

"No. Yes. I honestly don't know. Almost, I said nothing, for I'm not sure . . ." Pierre rubbed his chin with his hand. "I can only say—do not totally depend on their resources. Maintain your own resources, too."

"I thought I was. What about Uncle Manuel?"

Pierre started eating again. "Oh, he has been lying, too, but he's an old man, and so proud of his falsehoods.

Perhaps he's in with the police and their scheme, but more likely he has perhaps slipped a bit and the police are manipulating him. It's your grandfather I don't understand.''

''That's nothing.'' Reid dipped his finger in Pierre's syrup. ''I've never understood Granddad.''

Pierre held his fork at readiness as Reid licked his finger. ''I think you understand him very well. I think you two are as alike as two peas. And don't you think the way your grandfather seems almost anxious to be kidnapped is odd?''

''Anxious? He's not''—Reid swooped in for another drop of syrup and brought back only four little dents in his hand—''Ouch! Anxious.''

''Try it again and I'll use the knife,'' Pierre warned. ''I'll defend my waffle to the last crumb.'' Leaning closer to Reid, he complained, ''Your grandfather relies totally on his servants—traditionally the originators of extortion schemes—and he forbids excess security men. He ignores your warnings about Martin Security, when it wouldn't—shouldn't—matter to him who the security firm is.''

''He's just a cantankerous old man,'' Reid protested, but Pierre had planted doubts, and he wondered if that was the truth.

''Yes, but . . . You're right, I suppose.'' Pierre shrugged. ''It's all probably my imagination. Or mostly my imagination. You know, you're in charge here. Why don't *you* change the security firm?''

''Where did you ever get the idea I was in charge?'' Pierre protested. ''A man's home—''

''This is my grandfather's home.''

''Will you live here after you marry her?''

''No, I'm taking her house-shopping to find another place here in Houston—'' Reid stopped, realizing what he'd admitted.

''Marriage?'' Pierre said loudly, and Reid shushed him. In a well-oiled maneuver from their college days, Pierre dropped his fork and Reid dropped his napkin, and they both leaned under the table. "Marriage?" Pierre hissed. "Are you sure?"

"Don't rub it in."

"This woman—"

"Her name is Margaret," Reid said sternly.

"Of course, forgive me. This Margaret has tightened the noose around the neck of the most notorious flirt on six continents?"

"There are seven continents."

"You've *been* to Antarctica?" Pierre asked, his eyebrows shooting up.

"No, I haven't, and I'm not as bad as all that. You know I reached the age of good sense a damn sight earlier than you."

"Then all those stories I hear about you—"

"I've been celibate for longer than I want to discuss." The corners of Reid's mouth turned down. "I've been involved with two women since I was thirty, each time thinking I could stand to spend the rest of my life with them."

"*Non?*"

"Non. They never felt right." Reid raised his hands helplessly and dropped them. "I didn't know what was missing—until Margaret."

"Lucky Margaret, I'd say."

"Oh, I agree with you. Now, if only I can convince—"

Beneath their noses, a fork appeared. Slowly, like little boys caught in a misdemeanor, they raised their joined heads. Margaret knelt beside them, dangling silverware and napkin. Her quizzical eyes examined them as they reddened. Without a word, she pressed the necessary accoutrements into their hands and disappeared.

With mutual dignity, they sat up in their chairs to see everyone staring at them.

"How much do you think she heard?" Reid asked out of the corner of his mouth.

Pierre refused to speculate, leaving only a shrug to express himself and moving on to a subject of intense interest to him. ''Does this mean I can make a move on that little redhead who flirted with you so determinedly last night?''

''Take her—with my blessing. In fact, if you could get her to France with you for a couple of weeks, I'd appreciate it. I'm tired of the distractions Margaret sticks under my nose with the assumption I'll snap at them like a weak-minded fool.''

''Weak-minded? Hmm.'' Pierre scratched his chin. ''I wouldn't call you weak-minded. Nor even weak-willed. Perhaps you should press your suit with a little more strength.''

''Sweep her off her feet? Don't you think I want to? I'm so frustrated, I'm jealous of my own grandfather. Besides''—Reid snorted—''she's had enough defense training, she's liable to sweep me off my feet, and the landing would not be soft.''

''I'll hear the landing all the way to France.''

''I suppose you will.''

The door shut with a bang. ''What are you doing?''

Margaret jumped, knocking her head against the frame of Reid's bed. ''Ouch.'' She rubbed the spot ruefully. ''Did you have to sneak up on me like that?''

''Next time I enter my bedroom,'' Reid said, ''I'll make a lot of noise just in case you're crawling around on the floor . . . doing what?''

Sitting with her back against the bed, she explained, ''Mr. Jim and Amy are at Manuel's, playing pool and eating his wife's tamales. Nagumbi has disappeared—''

''He's doing some snooping for me.''

''Right. And Abigail has the day off. Everyone's out of the way, so I thought I'd come in here and have a look around.''

He seemed to be only an illusion as he leaned against the closed door of his bedroom; a face and hands that stood out against the dark wood. It accented the ruddy highlights of his hair and blended with the black jogging suit he wore. Yet for an illusion, he was too solid, too focused, and he sounded almost chilly when he drawled, "Find anything interesting?"

He was offended, she diagnosed, and perhaps with reason. "I should have asked if you minded," she said apologetically. "I'm just so used to going in and out of rooms as I please, it never occurred to me. But really, this was your friend's suggestion."

"What friend?" Reid snapped.

"Your French friend. Pierre." She couldn't restrain the smile that curved her mouth. "What an interesting man."

"Is he?"

"You know he is."

"Some women might think so."

"Most women might think so," she corrected, thinking of the way Chantal had fallen. "Those continental manners, the kiss on the hand, his pronounced accent—"

"That bastard."

His vehemence startled her. "He's nice!"

He stepped forward, and his eyes glowed with an unholy light. "He's worthless."

"He is not!" She stood and brushed the seat of her skirt. "We had a long talk about your grandfather and these kidnapping threats, and he gave me more suggestions than I've received from Martin Security and the entire Houston Police Force put together."

"Suggestions," he sneered.

"Yes, suggestions," she repeated indignantly. "He *suggested* I search for listening devices in *your* room and *your* study, because—"

Reaching out, Reid grabbed her hand and jerked her into his Epicurean bathroom.

"What are you doing?" she shrieked.

"Hush." Reaching into his deluxe shower stall with its pulsating shower head and its built-in seat and its array of soaps, he twisted the knobs until the water gushed out full blast.

Pitching her voice above the roar, she asked, "What was that about?"

"*If* my room is bugged, we don't need to tell any listeners that you're on to them."

"Oh." She thought about that, pushing up her sleeves to combat the increasingly steamy atmosphere of the bathroom. "You're right, of course. I'll go back in and search, and we'll remain silent."

Looking increasingly annoyed, he blocked her path with one arm across the door. "Running away again?"

"Running away?" She pretended that she didn't know what he was talking about, and smiled weakly. "No, I'm just doing my job."

"Your job description does not include treating 'the master's' "—his intonation was sarcastic—"grandson like he has a terminal case of cooties."

She sputtered a weak laugh. "Cooties?"

His grim mouth never wavered. "Cooties. In fact, it's been a week since my party, and during that time you have rejected me and everything about me. I try to talk to you, to get to know you, and you flee as if the devil's on your heels. I send you flowers; you decorate Granddad's study with them. I send candy; it ends up in Abigail's kitchen. I arrange to take Amy to the zoo; your daughter and I go alone while you go off to lunch. The only time I see you unaccompanied by your various guardians is if you're in a room and I trap you there."

"Like now?"

Abrupt and precise, he removed the bar of his arm. "Go."

Perversely, his permission made her stay. He crossed his arms over his chest, and he seemed taller than he really was—and that was too tall. Speaking slowly and carefully, like a trainer to her new tiger, she said, "I don't understand what you expect of me."

"It's what I *don't* expect of you. I *don't* expect you to act as if I'm about to jump your bones, when all I've been trying to do is ease you into a normal relationship."

"Normal?" she mocked.

"You know. Conversation, teasing, hand holding, walks in

the sunshine. The things that men and women do when they're approaching a merger."

Provoked, she said, "I don't want a merger."

"Call it a hostile merger." He sounded so pleasant, but he wore his barracuda smile. "It happens all the time. A big, bad corporation gobbles up a tiny little company, and together they cause a growth explosion."

She tried to slip past him, but she'd missed her chance. His hands grasped her waist and lifted her onto the counter with one easy motion. She swung her leg experimentally, warning him, and he said, "I just want to kiss you, darlin'. Would you incapacitate me for one little kiss?"

"Why shouldn't I?"

"For one little kiss?" he asked incredulously. "Do you think one little kiss will be that earthshaking?"

"No . . ." No, of course it wouldn't, and she had things to prove to him. If he wanted to kiss her, she'd let him. She'd provide proof of her own indifference to him. And prove to herself he wasn't the spectacular lover her unruly body expected. He leaned forward, slowly and carefully, giving her time to withdraw if she wished. He touched his closed lips to her closed lips, a dry kiss of mutual exploration. It excited her, woke nerve endings she'd decided were atrophied.

Maybe experimenting wasn't such a good idea, after all. Trying to slide off the counter, she said, "Okay. You've had your kiss."

His amusement mocked her. "You call that a kiss?"

"What do you call it?"

"A preliminary. Let's do this right, okay?"

"I suppose."

Making a yummy sound, he slid his fingers up the nyloned length of her leg to her knee. His other hand reached out and flexed around her other knee. "You're so sweet."

He said it so fervently, she should have been warned. Instead he stepped between her legs, and pulled her against him before she could complain. Her skirt rode up; the tile was cool and smooth beneath her thighs. It contrasted with the heat of Reid, close between her legs. He fit them together carefully, and she looked down at them, where they were joined but for the insignificant partitions of clothing, then up at him. His sherry eyes gleamed fire and pleasure, dominating her in a way that caused thorns of pride to goad her. Surely she could retain her composure; surely she could.

But her brain functioned at a subnormal level, clogged by the tide of hormones he incited. She felt dependent, vulnerable, and she shivered as one hand slid all the way up to her hips.

"I've waited for you forever," he vowed, wrapping his big hand around the nape of her neck. With his thumb, he lifted her chin. "I didn't even know what I was waiting for." His lips sipped at her mouth like a connoisseur tasting a well-loved wine. His teeth nibbled at her lower lip until she opened just a little, wanting another taste of him, forbidden though it might be.

He encouraged her, subtly coaxing until her tongue was in his mouth and she was on the offensive. Her hands tugged at his hair, her arms pulled him into her chest, and she moved against him as if he were a familiar and cherished lover.

Luxuriating in her aggression, he groaned and sighed, and the sounds of his pleasure jerked her from nirvana. How did he make her want what he wanted so cunningly? How did he shut off the well-primed defenses that kept her from disaster?

Reading her body language, anticipating her retreat, he tilted her, arching her back over his arm and taking command of the kiss. In one easy movement, he rendered her off balance in body and spirit, and her squirming accomplished nothing but to make her aware of the changes in his anatomy. She fought to keep her eyes open—a distraction to the most accomplished of kissers—but found her lids kept drooping. The most revealing of tiny sounds vibrated the back of her throat, and his hand found the arch of her neck and rested there, as if he were reveling in her reaction.

When he pulled back and looked at her, draped across his arm and stunned with pleasure, a peculiar expression crossed his face. In any other man, she would have called it love. That tender quirk of pride and delight alarmed her more than any other manifestation of desire, and like a rabbit burrowing from trouble, she ducked her head into his chest.

His voice was a rumble, an earthshaking event. "You're the woman for me, and I'll convince you of it with all the bricks and blocks and mortar at my disposal. I'll build an edifice of knowing in you that you'll never destroy with your fears and your skepticism."

SEVEN

"Oh, no, you won't." Margaret pulled away from the false comfort of Reid's arms. His hands tangled in her hair, and she could hear the *ting, ting* of her pins as they struck the tile. "No edifices for me."

His hand went to her cheek, and he stroked it. "Wouldn't you like to come with me and discover my secrets? I'm only a man, after all, and you might find what's between us isn't as cataclysmic as you fear."

He might be a man, but he wasn't *only* a man. And the cataclysm she feared shook her even now, after only a kiss. His face was a course in salesmanship, but she said steadfastly, "I'm refusing you."

He stared as if stunned, then shot backward as if he couldn't stand to touch her any longer. With a wealth of bitterness, he accused, "You'd care for a rabid dog and destroy a lover who's had all his shots." Reaching into the shower again, he adjusted the temperature.

"I have the right to refuse you," she said, sliding off the counter.

"Yes, you do. And I have the right to take a cold shower." He walked into the shower, slapping the door shut behind him.

"Don't be foolish," she yelled, hobbling over. Her skirt

sagged around her waist, and she absently acknowledged his mastery; when had his nimble fingers undone the fastenings at the back? "Your clothes . . ." She swung the frosted glass door wide, and found him glaring at her.

His jogging suit sopped up the water. His sweat shirt stretched, the elastic in his pants strained under the weight. "Run away while you can, little girl."

Wringing her hands, feeling foolish and quite unlike the rational butler she knew herself to be, she objected, "You can't expect me to leave when so much is unsettled."

He gestured grandly. "Then come in. Perhaps this cold water'll thaw a little of that frozen interior."

That made her mad, as mad as he seemed to be. "I must be frigid," she mocked, stepping in and stepping up to him. Cold water pelted her, spraying off his shoulders and around his face. "That's the only reason any woman could resist you."

"How true that is." With a grand gesture, he pulled his sweat shirt off and flung it through the open shower door at the mirror.

Water splatted all over the mirror, the sinks, the tile, and she scolded, "Now look what you did. I'll have to send one of the maids in to—" She faltered. The sunshine filtering through the window flattered him, imbuing his sparse body hair with the beauty of a great cat's coat. Her hands tingled, wanting to stroke him, but instead, she bent down, pulled off her one wet black leather heel, and tossed it after the sweat shirt.

"Now look what you've done." He imitated her in high falsetto. "I'll have to call one of the maids to clean up."

"God, you're a jerk."

He laughed with deliberate insolence and retorted, "God, you're a tease."

"I'm not!"

He laughed again, and she followed his gaze down at herself. Her jacket sagged about her shoulders, baring her bosom where the clinging white of a silk shirt hid nothing. Her black vest framed her breasts for emphasis. Her bra was obviously unruly, for one chilled nipple thrust itself above the cup and dared him to take notice.

He noticed.

He burned like an oil fire, unextinguished by the sluice of cold water drenching him. He controlled the flame with a mighty stillness, and his lips scarcely moved as he warned, "I'd run away now, if I were you."

The only sound in the bathroom was the rush of water and her own harsh breathing. She couldn't stop looking at his face, at the tense muscles and hot eyes. She couldn't stop looking at his body, lean and hungry for her.

Their chemistry exploded when put in contact, but still he denied himself what he could have so easily. He was impatient, but not unselfish, and something in her ignited.

The something seemed to be in her heart, and she might not want it, but it existed. It urged her, cajoled her, dared her to reveal a little bit of herself. An unimportant part of herself. For if she touched him, joined with him, surely that wouldn't mean she liked him . . . loved him.

He said again, "Go."

"No."

The words dropped into the stillness between them, breaking it like a stone breaks the ice on a puddle, and he moved on her before she could deny the impulse. Crowding her against the copper tile wall, he plastered his body against hers and kissed her with the finesse of a liberty-bound sailor—and she kissed him back.

"God," he breathed into her mouth. "Give me all of you."

His exhilaration poured more fuel on her flames. She tried to wrap one leg around his hips, but her skirt was too tight.

He tried to unbutton her shirt, but the silk was too unwieldy. His hands flashed to her neck, and the wet silk ripped with ease. A few buttons clinked on the floor, but most hung intact on the torn blouse.

Her excitement raced to meet his. "You dare," she

breathed, and in a grand gesture, flung off her jacket and shirt. As with all grand gestures, it went awry.

Her hands caught in the tight cuffs, but Reid jerked both buttons free for her, then stopped to stare and sigh. "Like a puppy's nose peeking out, begging me to pet it," he said, but the chuckle caught in her throat as he touched one trembling finger to that impudent nipple.

The contact jolted them both, and he groaned, "I can't wait." His palms spanned her waist and stroked the hose and the skirt all the way down her long, long legs. He slid back up her body and placed a lingering kiss on her plain white cotton underwear. The clothes spun over the top of the door, and as he looked at her, he groaned again. Groping behind him, he adjusted the water, bringing it to a comfortable temperature while his gaze absorbed her.

She was committed now. Committed to this act of love. She corrected herself. To this act of *lust*. There was no turning back, and she didn't want to turn back. Aware of her power over him, she pulled her headband off and shook out her hair with a challenging smile. Ducking beneath the water, she let it run over her until she was soaked, until the scraps of material she still wore revealed everything but hid too much.

Reid's expression was equally challenging, but unsmiling. Taking up the shampoo, he measured some of the creamy liquid into the palm of his hand. She watched curiously as he spread it between his hands and reached for her. The rich lather sprang to life under his fingers, freeing her blond hair from the restraints of gravity as he scrubbed it into a mass on top of her head.

Uncertain, she tried to take over from him, but he brushed her hands aside. "Relax," he whispered. "Feel this."

Sensuality, he forced her to realize, was not confined to the accepted erogenous zones. His fingertips fed magic through the nerves in her scalp, her neck, around the shells of her ears. His gaze followed a blob of shampoo as it drifted down the side of her neck. He followed it as it swept down her chest and then came to linger on the edge of her lacy bra. His eyes met hers once more, filled with a mixture of desire and a hard possession.

Plunging his hands into her hair, he brought forth a renewed lather and muttered, "This shampoo is an erotic tool unsurpassed by any mentioned in the Kama Sutra." Gathering drifts of fragrant lemon suds, he rubbed them on her neck, on her chest, on the one nipple that pebbled beneath his hand. The front clasp of her bra slipped open, seemingly by itself, and those torturing hands wandered to her stomach, down . . .

She caught his hand, and he grinned. "Let me." He rubbed shampoo on his own chest. "Here." Linking their hands, palm to palm, he rubbed their bodies together. Skin glided, flowed, in the most decadent sensation Margaret had ever experienced. It was like being massaged with mink or sable, but the massager was alive and rippling with muscle. The massager groaned and moved, and then, with a boldness that stole her breath, picked her up with a hand under each knee and wrapped her legs around him.

She was pressed against the wall; his hips undulated against her and she moaned, "Too heavy . . ."

"No," he sighed. "Saved myself . . ."

The sensation was too exquisite to endure. With smooth determination, he put her legs down and pushed her under the shower head. He scrubbed the soap from her hair, rubbed the lather from her body, took her panties from her hips and let them drop to the floor. As he rinsed himself, she shrugged her shoulders, and the bra slid away. Wiping the water from her face, he stared seriously into her eyes. "If we do this now, will we be parents in nine months?"

Margaret covered her mouth in surprise and nodded. She had forgotten that basic biology fact in the rush of pleasure.

Reid nodded back. "I'll take care of it." He peeled off his pants. Like a magician, he produced a package out of his pocket and showed her.

"Do you always keep them on you?" Margaret asked, aghast by the evidence of promiscuity in the man she was about to love.

"No, darlin'." Reid chuckled and eased her down on the tile seat. "Only when I hope to hustle one sexy, over-confident little butler." He followed her down, kneeling between her thighs. "Let me prepare you more."

"You can't. There is no *more*." His fingers found her, thrust into her, rubbed her, and she convulsed in sweet agony.

He laughed. The sound wasn't threatening or humiliating, but pleased and excited. "Help me," he commanded, tearing the foil and pressing the condom into her palm.

Her hands shook as she stared at the roll, then at him. His face was rigid with hedonism, waiting for her to decide, waiting for release.

"All *right*." She reached for him, pulled back, gathered her nerve, and laid her hand on him—and discovered the source of his heat and his hurry. It strained and pulsated and transmitted to her his urgency. No longer shy, she rolled the condom along his length, and Reid quivered with her touch.

"Look at me, love." Right above her, looking down at her, his eyes flashed a message of enchantment. "Now." He entered her easily. As her flesh swallowed his, an indescribable savor relaxed her muscles.

Then they were off, galloping away with the pleasure. He slowed for her when she shuddered, slowed when her toes pointed and her teeth clenched, slowed as climax after climax jolted her. Then he hurried off again, flying toward his satisfaction and never quite getting there. His voice cajoled, tantalized, whispered suggestions that tickled her ear as they teased her mind. His hands stroked, caressed, propelled her head to his chest, urged her mouth to taste him. His approval showered on her, like the water that splattered off his shoulders in a fine mist and ran in rivulets between his pectorals.

Their rhythm unbroken, he pulled her off the seat, sink-ing to rest on his bent knees. His hands steadied her spine as she took control, using her legs to drive the pulse of their lovemaking. His mouth caught her nipple and suckled eagerly: she slowed the demands of her body to savor it. The tendons of his shoulders strained beneath her hands as he tensed to match their separate tempos, but at last he gasped, "No more." Holding her clamped to him, he swung her onto the floor of the shower and began the powerful thrusts that signified his culmination.

Her back melted into the floor tiles, her feet clenched his spine. Drenched by spray, surrounded by rushing water, she sensed the peaking triumph burgeoning within her. She couldn't contain it, it was too grand, too overwhelming to mandate. In one titanic surge, she clamped her arms around him, her legs around him, her body around him. Sounds broke from her throat, uncensored by art or prudence: sounds echoed in her ears as Reid poised above her. Every muscle was devoted to their flowering: every movement amplified their elation. It was earthy sorcery, magic carnality, and for a moment they were lost in the mist of victory together.

Then she released him, and he sank atop her. Tiny aftershocks jarred her, and he encouraged them with subtle meanderings of his fingers, with deft rocking of his hips. She came to rest at last. Opening her eyes, she saw his shoulder jutted up, protecting her from the spray. She saw the copper tile surrounding her, felt the discomfort of the ceramic floor, heard the clamor of the water as it cascaded down the walls. Her limp hands fell away, her feeble legs slipped off him.

Reid leaned to one side and caressed the sun of her hair where it joined her face. "Next time," he suggested, "we'll use the trapeze." His voice reverberated through his chest, through her where they joined.

She blinked.

"It's a good thing we have a big water tank." Elevating himself, he stared down at them, at her, as if he savored the closeness.

She flushed with a sudden glow. He looked at her as if she were the most gorgeous woman in the world. As if she were a goddess of ancient Greece, with arms and head attached. As if she were the first woman he had ever seen.

His voice rumbled with tenderness. "Next time—"

Her attention snapped into place. "Next time? What do you mean, next time?"

He raised his eyebrows; his eyes smiled. "Just what I said."

"No next time. No way," Margaret said indignantly.

"You're mighty bold for a woman in your position." He nodded at their twined bodies, at her lax ease.

Her legs snapped to attention. "Please."

"Get off? Of course."

He removed himself from her body, and the physical pang of regret shocked her. He pushed himself up, resting on his hands and knees above her. His posture showed his reluctance to leave her; his eyes ate her as she slid from beneath his frame. Rising, he extended a hand to her. She gazed at the broad palm with indecision until he teased, "What are you afraid of? I've already done my worst." Reaching down, he grasped her wrist and hauled her up. "Or my best." Indulgent laughter curled through her hair, and he reached for the bar of soap. "I think I've fallen in love with the scent of lemon."

Planting her feet firmly, she tried to gaze at him, wanted to reason with him, but he turned her to wash her back. To the wall, she said, "You've had me now—"

"Amen to that." He rubbed her shoulders with soapy hands, rubbed her back, slid in twin circles on her buttocks.

"—and I'm sure you've discovered I'm just a woman."

"Not just a woman," he corrected. "My woman."

She swiveled on him, and panic closed her throat. If he had been angry or cold, she could have handled it. But Reid was simply amused and lenient, willing to humor her and sure he would get his own way. As he smiled and soaped his hands again, she protested, "I have a daughter, an impressionable child. We can't have sex whenever we—"

"Sex? That wasn't sex." He scrubbed soap down her arms, between her fingers, across the palm of her hand. "That, my unsophisticated darling, was the most magnificent mating since peanut butter and celery, melba toast and Brie." Leaning down, he lightly bit her nipple. "Yum."

"Unusual combinations," she choked.

"Yes, we are. But perfect together."

Her traitorous body shifted, eager to indulge itself even while her tongue denied it. "I don't want to be one of your women. I can't come running for a quickie every time you whistle. I'm a butler, a mother—"

"My woman," he repeated. He transferred his attention to the other breast.

Spelling it out, she said, "I cannot fornicate with you every—"

He interrupted her. "Do you know who encouraged me to come after you?"

"Your grandfather, no doubt," she said bitterly.

"Oh, no, my fabulous darling. I've heard urging and suggesting and downright nagging this last week, and it all started at the zoo."

Margaret's mouth snapped closed and the last remnants of passion fled. Drawing herself up, she said, "That's a terrible thing to say."

Reid leaned back against the copper-colored tile and folded his arms across his chest. "Take the bull by the horns, Amy said. No use waiting for Mom to change her mind, she said, because once it's set, only a federal amendment could sway it."

"You brought it up to her. You prompted her!" she cried.

He grabbed her arms and dragged her close, chest to chest. "I don't drag children into these kinds of battles."

His temper flared so hot, she felt scorched by the flame, but she boldly searched his eyes. What she saw there relaxed her suspicions and made her sorry. He looked hurt, as if she'd stabbed both his honor and his affection for Amy. "I know you don't. I apologize, but how did the subject come up?"

"You know your daughter; you know she's sharp as a tack and twice as bright about human relations as any psychotherapist. Is it any surprise that she's noticed what's happening between you and me?"

"Nothing's happening between . . ." She faltered; he looked so sardonic.

"This"—his gaze swept the shower—"was a hell of a passionate nothing."

Margaret sat on the balcony outside her bedroom and stared into the night. Venus shone just above the trees, bright and unblinking, and she cursed it. "Goddess of Love, indeed. Are you responsible for my behavior today?"

Oddly, she heard no answer. She had made a terrible, terrible mistake by opening the doors to her own sensuality. She'd put her body in the deep freeze for so long, she'd imagined it was solid. Now life was pulsing into the frostbitten parts, and it hurt. It stung, it throbbed, and she didn't want to have to deal with it.

Why did it have to be with Reid?

In some vague way, she'd imagined that she'd find another man one day and they'd marry. Her dreams had been of a mature love, gentle and kind and tender, without the peaks and valleys that characterized youthful passion. So what if she hardly qualified for the senior citizens' tour of Florida? At thirty-four, she felt as if she'd lived forever. Luke had been sick for so long. So wretchedly sick, and each day had been filled with midnight, and each week had stretched eternally. The young woman she'd been before had vanished in the night of illness. All her inner joy had faded; if it weren't for Amy, she thought she'd be terminally grim.

Now she'd made love with a man who thought he'd discovered sex. His eyes had glowed with fervor as he appreciated her body with hands and mouth. He'd made no secret of his heady arousal, yet combined his impatience with inventiveness and endurance.

He'd laughed when they made love. Laughed! As if sex was a joyful experience, as if he'd never been so happy.

Damn him, he'd driven her to impatience and inventiveness and rekindled the demands of her body—and, she feared, rekindled the demands of her own loving heart.

She groaned out loud, and from behind her Amy said, "Mom?"

Margaret jumped, half-afraid she'd been talking to herself and Amy had listened. Her normal serene voice hit a high note as she asked, "Yes, dear?"

"Are you okay?"

"Fine, dear."

"You sounded sick."

Margaret hesitated. What could she say? "I'm fine. I just sat on my foot wrong."

"Is it asleep?" Amy came eagerly onto the balcony. "Do you want me to massage it?"

Sticking out her stocking-clad foot, Margaret grinned through the darkness at her daughter. "Talked me into it. Shut the door behind you or you'll let the bugs in the house." The screen bounced against the frame, and Margaret winced at her daughter's enthusiasm.

Amy pulled up a chair and took her mother's foot into her lap. "You always do this for me when I have growing pains."

"I had 'em when I was your age, too."

"Did you have two parents when you were my age?"

The tone was innocent, the question was not, and Margaret considered it carefully before answering. "No, actually, I didn't. My parents were divorced. They treated me like a hot potato. 'You take her.' 'No, you take her.' Getting stuck with the kid was punishment."

"I'll bet you missed having two parents," Amy soothed.

She was like a bulldog, Margaret mused, grabbing hold of one idea and never releasing it. "That's why I always adored your daddy's family so much. So close and loving.''

"Yes, now I feel like I have two families," Amy said brightly. "Daddy's family and Mr. Jim's family."

The child was tenacious, but Margaret had a question she'd longed to ask, and the quiet and darkness around them eased her trepidations. "Do you remember your daddy?"

"Sure." Amy sounded perky and certain. "He was funny."

"He was that. Do you remember what he looked like?"

"Yes." She didn't seem to be so positive about that. "He was real thin, and his hands trembled when he held me."

Margaret didn't say anything, and Amy said, "I've seen your wedding picture. He was good-looking when he was young, wasn't he?"

He never had the chance to get old. Margaret wanted to say it, but what would that do but make Amy feel ignorant and uncomfortable? A child of nine can accept what her mother struggled with, and Margaret didn't want to destroy that acceptance. This was better for Amy. The girl's fading memory left her with no bitterness and an eager resolution to find another father.

"Do your feet feel better, Mama?"

Amy sounded anxious, sensing Margaret's abstraction, and Margaret leaned over and patted her hand. "It felt so good, I drifted off for a moment. Aren't you supposed to be in bed now?"

"I had to massage my mother's feet first."

Amy laughed as Margaret growled, "I knew I kept you around for something."

Amy didn't move from her perch on the chair, and Margaret thought, *Uh-oh*. When her daughter sat still, trouble was brewing. Maybe the dark made it easier for Amy to confess something, too. Maybe she hadn't come out just to urge marriage on her mother. In her most soothing voice, Margaret asked, "What is it, honey?"

"I've been wanting to tell you this for a while."

Now Margaret could hear Amy squirming, could see her movements in the glow of city lights around them. "You can tell me anything, dear."

"I know I can." Amy sounded strained. "But you're going to be mad about this one."

"I promise not to get mad."

"Promise?"

"Promise."

"Sir Gramps has left me his horse ranch in east Texas."

"What?" Margaret shouted, surging to her feet.

"You promised," Amy reminded.

Margaret just stood there. She knew her mouth was hanging open. She knew she'd failed to live up to her daughter's expectations of a fair hearing. But never in her life had she imagined . . . "Tell me about it," she whispered.

Amy's voice squeaked. "Are you mad?"

"No, I'm not mad." She took a deep breath and subsided into her chair. "Not much, anyway. Not at you, anyway. How did this happen?"

"Well, remember when I went to the stud farm last spring break?"

"Yes."

"I came back and told Sir Gramps how much I loved it and I wanted my own horse and all that stuff, and you told me to stop telling him or we'd have a horse grazing on the lawn, and it was against the law inside Houston."

"Right."

"Remember how Sir Gramps just laughed and said if you spread a little money around, nobody cares how much manure's in the grass?"

"Except he didn't say manure. I remember." Margaret reached up and massaged her own neck. She could see where this was going, and she wondered how she could have missed it before.

"Well, when I came back from California, Sir Gramps

told me he wanted to give me a gift. So he gave me the stud farm.''

"And you said . . . ?"

"Thank you," Amy said proudly.

Margaret began to chuckle. It was too much to suppose a nine-year-old would have the phrase "This is too much" in her vocabulary. "Dear girl," she tried to say, but the laughter just kept coming. "Dear girl," she tried again. "We can't afford to have him give you a stud farm.''

"Well, why not?" Amy sounded indignant, but not surprised.

"We can't afford to feed the horses; we can't afford to pay the taxes; we can't afford any of it. A stud farm is a rich man's toy."

"Oh, it's okay," Amy answered, very sure of herself. "Sir Gramps left me the money to pay for all that stuff."

Abruptly Margaret's laughter cut off. "What do you mean, he left you the money to pay for it? How much money?"

"I don't know, I didn't ask him. I was just so happy. But then I started thinking . . . maybe you wouldn't like it."

"An understatement if ever I've heard one."

"I'm sorry," Amy said, misery in her tone.

Margaret held out her arms, and Amy jumped into her lap. "Don't be sorry, honey. It's Mr. Jim all the way." She stroked her hand through Amy's short curls. "You're going to have to hold me in your lap if you grow much more."

"I *am* getting big, aren't I?" Amy asked proudly.

"You sure are. Whatever happened to that little baby I rocked?"

Amy laid her head back and looked up at her. "I'm still here."

Squeezing her tight, Margaret patted her daughter until she was sure Amy no longer worried about the "gift." Casually she asked, "When did Mr. Jim say you would get this gift?"

"After he died. He said he wanted to just give it to me, but he was . . ."

"Was what?"

"He said something really weird. I think he said he was baiting a hook with his will."

Amy was puzzled. Margaret was not. "That damned old—"

"Mah-om!"

"Never mind. I'll take care of it," Margaret assured her.

"Do I have to give it back?"

"You haven't got it yet. But yes, you'll have to give it back. At least now I know why Reid was so angry when he heard about that will." She swatted Amy's behind. "Bedtime."

Standing, Amy kissed Margaret. "Mom, we need to go get me some school supplies for my science project."

"Okay, honey. We'll go this weekend."

"Mom, I need to get started," Amy nagged.

Margaret sighed. "Is it going to be as messy as last year? I'll tell you right now, I'm putting my foot down when it comes to living plants."

"Okay," Amy said brightly.

"And no animals of either amphibious or reptilian extraction."

"Okay." The child's chipper enthusiasm dipped.

Margaret hugged her with all her might, instructing, "Call me when you're in bed and I'll tuck you in."

Amy made it through the door, and then she stuck her head back out. "If I had another father, he could tuck me in sometimes."

She slammed the door before Margaret could reply, and Margaret clasped her head in her hands. Who remembered the handsome, vibrant man she married? Other people had their memories. His father remembered his son, Lucius. His colleagues remembered their friend, Dr. Guarneri. Only she remembered him as her husband, Luke: talking with her, fighting with her, loving her. Those memories were fading, and she fiercely resented it.

She resented Reid.

She'd satisfied her curiosity about Reid, and she'd never let him take her again. But she was haunted by one question. She watched Venus set behind the trees and asked that heartless goddess, "How can I handle the fact *I* want to take him?"

_____ EIGHT _____

"Mr. Donovan, can I speak to you for a minute?"

Reid raised his head from the pile of work on his desk and the computer keyboard in his lap. "Of course; come in."

Reid watched with a cynical amusement as Cliff Martin sneaked through the study door like a substandard James Bond and eased it shut behind him.

"I hate to bother you when you're working."

"It's all right." Rubbing his neck beneath the casual open-necked tennis shirt, Reid gestured the security man into a chair. "My eyes are exhausted, anyway."

"I don't know how you can stand to sit there and look at one of them computer screens, anyway. They ain't safe."

"Really?" Startled, Reid asked, "Why's that?"

"Haven't you heard?" Cliff's eyes widened. "The rays off the screen'll make you sterile."

Reid blinked. "Gracious."

"There's all those viruses and stuff in the machines—"

"In the software," Reid corrected.

"Right. You just can't trust computers."

Reid leaned back in his executive chair and studied

Cliff. The man was wearing the same brown pin-striped suit he'd worn the first time they'd met, and it looked as if he'd slept in it every night since. The bags under his faithful hound-dog eyes were more pronounced. The smell of cigars hung heavy around him, and the telltale yellow stained his fingers. He seemed to have taken a plunge into ignorance, with his silly warnings about computers and their dangers.

But Reid couldn't ignore the taut shrewdness of the mouth, nor could he ignore Pierre's suggestion of corruption, so he said gently, "I make my living with these computers."

"Oh, yeah." Cliff fumbled in his pocket and pulled out the half-smoked stub of a cigar.

Struggling to remember that the man worked for him, struggling to remember that that was no excuse for excessive rudeness, Reid directed, "Not in here."

"What?" Cliff raised the wounded, infuriated, innocent face of a nicotine addict.

"You can't smoke in here."

Cliff's eyes slid to the smelly ashtray.

"Uncle Manuel and his pipe. Unfortunately, I don't have enough seniority over him to forbid his pipe." The words hovered unspoken in the air—*but I do have enough seniority over you.*

Dropping the cigar back into his coat pocket, Cliff dusted his fingers. "I'm quitting anyway."

"Good idea," Reid agreed. "What have you uncovered about the extortionists?"

"Me? Nothing. The police here don't take kindly to folks sticking their noses into official investigations. My job is just security; making sure they don't snatch your grandfather."

"Where were you when he was snatched?"

"Busy trusting the wrong people, I can tell you. I should never have taken that time off to go to my uncle's funeral." Cliff clucked his tongue mournfully. "I mean, I leave town for one day, and see what happens? This kidnapper's definitely an insider.'' He tapped his forehead. "Knows too much.''

"I'm afraid I have to agree. Have you found any incriminating evidence about the, er, insiders?''

"Oh, everybody has some *thing* that makes them a suspect. That footman, Simon, needs the money. He's going to school and working and sending home money to his mother. Abigail's in love with that Nagumbi fellow— maybe she's doing it to get his attention. Nagumbi . . .'' Cliff rolled his eyes. "That guy is strange, and—''

"He's beyond suspicion,'' Reid said firmly.

Cliff snapped to attention. "Of course. But it would certainly make my work a lot easier if we could put a few more men inside. Having one guy standing around dressed like one of the queen's guards might be entertaining for old—for Mr. Donovan, but it's tough getting good men who're willing to do it.''

"Money is a mighty incentive.''

"I know, but don't you think we could get a few more people in the house?'' Reid was already shaking his head, but Cliff persisted. "Just a few more people to beef up security? With only one guy inside and a couple lurking outside, I'll tell you the truth, I can't guarantee we'll always be able to keep tabs on your grandpop.''

"Mr. Donovan''—Reid stressed the name—"doesn't like the feeling of being trapped in his own home, and if we tried to bring more people in, he'd have all of them thrown out.''

"Can't you use your influence?'' Cliff whined.

"I'm combat-trained; so is Ms. Guarneri. You'll have to depend on us.''

"You, yes.'' He wagged a finger at Reid's nose. "I don't know about Ms. Guarneri. That's actually what brings me here.''

Reid raised a questioning eyebrow.

Cliff drew it out. "Are you ready?''

"Yes,'' Reid said shortly, gritting his teeth on the answer he wanted to give.

Cliff delved into his suit coat again, this time pulling a plain gold envelope from the inside pocket. In contrast to the rest of his person, this envelope was unmarked, uncreased, and clean. Pulling his chair closer to the desk, he opened it and pulled out several photographs. Half standing, he spread them out, one at a time, before Reid, and Reid had no more time for speculation about Cliff.

In the pictures before him, Margaret sat in various poses. Worried, smiling, serious, concerned, all her expressions were caught by the camera, as were the expressions of the two men she was with.

Jolted, Reid studied the snapshots with strained nonchalance. Masking his shock—but not soon enough, he feared—he leaned back and asked, "Well?"

"I thought this was something you should see," Cliff said. "Our little Miss Margaret seems to have more going on than she tells us."

Reid gestured to him to continue.

"She's been meeting these guys frequently for lunch."

"Only for lunch?" Reid asked, remembering the afternoon Margaret had taken off to go get Amy. She surely wouldn't involve her daughter with these . . . strangers.

"Yeah, only for lunch. I talked to the owner of the café. She used to meet them about once a week; she's kicked it up to two, three days a week."

"Who are the men?" Frost touched Reid's face, his words.

"Can't say. Sure are swarthy buggers, though, aren't they?"

Reid leaned over the pictures again, picking them up one at a time. "Yes, they are. Some kind of Mediterranean extraction, I'd say."

"You know how those foreigners are. Always organizing into gangs and blowing each other's heads off, when they're not kidnapping helpless old men."

"Do you have any evidence for what you're saying?" Reid peered up at Cliff, still leaning on the desk.

"Nope. That's why I brought this to you. Usually I can

find information on anybody if I try. Hell, I can tell you which breakfast cereal our Miss Margaret preferred when she was eight. But these guys are a total mystery, and that's not normal. They don't seem to have a job. I followed them. Don't seem to have a past.'' Cliff subsided back into his chair. ''As good-looking as those two are, I couldn't help but wonder if our Miss Margaret's had her head turned.''

Reid picked up one snapshot and examined it. Margaret stared back at him, all blond poise. She was smiling at the man across from her. Reid studied the man's perfect profile: tanned skin, flashing white teeth, dark hair falling gracefully across his forehead. Reid pointed to the bastard Margaret was smiling at. ''I don't see what's so attractive about *him*.''

''Neither do I,'' Cliff agreed. ''I can't see what's so attractive about his brother, either, but there's no accounting for women's taste. Every damn time our Miss Margaret left the café, those two guys had to fight off the females.'' Digging in his pocket, he pulled out the half-smoked cigar. ''Couple of damn Roman gods.''

''His brother?'' Reid stared at the other man's face, so similar to the other, so beautiful in its masculine way. There was Margaret, seated at their table, smiling at them without a wary tremble to her lips. He'd give half his fortune to have her look at him like that, and here she was, smiling at a couple of hoodlums. A couple of Roman god hoodlums. Absorbed in his agonizing appraisal, Reid never noticed as Cliff struck a match and puffed until the cigar glowed. ''How do you know those are brothers?''

''Well, look at them.'' Cliff stood up and shuffled through until he found what he sought. His stubby finger pointed at the two male faces, clearly visible in one photograph. ''If those two aren't related, I'm not Cliff Martin.''

Distracted, Reid frowned. There was a thought. Maybe this *wasn't* Cliff Martin. He resolved to have Nagumbi check it out—maybe that was what made all his instincts jangle. Fixing Cliff with his cool gaze, he assessed him.

Cliff stood, his stogie smoking between his fingers, and looked at his employer, but he hadn't the dominance to keep eye contact. He shuffled his feet, he stubbed out his cigar in Manuel's ashtray.

Reid shook his head. It was hard to believe this fool was anything but what he said. Returning to the matter at hand, he snapped, "Have you brought this to the attention of the police?"

"No, sir."

He leaned over to gather up the photographs, but Reid smoothly refused. "I'll keep these, if you don't mind."

"No. Oh, no, there's plenty more where those came from. I've got the negatives."

He curved his mouth; Reid supposed it was a smile. Cliff began to back toward the door, accelerating when Reid asked, "Why haven't you gone to the police?"

"There's nothing incriminating here, just suspicious. It'd take more than this to interest the police." Cliff hesitated at the doorsill. "I just thought *you'd* be curious. Something to think about as you shower."

Reid stared at Margaret as she picked up the papers Jim had dropped. Joking with his grandfather, she looked nothing like a criminal. Yet why would she be meeting strangers on the sly?

A clever cross-examination on his part had revealed nothing. She met friends at lunch, she admitted. When pressed, she said their names were Dommy and Jules—two androgynous names if he'd ever heard them. Reid rocked his desk chair back and forth in disgust. The woman felt no qualms about telling him to mind his own business when he pressed too hard, either.

Sifting through the information he knew about her had yielded nothing. Nagumbi confirmed that she was just what she said, a widow with a daughter, a butler with a degree in English literature.

He'd confirmed that Cliff Martin was Cliff Martin, son of the Kentucky security magnate. Reid just wished there were someone he could ask about Cliff's parting remark. What did he mean, "something to think about as you shower"? Had Margaret acknowledged their relationship to Abigail, perhaps? Bragged about shampoo as an aphrodisiac? Had Cliff heard through the grapevine? Did Reid's own bedroom hold no privacy, or was Cliff's comment a lucky shot in the dark? The answers left Reid uneasy and speculative, for there were no answers.

That left Reid with his instincts.

Examining his own acclaimed instincts revealed no discomfort, no suspicion of Margaret. True, his instincts clamored when he looked at her, but the clamor sounded like wedding bells.

That might be the problem. Maybe, just maybe, he couldn't see the warning signs for the stars in his eyes.

Margaret laughed with Jim, distracting Reid from his cogitation, and then smiled at him—nervously.

What did that mean? What did she have to be nervous about? Why did she persist on trying to slide out of the room when his grandfather needed her?

"Reid. Reid!"

Reid switched his gaze to his grandfather.

"Nice to have your attention at last, boy." Jim was looking annoyed. "Would you stop glaring at Margaret long enough to let her finish helping me clean off my desk? She's as jumpy as a grasshopper in a prairie fire. Turn those brooding orbs of yours to your work."

"All right," Reid agreed absently. He glanced at his computer screen, looked down to straighten the crease in his blue jeans, and glanced back up at Margaret. Damn, she was a fine-looking woman. Clad in that black and white butler's suit, she set his heart to thumping. But if it were up to him, he'd put her in pure teal blue, or perhaps in that marvelous African violet purple.

It bothered him that he daydreamed about her wardrobe. He was a man, with a man's distaste for shopping, but for her he'd traipse through every store in the Galleria with an open wallet.

Perhaps she had reason to meet these men, and perhaps that reason had nothing to do with extortion. Perhaps the loving in the shower yesterday couldn't keep her satisfied. Perhaps . . . Reid shook his head and muttered, "No." Without self-flattery, he knew that the steam in that bathroom hadn't all been from hot water.

"Maybe the extortionists have given up," Reid said, out of the blue.

Two heads, one white and balding, one silver as moonshine, lifted from their labors. Two pairs of blue eyes stared at him as if he were mad.

"Wouldn't that just take the cake," Jim said, and Reid looked at him sharply. It sounded—it *looked* as if the old man was disgusted.

"We can only hope," Margaret answered.

"No more notes," Reid observed.

"True. We haven't heard a word from the bastards." Jim rubbed his spotted hands as if they ached, and cocked his head to one side. "Maybe we could let up on the vigilance a bit."

"No." Both Margaret and Reid said it at once.

Their eyes locked, then Reid drew a breath. "No, it's not hurting us to keep our ears to the ground." Uncoiling himself from his chair, he said, "Come on, Margaret."

"What?" Margaret watched as he loomed over her. "What?" she said again, as he grasped her by the wrist and drew her toward the door. "Mr. Jim!"

"The boy's mad," Jim advised her. "Better do what he wants."

"In a pig's eye," Margaret huffed. She prepared to dig in her heels if he pulled her up the stairs, but he confounded her and dragged her down the hall to the kitchen instead. "I've got a luncheon date that I need to keep."

"With Dommy and Jules?" Reid queried.

"Yes! Yes, with Dommy and Jules. They're going to meet me out front and we're going to—"

He had no patience with this. "Too bad."

She tugged back on her wrist and almost jerked her shoulder out of her socket.

"You'll hurt yourself," Reid warned.

"Where are you two going so fast?" Abigail asked as Margaret flew past.

To Margaret, her friend was only a blur of green and pink feathers. "I don't know," she called back.

"To West University," Reid answered.

She was seated in his Legend, belted in, before she caught her breath enough to inquire, "Why are we going to West U.?"

"Remember our martial arts bout in the gym? Remember what you promised afterwards?"

Yes, she remembered. She remembered promising all kinds of things with clinging hands and open mouth, and she'd delivered on every promise.

"It's time to pay up," he continued.

"I—"

"We're going to look at houses."

"At a . . ." She grimaced. "Yes. I knew that."

"Oh, Margaret. The things you imagine," he teased.

She flounced around to stare out the window, and to see if she could spot her lunch dates. They weren't visible, but she wondered . . . Her conscience twitched.

She needed to speak to Reid. She didn't want to, God knew, but she had to speak to him. Turning her head in slow increments, she studied his profile. He looked rugged. Damn. He looked scary. He looked as if he could make the kind of scene she dreaded.

She turned her head back and then peeked around at him again. She opened her mouth, and shut it.

She didn't want to.

She had to. In a hurry, she said, "I've been meaning to talk to you."

"Okay."

She stared at him, speechless.

Glancing at her, he smiled briefly. "I'm ready."

"I doubt it," she whispered, adding aloud, "It's about your grandfather's will."

He grunted, although whether in response to her statement or as a reaction to the pothole he swerved to miss, she couldn't tell.

"It seems that Mr. Jim left Amy a considerably bigger bequest than he told me." She noticed her leg was jiggling up and down, and she laid her palm flat against it to calm herself.

"Oh, that." He sounded totally uninterested. "Yeah, I know."

"You know he left her the stud farm?"

"Yeah. His lawyer felt it behooved him to tell me about the bequest to A. M. Guarneri." His mouth quirked. "He was working on Granddad's orders, of course. I should have realized it sooner."

"Why?" she asked, fascinated.

"No lawyer of my grandfather's would ever release that kind of confidential information unless he wanted his license revoked and his reputation destroyed. Granddad would have him run out of town on a rail."

"So Mr. Jim's lawyer hasn't really been fired."

"Yeah, he's been fired. I fired him. It's just too damned bad nobody was listening except me."

The wry twist of his mouth told her he was laughing at himself. She guessed, "You fired him, and your grandfather rehired him."

"I fired him, but he doesn't work for me, so he didn't listen. He only pretended to. It was nothing more than bait to bring me here to meet you."

Margaret gaped. "You knew that?"

"It didn't take long to figure."

"Then Amy's bequest is a joke?"

"Not at all. Granddad *has* left her the stud farm."

"You'll stop him?"

"Me?" Reid swerved again, but not for a pothole. In honest amazement, he repeated, "Me? You think I can do something to change Granddad's mind? You think *I* want to be run out of town on a rail?''

''But that farm's got to be worth . . .'' Her imagination failed her.

''A lot,'' he agreed succinctly.

''Amy said he left her money, too.''

''Oh, that.'' He shrugged, watching her from the corner of his eye. ''Only about a million.''

As if she'd had the breath knocked out of her, she audibly dragged in oxygen. ''A million?'' she croaked. ''Dollars?''

''That's the way money is generally figured.''

He grinned, but she didn't see the joke. ''A million dollars? He can't go around leaving people a million dollars. He'll go broke.''

''That's true.'' Reid nodded. ''Why, if he went around giving out a million dollars once a month, he'd be penniless in about twenty years.''

''Oh, my God.''

''That's if he didn't earn any interest on his money, of course.''

''Oh, my God.''

''That stud farm could lose a million in a few years if we had a bad run of luck. This money will get Amy on her feet with the business, and if she decides she doesn't like it, I'll buy it back.''

''Oh, my God.''

He reached over and patted her bouncing knee. ''You lost the bet with me. Amy has to get to Harvard somehow.''

''Merit?''

''That's a strong possibility, too. Don't worry about it, darlin'.''

''But—''

''It'll all work out. Now look. Look at what I brought you to see.''

They pulled up in front of a brand-new Georgian two-story, with red brick exterior and a large front porch. The lot was wooded, and the house fit in among the trees as if it had been designed to do so.

Margaret wanted to protest, to hash this inheritance out, but Reid had clearly dismissed it as unimportant. She swallowed her words and stared at the house; not because she was overwhelmed—for how could one be overwhelmed while living in a replica of a sixteenth-century castle?—but because Reid seemed to expect it.

"How do you like the shutters? I had the builder paint them forest green."

Reid sounded concerned, and Margaret turned her head and studied him. His crisp, ironed denims made her want to laugh—who ironed jeans? His muscled chest straining against the white cotton T-shirt changed her laughter to the itch to touch, and hastily she said, "The color adds distinction. Did you say you were buying this as an investment?"

"I'm buying it, for sure. Nice neighborhood, huh?"

"It certainly is." The narrow street was lined with a grand mixture of houses. Big, new homes—like the one they sat in front of—rubbed elbows with homes from the forties. Trees shaded the street; hedges were mature and thick. A girl whizzed past on her skateboard, shouting rude comments to a boy in his swim trunks.

"A family place. My dog will have a great time in this yard," Reid said with pleasure.

"I didn't know you had a dog."

"I haven't yet, but I've always wanted one. Come on." He opened his door, stepped out, and seemed surprised when Margaret failed to wait for his assistance to alight. "You're too independent," he told her, taking her hand and leading her up the walk.

Margaret sniffed, offended. "Thank you for your critique."

Reid laughed back at her. "You're too thin-skinned, too. There are many, many things I like about you. Do you want me to name them?"

"No."

"I like to talk about them," he coaxed, opening the door with a tagged key from his pocket.

"No."

"Spoilsport."

They stepped inside and Margaret was struck by the smell of new wood, of mortar and wallboard dust. The entry and living room were tall, with vaulted ceilings to draw the heat of a Texas day. The light filtered through a skylight in the roof, through undraped windows and down the stairs from the second story. Rolls of carpet and pad lay about, waiting to be installed, and their shoes made tapping noises on the concrete floor.

"Come and look at the kitchen," Reid commanded. He retained her hand, but his desire to drag her from place to place seemed to have diminished. Instead he let her lead, directing her with nudges and encouragement.

"Very nice," Margaret approved, frankly bewildered but willing to play the game. "I like the cooking island."

"I liked it myself." He grinned, a close-trimmed lock of cinnamon-colored hair falling over his forehead. "I could do my famous pasta primavera in here."

"Ah." Gazing around with new eyes, she said, "You *are* going to buy it."

"I said so." He smirked. "There aren't any listening devices here."

She blushed at the memory his words invoked, but asked bravely, "Did you find any bugs in the mansion?"

"Not a one. Our extortionist missed his chance there. Come upstairs and look at the bedrooms."

He tugged, and she stumbled along behind him. No bugs. She never needed to be in his bedroom. That whole incident in the shower need never have happened. She couldn't dismiss the suspicion that Pierre had told her so Reid would find her there—but that was ludicrous. And try as she might, she couldn't suppress her thrill at the memory of that shower.

"Pay attention," Reid said, snapping his fingers in her

face as they climbed the stairs. "There are five bedrooms up here. Do you like it so far?"

"Nice." God, he confused her. So he wanted her professional opinion. He was buying this house. To live here?

Well, why not? He was a big boy, old enough to live with someone other than his grandfather while in Houston. She would have expected him to buy something a little more upscale—this house was nothing more than upper middle class. Actually, she would have expected him to buy a condo. This house required yard work and didn't have room for a maid. His midnight orgies would be interrupted by the security police, and the neighborhood kids would scrape their bikes on the paint job of his car.

Now, more than ever, she realized she didn't understand the workings of his mind. Up the stairs they went, making a flying tour of bedroom one, bedroom two, bathroom one, rec room, bedroom three, bedroom four. There they stopped.

"Here's where we'll put Amy." He waved his arm around the charming, rose-painted room. "Won't she just love it? It has its own bath. There's a tree outside her window, and if she's careful, she can climb right out onto its arms. I'll build a tree house." He stopped and considered. "I'll have a tree house built."

Covering her throat with her hand, she tried to subdue the choking noise that climbed from the pit of her stomach.

He turned his head and frowned. "Did you eat something that didn't agree with you?"

Her voice wasn't strong, but it was definite. "I'm having trouble swallowing."

"What's the matter?" Acting concerned—and he had to be acting, she thought hysterically—he stepped to her side and wrapped his arm around her waist. "Are you ill?"

"*What's the matter?*" Unexpectedly the question came out in a shriek. He jumped back; she was startled. Moderating her tone, she said, "What's the matter? You're talking about living together, and you ask, 'What's the matter?' "

"What did you think I was talking about in that shower?" he demanded reasonably.

She raised her hands in incredulity. "Sex?"

"Dammit, Margaret——"

"All right, *good* sex. I don't understand you. I don't understand you at all. Why are you acting like this? I'm your grandfather's butler."

He shook his finger under her nose. "If you call me 'sir' right now, I'll put you across my knee."

"Why shouldn't I call you 'sir'? You can't move me in here like the—the mistress of a Regency rake." She stuttered in her excitement. "Tucked in a little hideaway for your entertainment, not daring to poke my nose out——"

A spark of anger leapt to his eyes and died beneath the humor. "I would have never suspected it. You really have a vivid imagination, haven't you?"

She glared at him and then burst into tears.

In a flash, he enfolded her in his arms, and she didn't want to pull away. It felt comfortable here and she relaxed; relaxed enough to sob, "That's what Luke used to say."

"Your husband?" Alert, he stroked her head.

"He used to say if we could harness my imagination, we could light the whole west side of Houston."

The storm of tears was passing already, and he turned her with his arm on her shoulder and led her toward the master bedroom. "What did Luke think of your plunge into the stuffy world of butlers?"

"I did that after . . . after the funeral." She sniffed and wiped at her face. "I wanted a quiet job, routine and simple. The kind of job where I could raise Amy in comfort and stability."

There it was again; that word. Stability.

"I wanted to get away. After I paid medical bills, there wasn't any money left from the life insurance, so I borrowed from my father-in-law and moved to England and enrolled in Ivor Spencer's school.''

He smiled. "I bet Amy loved England."

"This is a nice room." She pointed to the windows set high in the wall, close to the cathedral ceiling. "Those should have stained glass."

"I'll make a note of it."

She ignored him, wandering into the sitting area and then into the bathroom. "Hey, you could play basketball in here." She stuck her head out the door and grinned at him. "It's almost as big as yours at Donovan's Castle."

Her nose was red, her eyes were puffy, her cheeks were tearstained. It brought such a welling of tenderness in him, he told her, "You're beautiful when you cry."

Surprise crossed her face. She ducked back in the bathroom and came out to allege, "That's not what that mirror in here says."

"Didn't Amy love England?" She disappeared back into the bathroom again like a bobbing ball. He heard the sound of toilet paper unrolling and a nose being indelicately blown.

"No."

She didn't reappear, and he stepped over a roll of carpet and one of carpet pad to reach the bathroom door. "I can't imagine Amy not enjoying England."

"It was a hard time for her." Testing the faucet, she found the water was hooked up. She leaned over the sink and sluiced her face until the worst of the redness was gone.

When she raised her head, Reid stood behind her. Their eyes met in the mirror. He smiled at her, and she sighed with resignation. "No towel," she complained, and he pulled the handkerchief from his pocket and offered it. Dabbing at her face, she escaped the confines of the bathroom with Reid on her heels.

"What happened, Margaret? What happened to Amy?"

She poked at a roll of carpet with her toe, and when she was satisfied with the results, she seated herself on the end. She sat erect, knees together, skirt twitched down, and he watched and analyzed. She didn't want to talk about it, nor did she want to attach too great an importance to it by refusing. So she sat like the perfect lady, all prissy and sweet, hoping the cracks in her composure wouldn't show.

Her voice almost didn't cooperate. It quavered for a minute, swooping low and then high, before moderating to tell the tale. "Luke and I had done everything to prepare her for his death, and she saw a lot of death in the hospital around her. So when he actually dropped his form—"

"What?"

A tiny smile lifted her lips, but she didn't meet his gaze. "That's what Luke told her he was doing. He was dropping his human form for another. Well, she comprehended her father's death only too well. So well, in fact, that she understood mortality at an age when most children still believe they can stop a moving car with their bodies."

"She was afraid she would die?"

"No." She raised one hand out of her lap and rubbed her temple. "She feared I would disappear, too."

Reid watched the betraying movement. This part of her story, she didn't want him to hear. Perhaps she didn't want to hear it herself. But more than that, she feared the growing destruction of the walls around her. He was breaching all her defenses. He sympathized, he really did, and if it were anyone else, he'd wait for the natural empathy that he knew would come. But with Margaret it was an impossibility. For how could he allow her walls to remain when his own were in shambles?

He sat down next to her, close enough so she could feel his warmth yet not touching—fostering, he hoped, the illusion of freedom. "What did you do?"

"It got so that I couldn't leave her with the sitter, couldn't go anywhere without her." She fell silent, remembering.

"You had difficulties, too," he guessed. "You had to

put aside all your own grief to tend to hers.'' Subtly she shifted away from him, and he was surprised. He searched her face for clues; why should the mention of her own sorrow distress her so?

Yet she gave him no time to analyze, rushing on with her story. ''At last, I did what I should have done originally. I sent for my father-in-law.'' A slight, fond smile crossed her face, smoothing the lines of strain.

''Is that the grandfather she visited this summer?'' he asked, deliberately defusing her wariness. ''The one with the shaving cream Twinkies?''

She laughed with pleasure and, it seemed to him, relief. ''The very one. He's a wonderful man. He kept her busy. They went all over London together, visiting the places he'd seen in World War Two and dropping their calling cards at Buckingham Palace. I still don't know what he said to her, but when he left, she was at peace.''

''And you?'' Shrewdly he checked her cautious face. ''When did you stomp your feet and scream at fate?''

The edges of her glossy composure crumpled just a little. ''Hmm?''

''When did you cry and mourn? You'd lost your husband, and you were at least fond of him—''

''I loved him.'' Her quiet sincerity passed his test.

''You loved him. He died after an illness. . . .'' He fished, wanting her to tell him about it.

She dropped her eyes to her lap, adjusted her fingers, ignored him. He waited, but she never looked up, and so he pushed on. ''He died and left you all alone with a child and no viable means of support and a huge medical bill. There must have been a time, in the wee hours of the morning, when you cried.''

''Of course there was.'' She said it too quickly, almost guiltily.

With a gentle finger, he lifted her chin and stared into her eyes, ''Have you never taken the time to finish the grieving process?''

''I have grieved for Luke every day since he left us,''

she said in fierce self-defense. Her arms crossed over her chest and she hugged them to her to shut him out.

Her gaze slid away from his. Her body language shouted rejection, but like a ruthless opponent, he ignored the unspoken and dealt with the actual words. "But that anguish should have eased by now. There are certain steps you must take to heal, to prepare to face life again. Are you telling me you haven't been angry at Luke for leaving you? That you haven't screamed at fate for the rotten deal it tossed you? That you haven't begged God to change what can't be changed?"

"I'm not trying to tell you anything." She enunciated clearly, clipped off each word with her teeth. "It's none of your business."

"I made it my business in my shower." Swinging one leg over the roll of carpet, he straddled it and placed his hands on her shoulders. He cupped them and rubbed them as if she were a horse and he the stable master. His voice oozed syrup as he reminded her, "Our relationship can't develop if you're stuck in the past. The time to free yourself from your unhappiness is now and—"

Her hands flashed up and broke his hold on her shoulders. Her gaze, before so timid, sought his in a fine fury. "I'm not unhappy!"

He fell back just a little, and she followed.

"I'm not unhappy; I'm not stuck in the past; and I sure as hell don't care what's healthy for our relationship."

"Now, dear." He sounded like an accountant placating his tyrannical wife, but she never noticed the inconsistency.

"You sit there, so complacent, a little rich boy who's never been unhappy his whole life long, and you dare judge me and my 'grieving process' as insufficient." Her finger tapped his chest; her nose bobbed so close to his, he could feel her heated breath. "You damned idiot."

Then she surprised him. He'd drawn her as he wanted, tapped into her pain and anger and released them. But the scene didn't continue as he'd envisioned. Like a growling cat, she reached over and grabbed his shirt at the tails, and jerked on it. She wanted it off; he did not, but he'd not taken into account that she was a mother.

"In my time," she panted, rising onto her knees on the rolled carpet, "I've wrestled a two-year-old for possession of a shirt, and you don't stand a chance."

Being compared to a two-year-old surprised Reid enough for her to pull his arms out, and the whole thing over his head. She tossed it down and went for his belt, and he grabbed her wrists. "What are you doing?"

He wavered between patience and amazement when she snapped his hold and jerked his belt open. "You figure it out."

"Margaret . . ." His voice trailed off. Her fingers wrestled with the button front of his jeans, and they caused a most miraculous change to come over his body.

It was too much to expect that she wouldn't know——her hands were pressed to the metamorphosis. She looked up in triumph. "Ha!"

He eased himself back on his elbows, trying to relieve the unexpected pressure. "What does that mean?"

"It means . . ." She opened the final button and inched her slender fingers inside his fly. "It means you're going to get what you have coming to you."

NINE

"Don't you want to initiate your new house?"

Her smile wasn't kind or generous or feminine. In fact, he decided, it looked downright predatory. "Our house," he insisted, but she reached inside his underwear to cup his flesh, and he forgot what it was he wanted to say. He fell all the way back, so the carpet supported his back, and his arms dangled off the sides. He heard her chuckle and he decided that sexual conquest was an ugly thing. He'd talk to her about it . . . later.

Those magic hands massaged his groin with a firm and gentle pressure, and when she urged his pants down, he raised his hips eagerly. She jerked his jeans, his underwear, down to his ankles, and there they stuck on his tennis shoes. She would have left everything where it was, but he grunted a denial and pushed his shoes off one by one. Immediately she stripped him of the trappings, and she flung it all aside. Crawling up between his legs, she smoothed her palms up the inside of his thighs, up his stomach, up his chest. He groaned at the fire she left behind, and when she laid her full weight on him, he thought he'd found heaven. Sweetness above, rough weave below; the scent of woman and wood and newness;

148

the rustle of leaves against the window and the rustle of clothing against his skin.

Dipping her head, she murmured against his lips, "Do you like this?"

Her voice was husky and amused and acted like a prod to his masculine pride. He wrapped his arms around her, prepared to roll off and land with her on the tail of carpet that flopped off the side of the roll.

He made a mistake and looked into her face. Satisfaction strengthened the smile on lips with a tendency to tremble. Vulnerability and success chased each other through her shadowed eyes. While one hand pinched his ear to hold him still, the other stroked through his hair as if she found comfort there. What could he do? He supposed he could handle being mauled by a woman—her mouth sank into his with a steady, delicate pressure—just this once.

God, her tongue drove him wild with its exploratory fervor. When she came up for breath and nibbled at his ear and then soothed the sting with that same tongue, he discovered his hand was under her skirt. He didn't remember putting it there, but her rounded cheeks wiggled when he stroked them, and he couldn't help but take that as encouragement.

Her hand was still wrapped in his hair, and he turned his head away when she tugged imperiously. She laughed again, nervously, as she tasted the cord of his neck and then found his nipple with her fingernails. "It's hard," she whispered. "Are you cold?"

He groaned. Finding the edge of her panties, of her hose, he skimmed his hand inside. Down the cleft, down until he could slip one finger inside her. "You're wet," he whispered back. "Are you on fire?"

She didn't say anything. She couldn't. Her head was tossed back, her teeth bit into her lower lip, and that sweet countenance of pain and pleasure possessed her face.

"So soon?" But he barely breathed it, unwilling to break the spell. Another finger found her, his thumb pressed against her, and like a firecracker in his arms, she exploded. He watched her face as he pushed her to her limits, judging when to release, when to resume, prolonging her climax for her rapture—and his own.

When at last she came to rest, he could wait no longer. "Help me," he instructed, sliding the underwear down her legs. She roused enough to help rid herself of the essentials, but not enough to deal with the intricacies of buttons on vest and blouse and skirt.

Reid struggled for a moment alone, then muttered, "To hell with it." Lifting her, he settled them together. What necessity couldn't do, the touch of bare flesh accomplished. Galvanized, she struggled to set her feet on the floor, one on either side of him. She raised up, and he could see the renewed sparkle in her eyes. He grinned at her, and groaned when she took him in her hands and fit them together. But she'd lost the edge of command, and as she struggled to take him into her, he raised his hips beneath her and thrust inside.

She gasped, her eyes half-closed.

He wanted to find the heart of her, push her to another cataclysm of joy, but the fierce stillness of her body worried him. "Did I hurt you?"

Wordless, she shook her head.

"Do you want me to continue?"

Her lids slowly lifted, and she stared at him as she shook her head again. Then, driven by the muscles of her legs, she lifted herself up, right to the point of despair, and sank down, bringing them back to heaven.

He witnessed her smile, so encouraged by his discomfort, and thought about how he wanted to explode into action. He said, "In a way, I'm sorry I took your edge off." He looked at her face in the dusty, silver sunlight; that structure of bone and expression that he loved. He looked at her body, encased in tie, shirt, vest, coat. He looked at her skirt, dangling at her thighs, and his hands went to her bare hips. He hiked her skirt to her waist, and he held her tightly as she came off him again, and back down. As she moved up and down to a slow and steady rhythm, he kept his hands on her, and when she tried to accelerate, his hands held her to a crawl. Her resistance to his guidance became more and more frantic, but he just smiled—or snarled—and said, "No, no. Torment should be a mutual pleasure."

The name she called him was no endearment, but it turned his smile into one of genuine delight. "Sweet talker," he said, and sucked in his breath as she reached behind her to prowl with her fingers between his legs.

Her persuasion loosened his grip on both her hips and his sanity, and suddenly she controlled the pace. The torment did indeed grow into a mutual pleasure, blocking his awareness of everything else. There was only Margaret, and more Margaret, and Margaret like sunlight in his soul.

The blotting of thought and emotion lasted only while her hormones danced in her veins. Reluctantly she returned to the reality of Reid beneath her, a large and open room around her, and a most embarrassing reflection of herself in the mirrored wardrobe doors. She gaped, horrified, and then more horrified when she met Reid's eyes in the glass. His slow smile burned the heat into her skin, and she couldn't tear her gaze away until the room tipped.

The floor rushed up in a padded thump, and he tucked her into the corner between his body and the carpet roll. It was then she realized her snare had gained her only temporary respite, and it had exposed her fabrication of indifference.

He smoothed the loose strands of hair out of her eyes. "How long has it been for you? Three years?"

"Not even a week," she answered saucily.

"Ah, you remember."

He sounded so satisfied that she grimaced. "I wasn't ever going to let you do this with me again, you know."

"Did I miss something? Did you *let* me do this with you?" His sarcasm was heavy and sure. "I thought you *demanded* that I do this with you. I could have sworn you ripped my clothes off and tossed me down, regardless of my wishes, and took your wanton pleasure—''

"Oh, shut up. My wanton pleasure seemed to coincide with your wanton pleasure, you know.''

"I know.''

She waited for him to say more, but he wisely didn't, and she decided this was a conversation she wasn't likely to win. She nibbled her lip, wanting to clarify to him that she wasn't always so wanton. "You're right. It's been almost three years since my husband died.'' Her thoughts arched back into the past, and she explained, "But it's been longer than that since I slept with a man.''

"Is that what you call this?'' His mouth curled tenderly. "Sleeping?''

"You know what I mean.'' Observing the pride that puffed him up like a peacock, she decided he didn't need to know too much. Her desire to avoid embarrassment seemed to bring with it unwanted side effects. She could have kept her resolution, too, if her traitor eyes hadn't filled with tears and the dastardly man hadn't pulled her into his chest. Her words were muffled and unstoppable. "The last six months Luke was alive, he couldn't function. I think that killed him as rapidly as anything. He loved sex. With him it was a joy to be shared, and when we couldn't share anymore . . . God, he just shriveled up and died.''

Reid warmed away her tears and her chill. His arms wrapped her body, his hands stroked her aristocratic back, and Margaret sniffled and rubbed her eyes across his shoulders.

"I guess you can tell I'm new at this.'' She raised her head and looked at him. "I shouldn't be reminiscing about my last lover with my new lover.''

Reid smiled using all his teeth, and Margaret wondered if she had annoyed him, but he corrected her firmly. "Luke is a part of you, a most important part. You don't live eight years with a man and not have some memories and some love you want to remember. I'm no fool. I'll never be jealous of a dead man, I'll only be jealous if you keep all those memories so tightly locked up, I feel they're a treasure I'm not allowed to sully with my mortal mind.''

"Sometimes . . ." She hesitated, but it had to be said. "Sometimes I almost like you."

"Well, we can't have that, now." He rolled back and held up one leg. A white sock still wrapped around his foot, and he pointed with mock disappointment. "Look at that. You didn't even knock my socks off."

Unwillingly amused, she smacked his shoulder and sat up. "I'll knock something else off if you don't watch your tongue." Glancing about, she located her underwear and hose, still together by some miracle. Too aware of his charming assessment, she shimmied into her clothes. She stood up, tucked in her shirt, found her shoes, and turned back to him, still on the floor. "Are you going to lie around buck naked all day?"

"Come here." He crooked a wicked finger, and for the first time she saw a resemblance to the mischievous Mr. Jim.

"Absolutely not." She laughed, but warily. "We can't hang around in an empty house."

He was still waggling that finger at her. "Why not?"

"You'll have rug burn on your rear," she pointed out, trying to sound sensible.

It seemed she failed. "Not if we follow my plan," he crooned, with his innocent shark-tooth smile. "Come here."

"We have to go back."

"Come here. I won't do anything."

"What kind of fool do you take me for?"

"A hundred kinds of a fool if you think you'll go back without coming here."

"I'll go back without you," she warned, sidling toward his pants—the pants that held the keys.

He just smiled and waited until she reached down to pick them up, then she was tumbling through the air.

She should give him one good chop across the Adam's

apple as he rested on top of her, but he smiled with such almighty delight, she didn't have the heart. She settled for exasperation. "Now what, you big jerk?"

"Now I'll give to you a little of what you gave to me." He nuzzled her neck. "It's been too long. I want to see those breasts."

"They look the same as last time." She wriggled beneath him as he tugged at her bow tie. "Kind of round with nipples."

"One can't be too sure."

His breath fogged her ear, and she began to lose her sense of direction. "We need to go back. Your grandfather—"

"Will be pleased as hell to know what we're doing."

"How's he going to find out?"

"Granddad?" He raised his head incredulously. "Sharpshooter Donovan? You think he won't *know*?" He raised his head further, his body still. "Listen."

She heard it, too. The scrape of the key in the lock downstairs.

"Mr. Donovan?" A man's voice floated up the stairs, booted footsteps echoed through the empty living room. "Mr. Donovan?"

"It's the builder," Reid groaned. He steadied her as she rose and straightened her clothes with rapid, precise gestures.

"Want me to go stall him?" she sassed.

"Wench." He stood up and stretched, and she couldn't help admiring the muscles that rippled and lengthened. He watched her watching him, and chuckled. "Who do you think would be the most embarrassed if he found us here, and me without a stitch of clothing?"

"I'll go and stall him."

Reid took her arm as they went down the walk, and she angrily shook it off. "Did you have to give me back my bow tie when you came downstairs?"

"How was I to know he'd wink like that?"

"I am mortified."

He pulled her around to face him. "I'm sorry. It's just that . . . I'm so conceited about you, about us, I want to shout it to the world."

She didn't seem to be at all touched by his pride. "Try to refrain." She stomped to the car and stood tapping her foot, waiting for him to open her door.

With a sigh, he turned to look at the house. Proposing to her there had seemed like such a marvelous idea, but she'd taken it all wrong. She thought he was propositioning her.

Before he could clear it up, she'd distracted him with her memories, then with her body. At the time, her rather forcible seduction of him had seemed like a good idea. Now he wasn't so sure. As a release of her anger, it had worked wonderfully. As a diversion from his questions, it had worked better—and who was in charge here?

How had she muddled his normally clear logic with the rewards of her body? No other woman had so affected him. It was that empathy between them, the empathy he'd used to tantalize her. Now he discovered it could be turned against him, and he wanted to curse and to cheer.

She's steering clear of the breakdown emotions, he told himself. She was too relieved to be away from the crying and too glad to laugh about her father-in-law. The upshot was, she'd never grieved for her husband. Amy's problems had overshadowed her own while the sorrow flowed naturally. Once Amy was healed, Margaret had her feelings firmly locked inside.

"Mr. Donovan, are we going?"

Reid peeked around at her, tapping her toe on the sidewalk. "Sure are, sweet thing." He strode down the walk and around the front of the car, and stopped. Etched on the hood was a long gouge in the paint. "What the hell?" He rubbed his finger on it and glanced up to see Margaret smirking.

"It looks quite similar to the time Amy scraped the handlebars of her bike along Mr. Jim's limo," she informed him. "That's the chance you take when you're around children."

Reid looked up from his desk. "Nagumbi, I have a job for you."

Nagumbi seated himself with the care that characterized all his movements.

Tossing the packet of photographs at him, Reid ordered, "I want to know who those guys are."

"Where did you get the pictures?" Nagumbi asked, placing them one by one in a line of the desk.

"Cliff Martin. According to him, Margaret has lunch with these creeps a couple times a week."

Nagumbi assessed the photographic evidence before his eyes. "Is that a reason for concern?"

"I don't know." Reid leaned back in his chair and rubbed his eyes. "I don't trust Martin, and as you've taught me, I never trust the information if given from an unreliable source. But something happened today that made me wonder."

Nagumbi raised one brow, and Reid nodded, familiar with his friend's method of conversation. "I took Margaret to the place in West U. and showed her around. When we left, I checked the rearview mirror, and there were these two guys"—he waved a hand at the photographs—"standing on the corner watching us drive away. Or watching me drive away with Margaret. They glared at me like I was a pervert."

"Did they follow you?"

"Not the way I drive."

"Did Ms. Guarneri see them?"

"I'd swear she didn't."

Nagumbi leaned back in his chair and steepled his fingers. "Unless she's a better actress than you give her credit for."

"I've thought of that." Reid shook his head. She'd been horrified, mortified, aghast, by the million-dollar inheritance for her daughter. If she was an actress, she was wasting herself in Houston—she belonged in Hollywood.

"I will check into this, as you require. In all actuality, this coincides with my own investigation."

"Of what?"

"After the return of your grandfather from the kidnapping attempt, I found the police report inadequate."

Reid found himself not at all surprised. "Pierre warned me. Have you unearthed any little discrepancies?"

"Quite a few. When I have a report which satisfies me, I will come to you at once. At the moment, I must satisfy myself with what is public record." He nodded with cold pride. "Of course, I am also maintaining an extra watch on the elder Mr. Donovan as my time permits."

"Which activity do you believe will reap the most benefit?"

"Public record, when used by officials correctly, is nothing more than another bureaucratic tool of confusion. I believe, knowing Mr. Donovan's propensity to do as he pleases, that an extra vigil over his movements would not come amiss."

Without hesitation, Reid ordered, "Do it."

"I'll seek him out at once. I still believe you should be aware that Ms. Guarneri may not be what she seems. Women are the bane of mankind," Nagumbi intoned, and Reid looked at him sharply.

"Abigail giving you trouble?"

"Such a little woman could hardly give me trouble." Nagumbi's expression never changed, and Reid wiped his grin away. "She is more of a nuisance."

"What's the problem?"

"She seems to feel that the two of us could . . ." He squinted in pained remembrance. ". . . could 'make beautiful music together.' "

"Perhaps you could."

"She is too young and too flamboyant. I'd soon bore her."

"She's old enough to know what she wants, and her

flamboyance is expressed only in her clothes and her cooking. Abigail's as solid as a rock." Reid swayed his chair back and forth and examined his friend. "She's wanted you for quite a few years. You could do worse."

Nagumbi's eyebrows lifted in a slow and dignified manner. "You seem to have given it some thought."

"I'd like to see you happy."

"Happiness is nothing more than a state of mind. I am content."

"No, I want you *happy*."

Nagumbi's face never twitched. "Ms. Guarneri seems to be involved with you in the manner in which you wish me to be involved with Abigail. Are you happy?"

Reid laughed softly. "I'm happy, frustrated, amazed, impatient."

"Wary."

"That, too."

"Shouldn't this love you tout so unsparingly defeat all suspicion?"

"Is that what love is? Sometimes I think it's a magnetism."

"Between two people?"

"Yeah. You know, it draws us, fighting, into this whirlpool—"

"Very attractive," Nagumbi said with calm distaste.

"Once we're in there, the colors and feelings flash around and confuse." Reid sighed. He'd wanted to propose to her at the house in West University; now he was glad he hadn't. This struggle between his emotions and his suspicions was ripping his heart, disturbing his mind. Was he thinking clearly? For the first time in his life, he doubted it. "I can't let love blind me to the possibilities. There's too much at stake here."

"I'm glad you still realize that." Nagumbi picked up the pictures. "You have no information on these gentlemen?"

"None. You'll have to start from scratch."

"And you believe I should give Abigail's claim on my attention credence?"

"Absolutely."

"Fascinating."

"Excuse me." Margaret stepped into the study, satisfied that her butler demeanor was fully restored, an able protection against the man with the sharp brown eyes. "Do you know where your grandfather is?"

Reid glanced at his watch. "Napping, I suppose. Doesn't he lie down this time of the afternoon?"

"Yes, but he's not there. I checked."

"Is there a reason for concern?"

He smirked at her as if he didn't quite believe her, as if she came in just to see him. What she hadn't wanted to tell him now seemed a necessity. "I can't find Amy, either."

"When did you miss her?"

"Just a few moments ago. She isn't where I thought . . ." Her voice trailed off. "I mean, she spent the night with a girlfriend, and I called to see when they were sending her home."

"And?"

"And they said they had done so three hours ago."

"While we were at the house?"

She wanted to cringe at the reminder. Not only had they made more than a casual "tour" of the house, but during that time her daughter had been unattended, and a mother's guilt knew no rest. "Apparently."

"Are these people reliable?"

"Of course." She knew she sounded huffy, but the fine edge of panic had begun to gnaw at her.

"All right," he soothed. "Did she come back here?"

"Abigail fed her lunch with Mr. Jim." She flexed her hands into fists, and he watched the betraying gesture.

"Then?"

"Then nothing. No one has seen them since."

Glancing thoughtfully out the window, he pushed his

cropped bangs back, and they sprang forward at once. "Have you checked the pool? You know Granddad still likes to toddle around the shallow end."

"They're not there." She followed his gaze out the window. "I'm afraid I'm being silly, but it just seems so *strange*. Mr. Jim wouldn't have sneaked out with Amy, would he?"

"Why do you say that?" He turned and examined her alertly.

"Oh, you know how he chafes at the restraint this whole situation has laid on him. He wants to go where he wants to go, when he wants to. And Amy . . ." She wrung her hands. "Amy could tease him into doing anything."

"I don't believe she'd ask Granddad to take her out when she understands the danger."

"I never exactly told her what is going on. All these kidnapping threats started after she left for the summer, and I didn't want to worry her when she got back. Amy's been nagging me to get her school supplies, but I've been busy. Until now, it never occurred to me she'd ask Mr. Jim to go with her." She felt breathless, afraid, and she massaged her neck as if that would ease the constriction. "I've been a fool."

"Have you checked to see if all the cars are in the garage? If the chauffeur is on the grounds?"

Slowly, steadily, she nodded her head. "That's really why I came in to see you. One car—and the chauffeur— are gone."

He rose from his chair, the superior lover transformed into the apprehensive grandson. "Damn that old man's hide. What do you suppose he's done now?"

"I don't know." She crossed her arms in front of her, recrossed them, recalled her dignity and dropped them to her sides.

"I'll call Cliff Martin; he assures me he's always available for conferences." Lifting the receiver, he punched the automatic dialer and asserted, "I'm sure this is all much ado about nothing."

"You're probably right. I'm just being fussy." An indefinable relief hit her as she put the responsibility in Reid's capable hands. He would handle this. He had a toughness to him, a confidence that reassured her.

He spoke into the phone. "Cliff Martin, please. This is Reid Donovan." He winked at her, and she weakly smiled back.

She smiled until he looked up and said, "I really don't appreciate being kept on hold this long." Tapping his foot, his expression changed from pleasant reassurance to impatience and then hostility. "Yes? What do you mean he's out of the office? Locate him for me. This is Reid Donovan. No, you don't seem to understand. I'm his primary client."

Drawn by uneasiness, she moved close to his side and put her hand on his arm. He nodded at her, his attention still on the conversation. The muscles beneath her hand stiffened. He braced his feet and shouted, "Out of town? How could he have gone out of town? Last time he left town, my grandfather was kidnapped. Who is it this time? His mother? Well, his relatives are certainly dying in droves, aren't they?" He hung up and turned a grim face on Margaret. "I'll call Uncle Manuel."

Hooking an arm around her waist, he sank down in the chair and took her with him. She didn't struggle; she wanted to be close. A cold emanated from the pit of her stomach, a twist of pain and fear. She snuggled into his chest, seeking warmth, and he pulled her even closer. Reaching around, he used the telephone with one hand and rubbed the other up her arm.

Like a native Hispanic, he dropped into Spanish as soon as the end answered. *"Hola, Tía Dela. Como está usted? Sí, bien, pero donde está Tío Manuel?"* He put his hand over the mouthpiece. "My aunt Dela has a soft spot for me."

Margaret could hear a flood of Spanish coming across

the wires, and Reid developed a frown. His Spanish got more insistent, more disgusted, and when he hung up the phone, he sat and stared at it. "What is it?" Margaret asked.

His gaze shifted to hers. "Suddenly, after years of communication, my aunt Dela can't understand my Spanish."

"Why?" Margaret whispered.

"I'd suspect she doesn't want to. She said she'd have Uncle Manuel call me. He got a phone call and he's out."

"Will he call?"

"Yes, she was positive he would." He wrapped his other arm around her. "It would seem you were right. Something stinks here, and we're not going to like it when we find out."

She strained back against his hold. "We've got to do something."

"Any suggestions?"

"There's got to be something."

"Let's wait for the phone call. I'm sure there'll be one. Now relax. You'll need to be clear-minded."

She didn't want to relax. She wanted to jump up and run around and be frantic. She wanted to fight or shout or . . . do anything. She'd been trained to handle situations like this, but she'd prayed it would never happen. Now a situation confronted her, and deep inside she wept.

He was right, dammit. All they could do was sit and stare at the phone in silence. Reluctantly she leaned back into him, her head beside his. She felt the little jump he gave when he thought of something.

Eagerly he queried, "Did you check with Nagumbi?"

"He isn't on the grounds."

He sighed with frustration. "I talked to him not two hours ago. Where is everyone? Does everyone know something we don't?"

"I'm so afraid they do." She shivered and crept closer. "I'm afraid they do."

The silence fell between them like a stone. They wandered alone in their thoughts, unable to lie to each other, unable to comfort.

"It's not true, you know," he said abruptly.

"What?" She was bewildered.

"It's not true that I'm a spoiled rich kid who never knew a moment's sorrow."

Lost, she cast about her mind until she remembered; hadn't she said something like that this morning? She'd been in a rage because he was poking at a sore spot, and she'd shouted at him. Was that what she'd said? She cringed. She remembered what Jim had said about Reid's parents. How could she have been so insensitive? How could she tell him she knew without him realizing how deeply Jim had confided in her?

"You think I'm crazy about my Granddad, and it's true. He took me in when the whole world fell around my shoulders."

Reid was picking his words carefully, and he wouldn't look at her, and she realized how uncomfortable he was, telling her this.

"I grew up in Seattle; did you know that?"

She nodded.

"It's a wonderful place. Mountains behind and the Pacific Ocean in front and hills and rain and fresh air. I love Houston; it's been good to me, but Seattle is a young boy's paradise. Camping, hiking, fishing. My dad and mom did everything with me." He drew a deep breath; it quivered, and her heart ached. "They died when I was eight. I wasn't like Amy. I wasn't prepared."

"But your grandfather took care of you?" she prompted.

"Yes, but it was tough. I resented him so much."

"Resented him?" Now she was astonished. "Why?"

"My folks were unpretentious. They weren't hippies, or even beatniks—they were the predecessors. My dad eschewed money and all it stood for, and my mother just wanted to educate the poor. I always knew my grandfather sort of . . . despised them." Now Reid's eyes met Margaret's, and a warm, amused communication passed between them. "I don't know how my dad got to be like that, but I suspect he'd found that money couldn't buy his father's attention and turned away from all the, er, 'trappings of wealth.' That's what Dad used to call it, with the emphasis on *trappings*."

"Then you got stuck with your grandfather."

"Yeah."

"What happened to your mother's family?"

"I wondered that for a long time after she died. I used to fantasize that my grandfather had used his influence to have them shipped to Siberia." He made a tunnel with his hand and held it to his eye, and with the other hand cranked an imaginary movie camera. "When they escaped, they'd return and snatch me from this stifling life of luxury."

"Gee, you mean that wasn't the case?"

He dropped his hands. "Smart-ass. My mother was an orphan. I guess marrying a woman with no family and no money was one of my father's rebellions that worked out well."

"Did they love each other?" The question just slipped out, and she rolled her eyes at her temerity, but he seemed to see nothing wrong.

"God, yes. We were a family, a magic circle where others could come and go and no one could intrude. They understood each other without a word sometimes, and I'd wonder how they did it." He turned his head in to his shoulder and wiped a tear off his cheek with a shrug, and Margaret pretended she hadn't seen it. "I missed them so much. I wanted my dad to toss me over his shoulder and fling me into bed, and I wanted my mother to tuck me in."

"When did you decide to give Mr. Jim a chance?"

"I never *decided*. But he transplanted me from a life of freedom in Seattle to a life of rich boy in Houston, and then did everything in his power to make me happy. I was such a snot about it." He groaned and shook his head. "I made him play G. I. Joe for two years. I loved watching his eyes glaze over with boredom, and then—''Reid poked her with his elbow''—he'd try and get up off the floor after his knees had been folded under him for two hours.''

''Reid!'' She was laughing, half-horrified.

He shrugged, clearly embarrassed at his younger self. ''I told you I was a snot. I resented him for being alive when my parents weren't. I scared myself when I began to love him, and I was really scared when the memories of my folks began to fade.''

''Was he kind and understanding?''

''Jim? Are you mad?'' Reid spotted the sparkle in her eye. ''Funny girl. He used to blow his top regularly and tell me to shape up, and then he'd go storming out. I'd wait to see if he'd abandoned me, but he always came back for more. After a while, my grudge waned. I just couldn't help it. I took pity on him and paid attention to what interested him. I made him so happy with my talk of oil stock and price per barrel.''

''No more G. I. Joe?''

''I gave it up.''

''Sounds to me like you grew up too fast.''

''If life hands you lemons, make lemonade.''

''Being a kid is demanding, isn't it?'' She sympathized, but his next words brought her to attention.

''Yeah, but it made me tough. Just like it's made Amy tough. How much tougher do you think she has to be?''

''What do you mean?'' She twisted in his lap and looked at him, amazed. He seemed to be serious, his eyes steady on hers, his mouth firm.

''Don't you think that you and I could make a home where she could relax that eternal vigilance and loosen that stiff upper lip?''

''What?''

''We've got a lot in common, Amy and I. We both lost our support too soon, and we wander through life being strong. I'm strong because I'm a man, because I'm expected to be. She's strong because if she isn't, you'll feel like a failure.''

Her indignation blazed. "What? Did she tell you that?"

"No."

She remained puffed with fury until the simplicity and surety of his answer sank in. "How do you know?"

"There are some things about Amy I recognize. At my party, she was unofficial hostess. For my grandfather, she's his support and companion. And she told me about how pleased you were with her progress in the martial arts."

"Every woman needs to know how to defend herself."

"I'm not arguing about any of it. Don't get me wrong, she's a very self-assured young lady. But she found out that being self-assured relieved your worry, and now she's just a little more of *everything* when she's with you."

The hostility bubbled up again. "You think you can help?"

"I think that she and I need somewhere we can go where we can shiver if we're frightened and cry if we're hurt and gather fortitude to face the world."

"I'm supposed to do all this for you?"

"No." A tiny smile tilted one side of his lips, and she knew he had her where he wanted her. "Amy and I will do that for each other, and in the process, do it for you."

"I can take care of myself."

"Of course you can."

"You're putting a guilt trip on me. You're saying if I don't move in with you, it'll be bad for my daughter. Where did you learn that? That's blackmail."

"Hey, babe, anything that works."

She leaped up, and he let her go. Her mind twisted, confused by what she'd been told, tumbling from its lofty butler fixation under the influence of the fears and the pain. She paced. He watched.

"Excuse me." Simon spoke from the door. He held out a large, flat envelope; his hand trembled. "I think this is important."

Reid rose, his eyes fixed on Simon with fierce intensity.

Margaret wheeled, snatched the envelope, and scanned the front.

"This is it," Margaret confirmed. She held it out to Reid, still sealed. "I know this is it."

TEN

Never removing his eyes from her, Reid took the brown envelope without touching her fingers. In a guttural voice, deep with agony, he asked, "What is this, Margaret?"

"A note." Wringing her hands, she stared at the envelope, waiting, waiting for him to tear it open. He stood like a statue, his hand outstretched with the note still in it, and so she explained impatiently, "From the kidnappers. Like the other notes."

The hand didn't draw back, but trembled slightly. She looked up, desperate to know what it said and not understanding his reluctance. In an instant she realized he hadn't yet vanquished all his suspicions. He didn't like it—it gave him pain—but her magnificent lover distrusted her still.

She didn't have time for hurt, only a flash of anger and a hissed, "Bastard." Snatching the envelope back, she tore it open.

She scanned the contents. She threw it on the floor. She twirled as if she would run out the door; she stopped as if she didn't know where to go.

Picking up the note, Reid read it, and with a well-restrained violence, shoved it in his shirt pocket. Picking up the phone, he punched the number for the Houston

Police. He demanded to speak to Mr. Morris, the police spokesman, and tapped his foot through several interdepartmental transfers before roaring, "Uncle Manuel? What the hell are you doing down there?"

His dear old uncle didn't sound feeble, as a retired police officer should. He sounded furious as he roared back, "I'm trying to get these yahoos in line. I leave the force and what happens? The whole damn place falls apart."

Like a ton of bricks falling on him, Reid realized what was going on, realized what he would have realized weeks ago if he hadn't been distracted by his hormones. In a frozen calm, he asked, "What have you done?"

What he heard made him shout, made him pace, made him want to take his grandfather and lock the old man in a dungeon. "—and you along with him," he told Manuel. "Your grand plan has netted the kidnappers two hostages, and by God, they'd better both be home and in bed before night falls, or I'll put you through Tía Dela's meat grinder." He slammed the phone, picked it up, and slammed it again for emphasis.

"The kidnappers have both of them," he said. "Both of them. Got off with them while they were shopping. The police don't know where they went. They were using—" He stopped and stared at her. "Margaret." His voice was stern, the voice he used when he commanded. The voice never failed him, but she didn't turn, she didn't flinch. "Margaret, it's time for us to talk."

He heard her whisper, "I've been through it before. I can handle it. I know what to do."

He stared at her back. She stood posed on her toes, her back straight, her shoulders shrugged up. Tendons stood out on her neck, and her arms were straight down her sides, the elbows so extended, they circled back a little. Her hands were rigid, splayed starfish of tension. He circled around her, observing her as if she were a statue, and what he saw in her face dissolved his distrust.

How foolish that brief touch of paranoia had been. All

of Margaret's world was bound up in Amy. All her maternal love and her fear focused on her only child. This woman would never have sent her child into danger, not for money, not for any reason.

Half-afraid to touch her, afraid she would shatter, he said gently. "The police already know about Granddad and Amy. They're working on recovering them now."

By moving only her eyeballs, she transferred her attention to him. "I've been through it before," she said with feverish conviction. "I can handle it."

"Yes, I know you can," he soothed. "Let's sit down, shall we?"

She stared at him, but she didn't seem to hear him. Moving with the slow patience of a wild bird trapper, he sidled up and put his arm around her. "Shall we sit down?"

"No." Her voice was expressionless, inanimate.

"Margaret, we can't just stand here."

"You sit down."

"No, that's all right. I'll stand here with you." Glancing around the room, he tried to think of something, anything, that would ease her out of her self-inflicted rigidity.

Everything looked so normal. His computer hummed, his books lay scattered on his desk. Propped on his end table was a snapshot of his grandfather and Amy, taken at his birthday party. In a neat stack in his organizer were the papers for the house in West University. There was nothing in here that would ease her. His instinct was to get her outside, out under the trees, out in the pool, anywhere where the sunshine would melt this tautness. "Let's go for a walk," he murmured.

She wavered for a moment, still on her toes. "A walk? A walk?" The amazed inflections in her voice made it sound like a new language. "Fine."

She released the strain that held her up on her toes and put her weight back on her heels. That made her the height he remembered, but nothing else about her seemed familiar. Easing her forward, he saw Simon and Abigail in the doorway, watching them anxiously.

"What news?" Abigail asked.

Still moving forward, slowly and steadily, he informed her, "Granddad's been kidnapped, and Amy with him."

Abigail groaned and put her hand over her eyes, but Reid couldn't allow anyone else to collapse. The household had to be up and running, and so he asked, "Would you make sure there's something light for them to eat when they come in?"

She dragged her fingers from her face and stared at him.

"It'll have to be something that can be put back until they get here."

"Of course, Mr. Reid."

She sounded normal, and he suggested, "A soup or a salad, maybe?"

"I know how to cook for an uncertain dinner hour," Abigail huffed, turning away. "I can take care of that."

"Thank you. That would be a load off my mind."

Reid pulled Margaret to a halt in the hallway. "Simon?"

"Sir?" With prompt attention, the footman stood at his side.

"Ms. Guarneri and I are going outside. I need a cordless phone with a hook for my belt."

"Immediately, sir." But Simon didn't move. He stared intently at Margaret.

"Shock," Reid explained.

"Do you want a blanket? Shouldn't she lie down?"

"I can't even get her to *sit* down. I'm sure the heat out there will warm her."

Simon nodded and disappeared, returning in a moment with the requested receiver. "It'll ring anywhere on the grounds," he told Reid. "Mr. Jim fixed it up. This one has an intercom. I'll buzz you if something happens in here."

"Thank you. I know I can depend on you to keep it together." He patted Simon's shoulder and moved Margaret toward the front door. Simon leaped to open it, and they passed out into the sunshine. The sweltering heat of August had given way to the bearable heat of September. Bearable, that is, in small doses and only when clad in shorts.

Reid passed a worried glance over Margaret, but she still seemed cold, frozen by possibilities. Unable to stand it, he stopped her on the porch and untied her tie, unbuttoned her collar. She stared blankly while he did it, moved obediently when he urged.

Where should he take her? They couldn't wander without destination around the grounds, yet to sit her down seemed a cruelty. She needed a distraction—hell, *he* needed a distraction. As they rounded the corner of the house, inspiration visited him. "Come on," he murmured. "I've got something to show you."

She didn't care where they were going, nor what he would show her, that was obvious, but he kept up a patter for the sake of normalcy. "This is not the way I'd planned to surprise you, but perhaps it's better. This is one of those things like a warm blankie or a favorite teddy bear." He opened the door to the five-car garage, and cool air whooshed out around them. Flicking on the light, he led her back past the cars and to the little door on the back wall. Carefully he opened the door to the storage room; the light was already on inside.

The smell of wet cedar chips rushed out, and Margaret crinkled her nose.

"Let me go in first," he instructed, and she waited docilely outside. He checked his guests, then called, "Okay, you can come in now."

Imitating him, she sidled inside. He watched her eyes widen, watched as the calm facade crumpled into delight.

"Oh, puppies." Her eyes shone, guileless with joy. "Where did you get them? Will the mama dog let me touch them? How old are they?"

"The animal shelter; if you're gentle; and about four weeks."

Moving with caution, she knelt beside the basket.

"They're precious, and all gold." She extended her hand to the mother and let her sniff it. "Are they golden retrievers?"

"Golden retriever, Irish setter, and then they ran out of room on the card."

She laughed, almost naturally. "Heinz fifty-seven," she crooned to the puppies tumbling about the basket. Clean, bright, inquisitive, they climbed over the sides and fell on their faces in their rush to be first to greet their visitors. The mother sat erect on the padding, watching with anxious eyes as her babies sniffed and chewed, but she made no effort to restrain them. Margaret sat down on the floor to grant them easier access and immediately lost a nylon to the sharp claws of one intrepid explorer. Scooping him up, she held him up to her face. "Hey, watch that." He bit at her nose, his teeth snapping in youthful vigor. "Oh, you're a stinker."

Another puppy climbed into her lap, snuggling into her skirt as if it were a hammock. A third pulled at her cuff. "Aren't they sweet? Are there five?"

"Yeah," he agreed absently, contending with his own tiny visitors. "They were going to put them to sleep, and I couldn't stand it, so I grabbed them all."

"What's your grandfather going to do with them?" She smoothed her hand over the soft and curly coat of the baby in her lap, accepted a nudge of the cool nose in her palm.

"Granddad? He's not going to do anything with them. I figured I needed a dog."

"A dog?"

"So I got a little carried away." He jerked his foot away from one little guy. "That's my shoe." He tucked his legs under him Indian fashion and rolled the puppy over in play. "I've got friends who have kids. When these little dickens are weaned, all my godchildren will be gifted with a puppy."

"How many godchildren do you have?"

"Four. That leaves Mama and one other for us." He

checked her face. "Do you think Amy would want to pick it out?"

She looked up at him, stricken.

"The dogs are for our house. Our house, the one I showed you today." She still stared at him, her eyes sick and afraid. "You and me and Amy and the dogs."

"Dear God." Like the victim of a belly cramp, she held her stomach and leaned over until her forehead touched her knees. "I don't know if I can stand this." The puppy in her lap whined for escape and wiggled away, and Reid leaped to her side.

"Margaret," he said hoarsely. "Sweetheart, it's going to be all right."

He leaned over her, wrapped one protective arm around her, and heard her moan, "I've been through it before, but this time I can't handle it."

The puppy who'd been in her lap and the one who'd snapped at her nose both whined in reply. One licked frantically at the side of her face; one rubbed her arm with his head. Reid dragged her into his lap.

"You've got to have faith, darlin'. Keep a little faith."

"Faith!" Her head jerked up and smacked him under the chin. "Faith. This is one of God's horrible ironies—again. Last time it was Luke. This time it's Amy. I marry a doctor who treats cancer, and he dies of cancer. I choose a career to keep my daughter secure, and she's kidnapped because of it." Her eyes blazed with a horrible light, so dry and wide, they looked as if they'd never shed a tear. Her bitterness exploded like a supernova.

"Your husband—"

"Died of cancer. At the very hospital where he fought to save lives. The best treatments couldn't save him, couldn't save him from the suffering. I loved him, and I watched him fade from two hundred pounds to one hundred twenty. I watched him lose his hair and his body control and saw him through heart failure and lung collapse. I watched him go into remission—twice. I listened to the doctors say they had it licked—twice—and he died anyway. It seems like I spent the whole three years standing in a hospital corridor waiting for the results of tests and surgeries and chemotherapies. Standing there with those damn fluorescent lights flickering. Looking up at those lights for all those hours while they took my blood and strained out the platelets and then passed it back to me. Sitting in a hard chair in the room and trying to pass strength through my touch to Luke. Seeing his face in that awful white light and finally knowing it wasn't going to work.'' She raised her eyes to his. ''Nothing worked.''

He looked down at her, and as he watched, the bitterness dissipated. Her face softened, her eyes filled with tears; a slow, soft pain bloomed and grew. The sobs shook her body long before they found an outlet in sound, and then she buried her face in his neck in convulsive agony. Her fingers clawed at his shoulders; she moaned as if she were dying, ''Now they've got my Amy. They've got my baby.''

He said nothing. He offered no comfort but for the firm press of his arms around her. This was what she'd been denying herself. This release of energy and grief would be a catharsis for her, and her words were a revelation for him. At last he had the explanation for her backward-stepping caution, for her suspicion of love and her dismay at intimacy. She'd gone every step of the way with her husband: bled for him, rejoiced with him, held him in her arms when he died. She didn't know if her heart could take the grief of loving, and she couldn't remember the joy. Her needs must be rejected for fear of attainment; if she loved, wouldn't she also suffer?

She hugged Reid's back, tried to pull away, and he cradled her. She clutched his neck, tried to pull away, and he held her. When she gave up trying to spare him, her tears soaked his shoulder, his chest. At times they ran down his arm. He dug out his handkerchief for her, and she cried until she wrung it out. At last the dreadful weeping eased, the time between bouts became longer. When she'd stopped, completely stopped, she rested on him, limp with emotion.

She kept her face turned away from him for a long time, but finally she sat back into his arm and looked up at him. "You are the most patient man I have ever met."

He examined the porcelain face, now blotched with red. "You look like hell."

"Thank you."

She didn't try to hide her face, he was pleased to note. She trusted him now, trusted him enough to let him see her when she'd been ravished by despair and know that he wouldn't turn away. "You've scared the dogs," he accused.

She lifted her head and observed the puppies, huddled close to their mother in their basket. "Poor lambs."

"You realize this changes everything."

"What?"

"I understand you now."

She shifted as if that made her uncomfortable, but she felt well enough to snap, "Have all your nasty little suspicions been vanquished?"

His feelings of affinity for the fragile, indomitable woman in his lap amazed him. "There's still some explaining to be done, but yes. You've vanquished me."

"That was never my intent."

"I know. Dammit." Delighted by her wry denial, he stroked the damp tendrils of hair away from her face.

"What did the police tell you?"

"It wasn't just the police. It was Uncle Manuel." He smiled at her, a crooked slash of humor.

Clearly, that was news to her. She hadn't heard a word in that office, hadn't noticed anything once she read the note. Her eyes rounded, her mouth dropped. "What was he doing down there?" The words lagged as she thought, and she sat up slowly. "What have he and Mr. Jim cooked up between them?"

"There's been this extortionist around town, preying on the elderly relatives of wealthy folks—"

"I know that," she interrupted impatiently.

He put his finger across her lips. "—and the police know who it is. Not that they'd tell me. But they haven't been able to pin the evidence on the turkey—he slipped through their fingers last time. But he's still operating, so they know he doesn't know that they—"

"Know." She waved a hand impatiently. "I get the picture. Go on."

"So with the help of my dear Uncle Manuel, my grandfather was recruited to be the sitting duck in a trap."

"That idiot old man," she breathed. "I should have realized he'd have his fingers in the pie. Wait until I get my hands on him."

"They've been throwing you at me, and me at you, as a blind to cover their activities."

"It's worked only too well." She bunched her hand into a fist.

"If it's any consolation, Uncle Manuel apologized for Amy. They never meant for her to be taken. They thought with the head honcho out of town, nothing would happen."

"Out of town?"

They stared at each other, and then Margaret reached into his soaked T-shirt pocket. Between her fingers rested the creased, tearstained note, and she held it to his face. "I could smell it when I cried."

He crinkled his nose in disgust. "A cigar. A cheap cigar that must have come from Woolworth's."

Looking as if she'd bit into something that tasted nasty, she said, "I was right all the time."

"As was I. Every time I looked in sheepish, stupid Cliff Martin's eyes, I thought someone much brighter was driving." Reid swore, angry but in control. "My instincts shouted at me, Pierre tried to warn me, but—"

"Mr. Jim, Manuel, the police—even my connections were lying to me." She scooted off his lap and stood, straightening her skirt.

"Your connections?"

"Oh, yes. I kept checking with detectives in the force because I thought the whole setup stank, and those trustworthy gentlemen assured me . . . Wait until I get my hands on them. They'll wish they'd never been born. I'll tell their father what happened, and he'll string them up on the clothesline."

"There'll be a lot of people dangling from that line."

"Of course," she whispered, her face clouded, "if anything happens to Amy, they'll string themselves up."

"She'll be fine. By God, she'll be fine." He plucked the note from her and opened it again. Aloud, he read, " *'What we have here is a failure to communicate. I want money for dear old Granddaddy, but I got the little girl, too. That should up the ante. And up your ante if you don't come through. I'll be calling you with instructions.'* It's not Granddad's printer this time."

"That's a relief," she said, but he paid no attention to her sarcasm.

"He's never actually kidnapped anyone before."

"What?"

He raised his head. "He's threatened to kidnap, and the victims have given the money. He's never actually had to take someone before."

"So he's an amateur. He'll be easy to challenge."

"Yeah, he's amateur, and nervous. It's been extortion before; now it's kidnapping with intent of bodily harm. Let's just hope he remembers his goal is to drain the swamp, now that he's up to his armpits in alligators."

Margaret nodded grimly. "How could the police have messed up twice in a row?"

"How could Cliff Martin have disarmed us enough that we didn't pursue our suspicions?" He went to the door. "He's sly and clever. Out of town, indeed."

Tilting her head, she asked, "You didn't tell the police we got a note, did you?"

"Why do you say that?"

"Because they aren't here to look at it."

"Give that girl a lollipop. The police would do nothing

but put it in their files, while it gave us the clue we needed."

She tilted her head and thought. "This means—" she drew it out—"that the chauffeur isn't really dead."

"What chauffeur?" he asked, confused.

"Remember? The unreliable chauffeur I hired? The one whom the police approved? I guess . . . I *know* he was put here to protect your grandfather. After that first kidnapping, the police didn't want you questioning him, so they said he was dead. He's not dead."

"He would have been if I'd gotten hold of him."

"Exactly." She smiled and nodded. "But it relieves my mind that nobody died for my mistake." Leaning down, she gave the dogs one last pat and walked to the door he held open. "What do we do now?"

"Nothing, much as it rasps me. If we had an inkling as to their location, we'd go after them."

She leaned against the doorjamb as if he'd taken the strength from her legs. "*We'd* go after them?"

He grimaced. "Pierre said that the whole police force was lying. He asked about corruption, insinuated—"

"You don't trust them even yet."

"Do you?"

"Well, I . . . yes!" She floundered. "They're the police! Private citizens can't go around trying to rescue people. Someone who doesn't know what they're doing might—"

"Mess it up?"

He captured her gaze, and reminded her without words of the colossal muddle the police had made of this whole situation. He said, "I can't help but wonder if someone in the police force is deliberately undermining the case, and even if they're not, they're doing a damn poor job."

The phone on his belt trilled, and the phone on the garage wall rang with it. They stopped in midstep, and he nodded toward the wall phone as he unhooked the receiver from his belt. Together they lifted the receivers; together they braced themselves for bad news.

"Donovan residence," Margaret answered.

The voice they heard was the last they expected. "Mama?"

"Amy?"

"Mama, listen—"

"Amy, are you all right? Speak up, I can hardly hear you." Margaret was gripping the phone so tight, her knuckles cracked, and she looked up to see Reid signal her.

"Amy, it's Reid. Where are you?"

"In a hotel room, downtown. I can see the big buildings from the windows. The street sign says Mount Phegley, and the cross street is Schmidt. There's a hotel there; he's got us on the third floor on the alley—"

"Who's got you?" he urged.

"That big, fat Mr. Martin." Amy sounded furious.

"That's what we thought, honey. Go on, tell us some more."

"There's a fire escape right outside the window—that's how I got out. I ran down the stairs and found an open window and crawled into this groaty room. I'm using the phone."

"Is he following you?"

"Not yet. He didn't see me go. Nagumbi broke through the door, and I went out the window and I heard a shot."

Amy's voice temporarily rose to a wail, and Margaret said, "Steady, girl."

"Who shot who?" Reid queried.

"I don't know," she said miserably. "I'm afraid it's Nagumbi. Cliff had the gun."

Reid rubbed his temples. "Nagumbi never carries one. I warned him— Go on, Amy."

"You've got to come and get Sir Gramps, and bring his pills. He's wheezing and he looks so white, and that fat man keeps telling him he'll shoot him if he dies."

"We'll be there as fast as we can," Reid promised. "Amy? Can you do something very hard for me?"

She didn't hesitate. "Yes."

"Get out of that room. Run down the hallway, make a lot of noise. See if you can get Cliff Martin to capture you again."

"No!" Margaret shrieked, but Reid ignored her.

"If Nagumbi's alive, he'll get to you. If Cliff Martin's alive . . . just don't tell Cliff Martin you called us. Don't tell him, or he'll move you and Granddad, and we'd never find you."

Amy sounded faint and faraway. "All right." Then her voice grew stronger. "I'll do it. I can't abandon Gramps, anyway."

"Go on, now, run," Reid urged. "We love you."

"I love you, too."

The line went dead, and Margaret whispered, "Oh, my baby."

He looked at her with sorry eyes. "It was the best I could do," he said miserably.

He was asking for forgiveness, and she had to give it to him. "I know." She walked across the garage and took his hand. "I trust you. I trust you more than I trust anyone." Knowing what he wanted, still she wavered. "You don't want to call the police, do you? We're going to do it ourselves, aren't we?"

"If it makes you uncomfortable, you could stay here."

"No!" she snapped.

"How about if we leave a message for Simon to phone in to the police in, say, two hours?"

"Well . . ."

Seeing the first signs of her yielding, he said, "You and I are trained in physical defense, and we have a stake in this kidnapping that the police can't imagine."

"When civilians get involved in cases like these, their emotions usually trip them up," she answered, telling him something she'd heard one hundred times. Her guilt appeased, she added, "On the other hand, we might be able to sneak in and take care of things without guns—and I'm so afraid my baby would get caught in the cross fire."

"We'll get them," he vowed. "This time it's our turn."

Her pure English stood out among the babble of different languages and accents. Her height made her extraordinary. But dressing like a ninja and skulking in the shadows attracted no attention in the east side of downtown Houston, Margaret discovered.

She was glad the black cap covered her blond hair, even though its enveloping cotton made sweat trickle down her back. She wished she'd taken Reid's advice and smeared combat camouflage on her face. In the alley, dark with refuse and thick with smoke, her pale skin shone only too clearly.

She coughed; she couldn't help it. "It smells like someone's cooking fish heads in motor oil."

"Yeah," he said distractedly. He leaned back against the dumpster and studied the building that rose in the twilight. "What do you think? Do you think that's the one?"

"I told you what I thought. Amy might be wrong about the floor she's on, but she'll never be wrong about the streets. That kid has a sense of direction, and she can read." Margaret looked up at the few unboarded windows on the fire escape. "I don't imagine she saw where she was going when she went up the stairs inside. She went running down the fire escape in a panic—she could have counted wrong. After all, there are two sets of stairs to get to the fourth floor because the bottom floor of the fire escape doesn't have stairs. You have to lower the last set of stairs from above."

"Perhaps that could have confused her," he acknowledged. "Very well, we'll climb up to the fourth floor, but quietly. If we've made a mistake—" he smiled at her, a wry twist of his mouth—"I'd just as soon not be shot by some anonymous room holder."

His smile made her feel better. This whole thing was making her feel better. Her heart pounded, her breath came in little gasps. She was sick from the threat to her child, but the action stirred her blood, and the confidence she felt in her partner was like a shot of caffeine. This was what she needed: not fear-filled hours waiting for a call from the police who had failed her so far, but her own personal chance to bring Cliff Martin to his knees.

The police would say she was taking ridiculous chances with her life and her daughter's, but the specter of a stray bullet haunted her. She knew she was trained in defense; she knew Reid's training surpassed her own. They were prepared to sacrifice themselves; their families were inside with that villain.

"Come on." Reid touched her arm.

She followed him to stand below the fire escape beside a boarded-up window.

"Up you go." He boosted her up onto the metal lid of the dumpster and followed her up. The fire escape still hung beyond their reach, and he instructed, "Put your foot here."

Laying her palms against the aging brick, she placed her foot into the saddle of his hands. With a grunt, he hoisted her above his head, and she grabbed the iron platform above. He took his hands away and she dangled, revulsion on her face. "I grabbed somebody's chewing gum."

He kept his voice low and unsympathetic. "You shouldn't slip."

She walked her hands down to the corner where no railing would stop her and swung herself up with her arms. The discolored woven-metal platform where she rested made her ill, and she looked at her hands. "Give me the gum," she muttered. Untying the stairway, she prepared to lower it.

The stairs creaked and moaned in rusty distress, no matter how carefully she maneuvered them. "Quiet," he ordered in a hush.

"Rain and only the Lord knows what have glued these

things together. Damn.'' She jerked her hand back. ''I pinched it.''

''Bleeding?''

She shuddered. ''Gangrene's a possibility.'' She shook the scarlet drops away and leaned into her job again.

He gestured once, emphatically. ''Get back.''

She put her spine against the building, keeping her head down. Above her, she could hear a window opening in jerks, the painted wood swollen with humidity. She could hear a plaintive child's voice—her child's voice.

''I'm hot.''

And the snappish answer from the man leaning out—Cliff Martin. ''I opened the window again, kid.''

''Have the cops arrived yet?'' Amy's clear voice floated out into the evening air. ''It's eight-thirty. They'll be here soon.''

''Oh, did you set up a timetable?'' Cliff sneered.

''No, but a stupid kidnapper like you could hardly have fooled them for long.'' She sounded calm and logical, not at all frightened.

''Your confidence in me is overwhelming.''

Cliff turned away from the window. His voice was fainter, but Margaret could still hear Amy. ''A smart kidnapper would have brought Sir Gramps's pills. A dead corpse won't do you a lot of good.''

From deeper in the room a voice quavered, '' 'Dead corpse' is redundant, Amy. All corpses are dead.''

Margaret straightened. Mr. Jim was still alive, and Amy was not terrified—if only she'd stop needling Cliff Martin. That was terrifying in itself. She looked down at Reid, and an urgent communication passed between them.

Her baby was right here. She could almost touch her.

His grandfather was right here. He needed Reid.

Margaret grasped the stairs again, lifting them with a strength she hadn't possessed before. Only a few screeches of distressed metal disturbed the evening. The sounds were absorbed in the constant tumult of the city: the sounds of the freeway passing close by, the shouts of the hoodlums as they took to the streets.

Reid bounded up, and mouthed, "This is it."

She nodded. She looked down at her hands. They were grimy with her efforts. A tremor reflected her excitement and her fears. She looked up at Reid.

He, too, stared at her hands. Picking them up, he found the place where her skin had been pinched open and blood still oozed. He brushed it lightly with his finger, then raised it to his mouth. He sealed the area with his lips and sucked hard. Tears sprang to her eyes and she tried to jerk away, silence accentuating her pain. He kept a steady pressure until he lifted his mouth and spit the blood to the street below. "No gangrene," he whispered, folding her palm tight together.

She nodded, not knowing whether it was an order or a comment, knowing only that her tremors had stopped. She took the first step up, then another. Climbing the stairs with stealth and an ever-increasing speed, she fed her excitement with outrage. She focused on that window on the fire escape, her thoughts primitive, vengeful.

She was aware of Reid climbing half a step behind her, making the turns, going to the rescue. She never looked at him, yet she never forgot he was there. He was her accomplice. He had his own concentration, which she would not break.

The fire escape outside the window was as gray and flat and dirty as the rest of the building. She stood there, and her eyes gleamed. Inside was her baby. She had to enter. She had to save her child. Wanting to get in, unable to wait, she shot through the open window like a bullet from a revolver. She saw Reid's arm fly out to stop her—too late.

Inside, she dropped into an attack stance, but it was useless. Useless.

Cliff Martin held a gun to Jim Donovan's head and smiled.

ELEVEN

"Well, if it isn't the Karate Kid—or perhaps Albert the Butler?" Cliff sneered.

The red tide of fury subsided, but the throbbing in her veins intensified.

Reid climbed through the window behind her. "I tried to stop you," he murmured.

Cliff Martin kept the gun cocked at Jim's head. He gripped Amy's shoulder so she stood in front of him, at the foot of the sagging bed. There Cliff was protected by the human barricade in front and the wall behind.

The hand holding the gun trembled, and Margaret understood Reid's comment about untested kidnappers. It didn't matter if the gun discharged beneath a shaking finger; Mr. Jim would be just as dead.

"Hi, Mom." Amy sounded matter-of-fact and unafraid. "I like the black outfit."

Margaret's eyes narrowed. Amy was, as Reid had pointed out, brave and self-assured. But her baby's lower lip quivered and she chewed it with her teeth. Margaret ached to hold her and hug her and tell her it was all right.

She ached in a different way, too. Anger bubbled in her, an anger to match the sorrow of the morning, to match the passion of the week. She wanted to smash Cliff

186

Martin. She wanted to see his face bruise beneath her fist. She wanted to see the police taking what would be left of him away.

She couldn't do any of that. She had to contain herself when she wanted to scream and rage, and that made her even angrier. She settled for a tight smile. "Thanks, honey. I'm grateful for the chance to wear it before Halloween."

Amy looked almost diverted. "Are you going to rescue us before the cockroaches eat my shoes?"

"Are they huge?"

Amy indicated with her hands the length of the roaches, and answered flippantly, "Everything's bigger and better in Texas."

"Did you bring my pills, son?" Jim asked.

Margaret transferred her burning gaze to the old man, and her fury burned hotter. He was pale, his hands shaking in his lap. An unhealthy sweat dotted his forehead and plastered his hair into a wispy gray paste. The man for whom dressing was an effort found it a strain to be kidnapped.

Beside her, Reid held up a prescription bottle and took a step forward. "Here they are, Granddad. Let me just give you—"

"Don't move again," Cliff ordered.

Reid froze, and Margaret placed her hand on his shoulder. She stared at the gun touching Mr. Jim's head. If only Jim could reach up and bat it away. Useless aspiration; he obviously was doing all he could just to sit up.

In slow motion, Reid took his step back. "Next time you decide to be the bait in a trap, Granddad, make sure you have these pills along for the ride."

Turning her head, Margaret looked at Reid. His face was impassive, his voice smooth. But she recognized the signs in him. Anger. An anger to match hers.

Mr. Jim laughed, and coughed. "Figured it out, did you?"

"None too soon," Reid agreed. "The cops closed in so quickly last time."

"Last time I wore a homing device."

Cliff jumped and barked. "What?"

"Didn't your hired gunmen tell you?" Jim sneered. "Or were they so busy running, they didn't stop until Mexico?"

"So that's why they didn't finish the job," Cliff said.

Reid didn't like the way his grandfather baited the man with the gun, but he couldn't resist a jab of his own. "I hope you didn't pay them ahead of time."

Cliff scowled. "Only half."

"Oh, that's good business sense. If you want something done right, you have to do it yourself, right, Martin?" Jim turned back to Reid and Margaret. "The two hired hands realized I was a live microphone when they ripped my shirt looking for money and found the recorder. They just wouldn't believe it was an outside pacemaker." Margaret shook her head in reproof, and he pointed a trembling finger at her. "Remember how you questioned me? About my torn shirt? About the wires dangling from the wheelchair? You gave me a bad turn when you insisted on sending the wheelchair to be fixed. Good thing you two were so involved with each other."

"Lucky break for you, Granddad," Reid said.

"Lucky break, indeed." He took a rasping breath. "I planned every bit of it. I took one look at Margaret and I knew she was the woman for you, and I knew you'd give me a lot of entertainment before it was over."

"Always ready to please." An unwilling admiration swelled in Reid. His grandfather was obviously suffering, yet still feisty enough to needle his kidnapper—and that scared Reid to death. "So you refused to wear a homing device anymore?"

"Right." Jim's voice faded, his energy exhausted. "Those idiot cops couldn't be trusted—"

"Not to move in too soon," Reid guessed. "So it

wasn't sabotage. They were just too anxious to rescue you."

"Sabotage? What made you think sabotage?" Jim cocked his head. "Is that why the police aren't here?"

Reid ignored the reproach and said to Cliff, "The man needs his pills."

"The man can die for all I care." Cliff's hand shook harder beneath Reid's hard stare. "He's the bait in a trap? A trap to catch me? Well, you haven't caught me yet, and I'll bet you didn't bring the money."

"You're right. I didn't bring the money." Reid's voice smoothed and urged, "But think, Cliff. Think about it. There's a difference between being arrested for extortion and being arrested for murder. You don't want to shoot my grandfather."

"Oh, don't I?" Cliff twisted the gun slightly. "Maybe I want to shoot them both."

Amy turned and saw the gun pointed at her head, and when she turned back to her would-be rescuers, the fear in her eyes made Margaret gag. "Mom," she whispered. "I really don't—"

A sharp rap of knuckles on wood made them all jump. Everyone stared at the door, wavering in the grip of uncertainty.

"Did you order room service?" Reid asked Cliff, his eyes sweeping the peeling paint, the ragged sheets.

Cliff glared, his piggy eyes rounded with the panic of a fugitive. A second knock sent his gun to swinging. "Go answer it," he told Margaret. "You're the butler. Get rid of them."

Margaret nodded, but the visitors had lost their patience. One kick, and the drooping door flew open. Two men in black leather jackets stepped across the threshold in unison. Two men sized up the situation at once; two men nodded at Margaret's pleased exclamation, at Amy's cry of relief.

In one appalling second of communication, Cliff and

Reid exchanged a glance, then Cliff said, "Well, there they are. The kings of the luncheon."

The men from the photograph stood there, the ones who ate with suspicious regularity with Margaret. They slumped like bored tourists, barely twitching.

Emboldened, Cliff asked, "Who are you guys, anyway?"

One man pulled the toothpick from his mouth and tossed it down. The other stuck his hands into his pockets and answered laconically, "We're part of the special forces for the Houston Police Department."

Cliff didn't seem to understand, so the man expanded in a pure Hollywood accent, "You know, undercover cops."

"Detectives?" Cliff squealed. Raising the gun, he touched Jim's head with it. "I'm going to blow him to bits."

All action stopped, put in painful suspension by the hopeless monotone of his voice. Only Amy moved, twirling slowly on her toes until she faced Cliff. She looked at him, and what she observed decided her.

In a blur, she arched off the floor. The edge of her foot jerked up in a slicing kick. She made contact with Cliff's groin, and Cliff screamed and dropped like a rock.

"Amy!" Margaret cried, starting forward. But the two detectives were too fast for her. With a speed belied by their previous lethargy, they snatched Amy away. In one smooth movement, they plucked the gun from Cliff's hand and handcuffed his wrists behind his back.

Still fighting, he rose to his knees, and that was all Margaret could stand. Her fist flashed out. Blood gushed from his nose as he fell backward, and one of the cops grabbed her from behind.

While she struggled, Reid stepped into the fray. He picked Cliff up by his collar and held him close to his face. "Listen to me," he said loud and clear. "The justice system is too lenient; we all know that. But I've got money, I've got influence, I've got favors I can call in. I'm going to make sure you stay behind bars forever.

I'm going to know you're dating the biggest bully in the prison.''

Cliff wasn't out of it yet. He lifted his head again. ''My father's got money, too. You can't keep me in prison.''

"Do you think your father's going to bail you out?" Reid asked incredulously. "He owns the biggest security firm in America. You're an embarrassment to him.''

"I had to show him." Cliff's mouth opened wide to yell, but a sob came out. ''He owned half of Kentucky by the time he was thirty—I'm going to own half of Texas.''

Reid dropped him, wiping his hands on his pants as if he'd been holding a slug.

"There's a bit of competition here in Texas," Mr. Jim said.

Reid looked up from the bloody, bawling Cliff to see his grandfather try to smile at him.

"Pills?" the old man whispered.

"Of course." Reid ran his hands over his pockets, but nothing was there. He looked wildly around for them, and realized the room was crowded with men and women in blue uniforms. He looked some more and found Margaret huddled over Amy, hugging her and crying. He found the two undercover policemen over the top of Margaret and Amy, rubbing their backs and making comforting noises. The noise level was incredible, and Reid had heard none of it. He'd been so intent on controlling his desire to kill Cliff Martin that he'd been totally oblivious.

"Pills?"

That hoarse whisper nudged his again, and he hollered to the room, "Stop!" The swirl of movement halted, the noise died. Policemen stood with their pencils suspended above their notebooks, Margaret and Amy wiped the tears from their cheeks. Only Cliff continued to cry in loud, braying sobs.

"We need to find Granddad's pills. I dropped them."

"In here?" It was one of the undercover cops.

"Yes, in here. I held them in my hand before you came in."

The police all lifted their feet, one at a time, and shook their heads. One of the black-jacketed policemen dropped to his knees beside the bed and shined his light beneath. "Here it is," he called. He waved his hand in the air, and someone put a nightstick in it. He rolled the brown bottle out and gingerly picked it up. Dust fell in coils as he wiped it off with his handkerchief, and his mouth twisted as if he tasted something nasty.

"Make sure it has the right name on it," he advised as he passed it to Reid. "As long as it's been since they've cleaned under the bed, it could be anybody's."

Reid took it between two fingers. "It's Granddad's," he confirmed. "Can we get an ambulance for my grandfather? I'll want him taken to the medical center."

"Yeah." The slouching detective nodded to one of the uniformed police.

Reid turned to ask for water, and found a glass thrust into his hand. Right at his elbow stood Margaret, pale and serious. "Nagumbi's out in the hall," she told him. "He's unconscious, but the police have bandaged him up. They say if he hasn't lost too much blood, he'll be fine."

He smiled his thanks back at her. Armed with water and pills, he marched to his grandfather and found Jim had Amy wrapped in one arm.

The weak, old voice was scolding, "If you ever scare me like that again, you'll find out what spankings are for."

Amy promised, "Next time I'll let him shoot you."

"She's got you there, Granddad." Reid shook out two pills and held the glass while Jim drank. Then he enveloped Jim and Amy in a hug. "I'm so glad you're both safe."

Amy wrapped her arms around his neck and squeezed hard. "Me, too."

"Where'd you learn that kick?" Reid queried.

"I learned the kick at my class." She grinned. "I learned where to kick from my mom."

"I'll watch myself," Reid promised, with an amused glance at Margaret.

There was no response from Jim, and Reid checked him with sharp eyes. The old man had his head leaned back and his eyes closed. Reid wrapped a supporting arm around him. "Do you want to lie down on the bed while you wait for an ambulance?"

Reid was able to gauge how bad Jim felt by the fact he didn't object to an ambulance. He only said, "On *that* bed? They'd have to delouse me at the hospital."

Two ambulances arrived within fifteen minutes; one for Jim, one for Nagumbi. Margaret oversaw the loading of Jim; Reid oversaw the loading of Nagumbi. His friend was conscious now, and swearing about the pain in plain, precise English. Reid thanked Nagumbi again and again, assuring him that his help had led them to the rescue.

The police questioned Reid, Margaret, and Amy briefly, then the three of them found themselves on the street. Night had fallen, but the place was alive with floodlights, police cars, and curiosity seekers.

The undercover policemen strolled up. One had a new toothpick stuck in his mouth. The other slouched, yet when he looked up, his eyes were piercing. Pulling his hand out of his jacket pocket, he offered it and said, "Dom Guarneri, at your service."

In the process of extending his hand, Reid froze. "Guarneri?" he croaked.

"Yeah. And this is my brother, Julian."

"Guarneri. Margaret's brothers-in-law?" Two heads nodded in unison, and Reid reached out and caught Dom's hand and pumped it. "You don't know how happy I am to meet you." He grabbed Julian's hand and shook it, too, although it had never been offered.

The brothers exchanged glances. Dom, who seemed to be the spokesman for the two of them, agreed with patent disbelief, "Yeah. Well, we thought maybe you'd want to ride with us to the station and fill us in on the events of the day."

"I'd be glad to. Glad to."

He turned back to tell Margaret where he'd be, and bumped into her standing at his back. "Margaret, I'm going—"

"I heard." She stared hard at the Guarneri brothers. "I imagine you'll be wanting my testimony, too?"

"Not right now, Margaret." Dom reached out and hugged her, and she stumbled, annoyed with his affectionate display and displeased about something. "You go take care of Amy."

"You'll need her testimony, too," she protested.

"Later. Right now you just take her home."

She broke away from his restraining hand and stared right into his eyes. "According to police procedure, you'll need to question us right away. In depth."

"According to police procedure," Dom answered right back, "you were supposed to call us as soon as you found out where they were keeping Amy."

Margaret grimaced. "Ugh."

"Yeah, ugh. What's Pop going to say when he finds out you tried to take on a criminal without notifying the police?"

"Didn't Simon call with the message?" Margaret asked.

Dom pointed his finger at her. "That's not going to get you off the hook, Margaret. We've told you one hundred times, when civilians get involved, their emotions make them do stupid things. And you did, didn't you?"

She glared at him before she admitted, "Yes."

"You jumped through that window without thinking, didn't you?"

"All right. Yes."

"Women!" Dom snorted. "You'd think anyone who'd been in our family as long as you have would have better sense. So we're going to take Mr. Donovan with us and talk to him a little bit. We've been wondering about him ever since you stood us up to go look at that house in West U."

Margaret blushed, but didn't let her embarrassment stop her. "If you're doing what I think you're doing—"

Julian spit the toothpick on the sidewalk. "Don't worry."

Dom hooked an arm through Reid's. "We'll take good care of your boyfriend."

"Boys," Margaret warned. "I'll tell your father on you."

"First you'll have to tell him you withheld information by not telling us about that note Cliff's been sobbing about," Dom said.

"Damn you, what would Pop have done?"

"Don't swear. It's not attractive in a lady." He wrapped his arm around her neck so she was stooped and twisted. "Besides, what the old man would do has nothing to do with it. He took care of Amy this summer and that time in London, just like he takes care of his grandkids, but he's no wimp. He's a gumshoe himself, and you know what he thinks of a woman doing a man's job."

"Chauvinists," she snarled.

He knuckled her head, shrugged, and released her. "Hey, who do you suppose taught us how to behave? We'll catch you later, sis."

They walked away from the still-sputtering Margaret. Julian got in the driver's seat of a plain, black sedan. Reid slid into the middle of the front seat, then Dom got in beside him. Julian drove off with a squeal.

"Do you think she'll chase us down?" Reid asked with interest.

"She's a determined woman." Dom twisted in the seat and checked behind them. "She'll do what she wants to do, and to hell with what's proper." He twisted back and stared at Reid. "Which brings us to the question: What are your intentions with our sister-in-law?"

Margaret paced through the entryway. She'd reassured Simon and Abigail and the rest of the help, telling them an abbreviated—and funny—version of the fight and rescue.

She'd helped her daughter prepare for bed and tucked her in with the heartfelt gratitude of a mother who'd almost lost her finest treasure. She'd called the hospital and received a reassuring report on Mr. Jim.

She'd showered, washing the reminders of the afternoon off her hands and her body. She'd changed into a soft cotton jumpsuit of faded blue—and now she paced.

Reid should have been home hours ago.

What had the Guarneri brothers done to him? Visions of Reid walking back to Houston on a dark and lonely road haunted her. She knew those boys, had known them for more than ten years. They loved her, and she loved them. She'd been the sister they'd never had. They'd moved to Houston to be with Luke during his illness, and to protect her from the vicissitudes of life. Although they'd let her move to London on her own, she'd known she had only to call to bring them running—and Pop had had a time convincing them to let him come and help her on his own.

The sons of an Italian immigrant policeman, Dom and Jules had been raised to be tough and resourceful. Their old-world values could hardly condone the cohabitation of their treasured sister with any man, and they had a distinct lack of reverence for money and the power it could bestow.

So she paced, and worried.

When the intercom buzzed at midnight, and the security man at the gate announced their arrival, she flew out the door and waited on the front step. As the black sedan pulled up, her anxiety made her shiver and rub her arms.

From the driver's seat stepped a stranger, a policeman in partial uniform. She stared, and he tipped his hat. "Off duty, ma'am," he said, as if that explained everything.

From the far side of the backseat stepped Julian. He was smiling, a rare and foolish grin. From the near side stepped Dom, cackling like a hen.

Margaret squatted down and squinted through the open doors of the car, trying to confirm her suspicion of foul play. When she couldn't see Reid in the feeble light of the overhead, she accused, "You dropped him, didn't you?"

"What . . . ?" Dom wheeled around and noticed her for the first time.

"Where did you put Reid?" She advanced on Dom, her fists clenched.

"Oh, hi, sis." Dom threw his affectionate arm around her shoulders and made kissing noises in the vicinity of her ear. "How are you?"

His boisterous affection notified her even before his breath struck her in the face. "Whew." She fanned her hand in front of her nostrils. "How much did you guys drink?"

That seemed to bring out the hysteria in the Guarneris. They laughed and laughed. Julian stumbled around the car, hanging on the fenders, and repeated her question to his brother, and that set them off again.

Margaret failed to see the humor. She stood and tapped her toe and waited for the hilarity to die down. "What did you do with Reid?" She emphasized one word at a time, and quickly thrust her fist in their faces. "If you start laughing again, I'll show you how proficient I've gotten in my self-defense classes." She glanced up at the driver, and he shook his head.

"They just called me to drive, not defend them. Ma'am, you can do just what you want."

Julian held his hand over his mouth and snorted, but Dom collected himself enough to say, "He's right in there."

His unsteady finger pointed in the general direction of the car, and she demanded, "Where?"

"There. On the floor of the backseat."

"Did you beat him up?" she cried, horror-struck.

"Naw." He waved his hands in wild negation. "Come on, Jules. Let's get our sister's boyfriend out of the car. She's worried about him."

Like little boys, they made smoochy noises in the air and sighed in their imitation of a lovelorn lady. She growled, and together they lunged at the door of the backseat. From inside, Margaret heard, "You'll just have to carry me inside. My feet are no longer connected to my body."

Compared to the mumbles of the Guarneris, the voice was clear and strong and articulate. She could hardly believe that the Reid she heard could make such an inane statement. The Guarneri brothers thought it was another reason to giggle, and giggle they did as they pulled at the passenger on the floor of the car. Her eyes bugged as first Reid's feet, then his hands, flopped out. He was bent forward like a Raggedy Andy in a rocking chair, and he lifted his head from his knees and smiled at her. "Hi, Margaret. I bet you'd like an explanation of this."

Margaret was a swirl of conflicting emotions. First the relief hit her. He wasn't somewhere hitching a ride with the leader of the chain saw massacres. He wasn't in a boxcar heading for Mexico. He wasn't in an emergency room having them set any bones.

He was safe.

Well, hallelujah.

Now the outrage hit her. She'd been home, worrying her keister off, and he'd been out cruising the bars with her hard-drinking brothers-in-law.

That son of a bitch.

Frigidly she replied, "I'd say the explanation is obvious."

Dom and Julian tugged at Reid's hands until he tumbled out of the car. They caught him before he hit the ground and hoisted his arms around their shoulders. His feet did a little dance; his knees gave way one at a time. His resemblance to Raggedy Andy increased with every step he couldn't make. But his voice was still clear and pure. "Now, Margaret, I know what you're thinking, and it isn't true."

Dom added his earnest agreement. "No, it's not. Come on, Julian, let's get him up the steps."

Reid continued, "They suggested we go talk it over at a bar, and I agreed."

"Upsy-daisy. Lift those legs. Hey, Web, give us a hand here."

The driver came to push from behind, and still talking, Reid began the slow ballet up the steps. "I told them I don't drink, but they insisted on buying me a beer."

"Have you ever heard of a Texan who doesn't drink beer?" Dom asked, and Julian shook his head in wonder.

"I didn't want to make them mad, so I drank it."

"One little, teeny beer." Dom raised his fingers to show her how little and teeny it had been, and Reid slid back a step.

"The reason I don't drink, see, is because I can't tolerate liquor in any form."

"Right." Her disbelief obvious, she stepped back and opened the double door to allow the procession in.

"Don't be that way," Reid begged. "Have you ever seen me take a drink?"

She thought back over the time she'd known him. Then she thought again. "Well, no."

"There's a very good reason for that. At our dinner parties, water flows like wine. You'll notice my grandfather never drinks, either."

"No kidding," she scoffed. "The doctors are hardly going to suggest that."

"He never drank when he was young, either. Found out he couldn't hold his liquor the hard way, on an oil rig. He decided to ride that sucker. You'll have to ask him to tell you that story someday soon." Reid laughed. "It's a corker."

"Sounds like it. How many beers did you have altogether?"

Dom answered that, clearly unbelieving. "Two beers." This time it was Julian who held up his fingers, indicating two. "*Two* beers. And he talks like this. His brain works fine, his mouth is a wonder. His body—" He sliced his hand across his Adam's apple. "Kaput."

"We had a marvelous conversation," Reid said. "My bedroom's up the stairs."

The group stopped and gaped at the winding stairway.

"No."

"Forget it."

"No way."

They turned and headed for the study, the home of the closest couch, but Margaret said, "No, no. We'll put him in Mr. Jim's room. It's on the ground floor. This way."

She led them, switching on lights as she went, but the procession halted before the Mickey-and-Reid portrait hung with pride in the main foyer.

"Hey." Dom jiggled Reid in delight. "I never realized you knew Mickey Mouse personally."

Reid raised his bleary eyes to the painting, and his lips curved in a openmouthed smile. "Doesn't everyone?"

They stumbled down the hall, bumping the Ming vases and joggling the tapestries. When they reached Jim's room, she went ahead and flung the comforter down to the foot of the bed. "Put him there," she ordered, and the three men picked Reid up and bodily tossed him on the mattress.

"Fabulous." Margaret surveyed the disheveled marvel of a man and asked, "Reid, do you want me to undress you?"

Reid lifted his head and smiled widely, but Dom and Julian vetoed it immediately.

"No, no."

"I don't think so."

In unison, they climbed on the bed and began to tug at Reid's clothing. Reid moaned at their less than gentle ministrations.

"If my body wasn't numb from the neck down, I'd be horribly upset about this."

"If we believed your body was numb from the neck down," Julian retorted, "we'd let Margaret undress you."

They all stared at the usually silent Julian, and Margaret began to chuckle. "I'm glad someone thinks it's amusing," Reid huffed.

Collapsing into a chair, she watched as they stripped him to his shorts. "At least that makes it a profitable evening."

"Oh, it's been very profitable," Dom assured her, jerking at Reid's shirt. "We've had a long talk with this feller here. Questioned him about his intentions, found out his plans. Our father will be proud of us."

"Be sure you go home and call him," Reid ordered. "You promised you would."

"You want them to call my father-in-law?" She was dazed and suspicious. "He's liable to come out here and clean your clock."

"Naw." Dom hopped off the bed. "Pop'll be relieved to hear you've got a man. He worries about you, you know."

"A dependable man, too," Julian said.

She sat forward and clutched the arms of the chair. "All right, what's going on here?"

"We're happy for you." Dom shrugged, and Julian imitated him. "This guy will take care of you for the rest of your life."

She leaped up and hotfooted it to the door. "I don't know what you're talking about."

"Sheesh," Julian said in disgust. "Women sure can be dense."

"I don't want another forever-man," she denied. "I'm not about to get involved."

"Like you could help it," Dom hooted. He flipped off the light as he left the room. "Come on, Julian. The evening's young. Let's go find us some babes who don't think so much."

Sputtering, Margaret followed them out to the front steps. Resigned to her idiocy, they patted her back and kissed her good-bye. Their driver opened the door for them, and with a flourish, they leaped in and rode away, leaving a very confused woman staring after them.

"What do they mean, as if I could help it?" she asked the night air. "I don't need Reid Donovan." She stomped back into the house and slammed the door. "I don't need any man." She hovered in the entry, undetermined, but she had to make sure. "He's just the man I'm sleeping with, that's all." She crept down the hallway and stuck her head in Jim's room.

Reid's breathing sounded soft and even, and she sneaked up on the side of the bed. In the light from the hall, she could see him. He lay on his back, his arms thrown out, still in the same angle they'd left him.

She frowned. That spread-eagle position couldn't be comfortable. Moving slowly so as not to disturb him, she brought his arms into his chest and his legs together. She eased him onto his side and smiled fondly as he sighed and snuggled into the pillow.

What a beautiful man he was. She hesitated to cover him for the pleasure of gazing on his body. His legs were corded, powerful from exercise. She knew what the boxer shorts concealed, and the memory made her misty with nostalgia. His chest tempted her with its rippling muscle and smooth skin. His face pleased her with its authoritarian angles and dark-bearded shadow at the chin. Her fingers couldn't resist the enticement. She stroked the rough bristle. She caressed his sharp cheekbone, slid a fingertip across his eyelid. Brushing his short bangs away from his forehead, she whispered, "We're just using each other, aren't we? I don't know how the boys got the idea that you were a permanent kind of man, but you really have them fooled." She chuckled and pulled the covers over his legs. "I don't need you, and you don't need me, and that's the way I like it." She tucked the blankets up to his chin and went to the door. Adjusting the rheostat so the ceiling fan barely circled, she crooned, "You won't hurt me like Luke did."

From out of the darkness, Reid spoke. "You mean," he asked, "if I were ill, you would abandon me?"

Margaret froze, but he said nothing else, and she shut the door behind her. But she couldn't shut the door on the question. Nor could she shut the door on the pain in her heart when she thought of vital, dynamic Reid Donovan struck by sickness.

Would she abandon him then?

Oh, God, she didn't want to know.

TWELVE

Margaret leaned her elbows on the kitchen counter. The seat of her stool swung back and forth in a quarter circle. Propelled by her hips, the rhythmic sway denoted the restlessness that had plagued her since the tumultuous events two weeks before. "What do you think the world would be like without men?" she asked Abigail.

The cook squirted dough onto the cookie sheet. "Oh, I don't know. No crime. No crooked politicians. Just a lot of fat, happy women."

"Now, that's not true." Margaret slid down until her chin rested on the cool tile. "There'd still be a *little* crime."

"Why're you wondering?"

"I was just thinking that men are only good for one thing."

Abigail laughed. "You talk just like a husband."

"I suppose." Margaret sounded wistful. "Isn't it fair to just want a guy for his body? Just once in my life?"

"Anybody I know?" Abigail peeked up from her work. "I can't see that Mr. Reid would object to being hungered after."

Margaret snorted, not saying anything. The swing of

her chair grew wider, and her lower lip stuck out like a sulky child's.

Abigail put down her cookie press and put her hand on her hip. "Does he?"

"Reid Donovan is a jerk."

"That's what you said the first time you met him. You mean you haven't changed your opinion yet, girl?"

"He's a jerk for different reasons now."

"How can you say that? He's been dancing with you every night. He takes you to the ballet, he takes you to Tony's to dine with the celebrities, he's kissing you in the corner every time I turn around. He and your kid are absolutely nuts about those damned mutts, and they spend hours together. Those Guarneri men are hanging around all the time with their feet on the furniture, eating us out of house and home. Come on," Abigail coaxed. "Tell Aunt Abigail the problem. You should have the glow of a woman in love, and instead you're just moping around here. What else do you want?"

"He wants to get married." This was pronounced in accents of doom.

"Well, that sounds like a good idea to me, seein' as how you act like an old married woman who's had a fight with her man. But what can he do to you if you don't want to get married? Torture you?"

Margaret rolled her eyes up, and the swing of her stool became more pronounced. "He has his methods."

"Like what? Thumbscrews? The rack? The worst he could do is—"

Margaret's shoulders's slumped.

"The worst he could do is . . . oh, dear." Abigail covered her face with her flour-dusted hands and began to chuckle. "You poor thing. You poor, poor thing."

"What?" Margaret snapped. "You think you're so smart. What do you think he's doing?"

"I don't think, I know. I'm surprised I didn't think of it before. You think I don't recognize the signs of sexual frustration? I've been there for the past few years myself,

and I didn't have a man chasing me into corners and
raising my blood pressure. That man is crafty.'' Abigail
shook her head in admiration. ''He is crafty.''

''He's a jerk.''

''Oh, I'll go with that, too.''

''I had just decided to give him everything he wanted.
I decided to sleep with him, take what he's offering with
both hands—'' Abigail snorted, and Margaret shook a
finger at her—''and enjoy it. Now he's changing the
rules.''

''Maybe he's not changing the rules. Maybe you should
have asked for all the rules before you started playing the
game.''

''You sound like Reid. Everybody's against me,'' Margaret said petulantly. ''Everyone's nagging me to give in
to Reid. Even my own daughter's turned traitor.''

''You're just jealous because Amy has more money than
you do.''

''Damn.'' Margaret slapped her hand on the counter.
''Does the whole world know about that legacy?''

''Certainly everybody knows who was standing within
a half mile when you were yelling at poor, sick Mr. Jim
about it,'' Abigail said reproachfully.

Margaret avoided Abigail's eyes. ''Well, for one thing,
he paid his lawyer to call Reid and tell him about it.''

''Why would he do that?''

''Because that crafty old—''

Abigail cleared her throat.

''—man knew Reid would come running to find out
who was taking money from his grandfather. He knew
Reid would assume I was A. M. Guarneri in the will. He
knew I'd be the one who got the brunt of Reid's attention.
And you know what I think?''

''What?''

''I think he hired me with this whole setup in mind.''

''Girl, you have a great imagination,'' Abigail chided.

''No, listen,'' Margaret said. ''He said he wanted a great-grandchild. I think he was just looking around, checking the possibilities, and here I came, all innocent—''

Abigail shook her head with sad resignation. ''You have gone over the edge.''

''Maybe,'' Margaret said grudgingly. ''All I know is that the lawyer who set up the will is working for Mr. Jim again. I went by the study and I heard the lawyer and Jim and Reid laughing, one of the smug masculine laughs, and the lawyer said, 'I needed the vacation.' ''

''You have your ear pressed to the door?'' Abigail asked, her fist resting on her hip.

''No, they didn't even shut the door.'' Margaret's voice rose. ''They didn't even care if I heard them. They saw me walk past and laughed even harder.''

''Don't you shout at me. I'm not old and sick like Mr. Jim, and I'll shout right back,'' Abigail told her with fire in her eye.

Subsiding sulkily, Margaret protested, ''Well, he shouldn't have left Amy so much more money than he told me.''

Abigail waved one hand expansively. ''It's peanuts to him. He loves that little girl, and his will is his own business. I don't see why you need to be sticking your nose—''

''All right.'' Margaret slashed her throat with her finger. ''So sue me. I shouldn't have hollered at Mr. Jim. Even my brothers-in-law tell me to mind my own business. Even *they* think Amy's mature enough to handle a fortune.''

''What do you think?''

Using her thumbnail, Margaret traced the grooves between the tiles on the counter.

''Hmm?'' Abigail insisted.

Margaret mumbled, ''I suppose that wealth won't spoil Amy.''

''Because you raised her correctly. Everyone's noticed your daughter's more mature than you are these days.''

Giving in to irresistible temptation, Margaret stuck out her tongue.

"See?" Abigail said. A bell chimed in the distance, and she wiped her hands on her apron. "There's Nagumbi, summoning me once again."

"It's five o'clock. Shall I send out for dinner, or will your master let you out of his room in time for you to fix it?" Margaret asked sarcastically.

"The man's been shot. Have some compassion," Abigail chided. But the dimples appeared and disappeared on her cheek as she smiled and then tried to hide it.

"Oh, right. One crummy little bullet hole in the shoulder and he spends all his time in his room with the cook."

"I'm feeding him healthy foods."

"Is that why you didn't come out for twenty-four hours last week? I could have sworn you were starving him."

"He was showing me his stamina," Abigail said loftily.

"His stamina?" Margaret cackled. "That's a new word for it."

"You're just jealous," Abigail said with lofty disdain, walking out the door. Sticking her head back in, she added, "And horny."

"And horny," Margaret mimicked. She made a face at the now empty doorway. Damn Abigail for being so clever. Damn Reid for addicting her to the delights of his flesh and then tormenting her with its withdrawal. What was it he'd said . . . ?

"No, Margaret." He had taken her hands from under his shirt and held them pressed together in front of him. "We mustn't anticipate our wedding day."

"What the hell do you mean, we mustn't anticipate our wedding day?" She had grabbed his belt as he edged away from her on her couch. "What were we doing before?"

"What we did before Granddad and Amy were kidnapped is something that never should have happened, and won't happen again until we're married."

"Are you crazy?" She glanced around her little living room as if the answer would pop out of the walls.

"Not at all. I've never wanted to marry a woman before; I didn't know how to behave correctly. But that's all over. Now I know what to do." He watched her closely as he made his grand announcement. "I'm going to court you."

"Court me?" she asked in a daze. "What do you mean, court me?"

"Convince you through mutually pleasant means you want to marry me and consummate our relationship within the bonds of matrimony."

"What was all this?" She spread her hands to indicate their present dishevelment. "You certainly led me to believe we'd be 'consummating our relationship' "—she spat the words—"this evening."

"This is one of the mutually pleasant means I was speaking about." He tucked in his shirt. "I agree, we got a little carried away. But the emotions of the past few days contributed to that, I suppose. After all, it's not every week we confront a kidnapper."

She stared at him, still not believing this new development. Searching her mind for some way to counter his ridiculous logic, she stuttered, "You haven't asked me to marry you."

"I was going to," he assured her. "But every time I started, it was the wrong time. I planned to ask you at the house in West University. I planned to show you the puppies and ask you. So I've decided to let you do the asking."

"What do you mean?"

"I'd say that was clear. I'm buying a house just for us, I got us a dog, I love your child. I've done all the offering; now it's your turn to offer for me. If you want me, you're going to have to ask me." He nodded.

"I don't believe this." She sagged against the arm of her couch. "You want to marry me, but I have to ask you?"

"That's it," he said approvingly.

"And if I don't ask you?"

"Then you can't have me."

She clutched one of the pillows tight in her fists and

thought it an inadequate substitute for his neck. "You're going to be mighty frustrated."

"So are you." His lascivious wink made her wrap her fingers around the pillow and wring it. "Once I broke down your walls, I discovered a very easy woman."

"What?" She sat straight up.

"Oh, come, darlin'. I know you're not likely to become the town nymphomaniac, but with me, you're a pushover."

"*What?*"

Leaning forward, he ran his hand up her thigh as he nuzzled against her ear. She knew what he was doing, and why, and she tried to remain untouched. But it didn't seem to matter. She melted like a snow cone in a heat wave. When he pulled back, she was clinging to him, and he said, "See?"

Her eyelids fluttered open, and she looked at the man above her. "You're trying to control me with sex," she accused.

"That, too." He smiled, that all-teeth barracuda smile, and jumped back before she could hit him.

"You bastard. Is that what you told the Guarneri boys?"

"Yep."

"It's okay," she reassured. "You can back out on it. You can tell them you were drunk."

"On two beers," he reminded her.

"You'll stick with that story through thick and thin, won't you?"

"You believe it, too, don't you?"

"Yes," She was disgusted. "I talked to your grandfather when he got home from the hospital, and he told me the oil rig story."

"That's my girl." He stood up and away from her and strolled to the door. "After you propose, we'll try making love a new way."

She cocked her head inquiringly.

"In bed."

"Say, that *is* an idea." She didn't try to contain her sarcasm.

"Just don't take too long to propose," he warned. "Or I'll be forced to turn up the heat."

She was quick enough to smack him in the back of the head with the pillow and shout, "You owe me one hundred fifty bucks for the two bets you lost," but that had been a temporary satisfaction. He'd stuck with his resolution. All the black lace garter belts in the world hadn't changed his mind. He'd walked out on her seductive striptease. Sexy underwear, then no underwear, earned her a swat on the behind and an order to get dressed.

Now she was reduced to constant exercise and cold showers. She got a momentary feeling of achievement every time she ran into Reid in the gym or the pool. She wasn't the only one who was suffering, but he was holding up much better than she. He had a goal in mind, and he relentlessly pursued it. She had no goal but escape, and that was not a goal—only an avoidance.

Trouble came during the day, when Amy brought her patterns and cloth swatches and asked which one would be appropriate for a bridesmaid's dress. And again when Mr. Jim talked to Manuel, in loud and longing tones, of his great-grandchild and how he longed to see it.

Trouble came at night, when she lay in bed and remembered, in vivid, Technicolor reruns, just how good Reid had been to love. Lust was a pallid word for what she felt. After every date, his kisses, his caresses, moved her to a frenzy. She was always gasping, desperate, when he pried her hands away from his body and left her in a puddle of desire.

When she slept . . . the dreams would make a sailor blush.

She walked around trying to scratch an itch she couldn't seem to reach.

The other servants jumped when she snapped at them, not understanding her foul mood.

But now they'd understand. Abigail would make sure of that.

With a sigh, Margaret slid off the stool. She'd go and exercise again.

•

Pool or gym? Margaret debated as she clattered down the stairs to the gym. With a shrug she opted for both. Perhaps if she was tired enough, her dreams would be quiet and restful. It had never worked before, but it should, dammit.

Flipping on the light, she rummaged through the closet for her swimming suit and her shorts. It made her angry that her body, which had been trained to obey her, should now obey Reid. Who did he think he was, anyway?

She snatched her clothes out and slammed the door shut.

Making all the rules, changing all the rules, being the perfect jerk one minute and the perfect gentleman the next. Laughing at her because she was off balance. Trying to convince her that she should ask him to marry her when nobody had said one word about love. He'd hinted that he cared. He'd hinted that if he could take the chance on her, she could take the chance on him. But he'd never reassured her.

She kicked off her shoes.

He made her so mad. So smug and sure he could manipulate her.

She took off her jacket.

The constant highs and lows were making her dizzy— she, who'd been level-headed for so long.

She started to unbutton her vest, then stopped and stared at her hands. They looked so . . . so flesh-toned. She must have gotten too much sun.

She jerked off her nylons.

Her legs. They looked so . . . so colorful. Usually her whole body glowed a sickly white beneath these fluorescent monstrosities. Usually—she looked up and did a double take.

"What? When? Why?" She stammered to a stop. There

was no one to answer her questions, and she didn't even know what to ask. Above her, on long tracks set on the ceiling, were lights. Real light bulbs inside real frosted peach glass covers. The fluorescent tubes that had so bothered her were gone, removed with nary a trace. She strained her eyes, circling below the spot where they'd been hung. Nothing. Whoever had removed them had done a marvelous job. Sniffing, she detected the smell of paint and plaster.

"Well." She sat down on the mat and stared up. Then she lay back on the mat and stared up. "This is amazing," she told the ceiling. "Why do you suppose he did that?"

She knew who'd done it. She even knew why. He'd done it because he remembered how she hated fluorescent lights. He understood what they reminded her of. He knew she thought of hospitals, of death and misery, when she saw them. He knew, illogical though it might be, she'd never shake that association. So like the arrogant jerk he was, he'd changed the lights, without a word to her, without any thought to the cost or the trouble.

The man wanted her to be happy.

Admitting that Reid was a thoughtful arrogant jerk put her in a difficult position.

The position of having to propose. Why should she, really? When she offered him marriage, she'd be giving in to a man already too indulged. He was spoiled. He was audacious. He radiated sensual magnetism, and women fell like ninepins at his feet. She'd be falling, too, just like the rest.

But at least when she fell, it would be with such a thump and wallow, he'd never see another woman beneath him—in any manner. Her eyes narrowed as she considered the women who wanted him.

He was a charmer, true. That brown-red hair, cut too short; those sherry eyes, liquid with expression. That slashing bone structure that wasn't handsome, but so striking. It wasn't his looks that brought the women to attention. The heat of his gaze, his open appreciation, the way he focused his whole attention on the woman of his choice. Those were the reasons a woman wanted him.

What a ghastly man he had been these past weeks. Pushy, obnoxious, protective of his grandfather. Suspicious of her, and she wasn't sure if she'd forgiven him for that. Asking questions just to torment her, and succeeding only too well.

If I were ill, would you abandon me?

How cruel to make her face the fears that ruled her life. That one question had torn the blinders from her eyes, had forced her to face the truth. If Reid were sick, she could run to the ends of the earth and never escape the pain, because she loved him. Loved him with the hot pleasure of a girl, with the calm sureness of a woman. Loved him enough to trust that the joy of their lives would overcome the adversity.

That was something else he'd returned to her: the memories of Luke, alive and healthy, with no shadow on him. Because of Reid, she could remember Luke with a sweet sadness and not a tearing pain. All because of Reid.

That man, that swashbuckling barracuda of a man, was kind and loyal. He wasn't a one-dimensional leader, with a single-track mind. He was a colorful, multitalented genius who was the other half of herself.

So all right. He'd won. But she would win, too, and in more ways than one. She'd have her man, to care for and cherish. She'd have a father for Amy; one who fostered a sense of family in the child and never displayed jealousy of the Guarneri family.

If anything, he got along with them too well.

Grimacing, she picked up her jacket and shrugged it on. Her brothers-in-law would celebrate tonight.

As she prepared to surrender, her restless body proclaimed victory. She'd roped and tied a man who celebrated sex. After they married, she'd take him to bed and work him until he screamed. She'd show him what a real woman could do when faced with an irresistible force. In fact—she held her nylons between two fingers and debated, then flung them aside. Maybe if she caved in and proposed right away, he'd cave in and she'd get lucky right away. Chuckling, she checked her tie and put on her shoes.

There. If she was going to propose, she'd do it right. Trotting up the stairs and down the hall, she stopped at the first bouquet she liked. An eclectic mixture of lilies and ferns, it graced the entry with its lofty beauty. She lifted the flowers out of the vase and wiggled them to rid them of the excess moisture. Water dripped all over the solid wood floors, but she was beyond caring. With an elegant flip, she shook out a lace doily and wrapped the stems. Clearing her throat nervously, she walked to the study door and lifted her hand to knock.

Before her knuckles made contact, a loud banging shook the front doors. Startled, she glanced around. Where was Simon?

No one was in sight.

To arrive at the front door, visitors had to be allowed in the gate by someone in the house. So how had a stranger managed to sneak up the driveway without being apprehended by the still vigilant security? There should be someone here to greet . . . whoever it was.

The pounding came again, and Margaret marched to the front door. Two weeks before, the press had swarmed over them, tramping on her lawn, kicking over her flowerpots, demanding interviews and photo opportunities. In the way of news, the Donovans had become an old story, but lingering caution made Margaret peer through the peep hole. Through the convex glass, she could see a distorted face peering back at her.

A smile broke across her face, and she jerked open the door. "Pierre! What are you doing back in Houston? Chantal! How was your trip to France?"

Chantal looked totally enchanting, of course. Her rayon shorts outfit, so appropriate for the Houston autumn, flattered her figure and enhanced her visage. Her battered suitcase rested beside her expensive briefcase at her feet.

"France was wonderful, but too brief." She bent a glance of unholy amusement at Pierre. "If only we hadn't been called back early."

Wedged between his suitcase and his briefcase, Pierre glared at her, but replied to Margaret. "I came back to do a favor for a friend, and to go to a wedding."

He looked so acutely uncomfortable, Margaret smiled. "Your own?"

"Comment?" he asked blankly.

"Your own wedding?" Margaret indicated them with a wave of the hand. "You're acting so oddly, I thought that you and Chantal—"

Pierre relaxed and exchanged an understanding glance with Chantal. "We are just, as they say, good friends," he interrupted with a grin. Then his grin faded, and he wiped his hands on his pants as if the palms were sweaty.

Margaret held the door wider. "You're hot, and I'm a dreadful hostess . . . I mean . . . butler. Come in."

Shifting from foot to foot, they made no move to enter. They kept nudging at each other until Chantal said, "You said you'd ask her."

"Ask me what?" Margaret queried.

Pierre rolled his eyes heavenward and muttered a few words in French, then said aloud, "Are you Amelia Margaret Guarneri?"

Startled and confused, she agreed, "You know I am."

Leaning down, he drew an envelope out of his briefcase. Margaret accepted it and looked inquiringly at him.

He drew a deep breath, as if bracing himself for some unpleasant duty. "I've been asked, in my capacity as a law officer, to present you with this summons to court."

Her mouth dropped open, and she stared at the unopened envelope drooping in one hand and at the flowers drooping in the other. "What for?"

Taking several rapid steps backward, Pierre told her, "Reid Donovan is suing you for palimony."

Margaret lost her dignity. "What?" she shrieked, advancing on him. "He's doing what?"

"Reid Donovan is suing you for palimony," Chantal repeated kindly. "Will he be bringing a patrimony suit against you soon, too?"

Like an avenging fury, Margaret rounded on Chantal. "What kind of smart comment is that?" She saw the camera Chantal held. "What are you doing?"

"Recording the fact the papers were served on you." Chantal smirked. "Maybe I'll sell that picture to one of those sleaze magazines. I could get good money for it."

"Maybe your heirs could," Margaret snarled. She extended her hand, palm out. "Now, give me that camera before I smash it."

"What will you do if I give it to you?" Chantal mocked.

"Smash it."

Chantal tucked it behind her back. "No way. Reid, I'm glad you brought suit against this woman. She obviously has violent tendencies."

Flinging herself around, Margaret confronted Reid. He stood in the open door, wearing a black suit, a white shirt, and the reddest power tie she'd ever seen. "Something tells me," she said, clutching the lilies with white knuckles, "you were expecting this."

He ignored her, smiling at Chantal with his most innocent smile. "I see Pierre told you about my suit against Ms. Guarneri."

"Yes, and I think it's shameful the way she's treated you." Chantal clicked her tongue. "Just shameful."

Margaret suddenly realized it was a joke. It had to be a joke, and she chuckled weakly. "Stop this nonsense right now. You've had your laugh. Now let's go in and sit down . . ." Her voice trailed off as three pairs of eyes reproached her.

Pierre shook his head. "The summons is real."

She looked doubtfully at the envelope.

"Read it," Reid advised.

Tearing the seal, Margaret skimmed the convoluted legal document. She'd never seen a summons before, but this certainly appeared to be genuine. Bewildered, she asked, "Why would you bring a palimony suit against me?"

"Yeah, Reid." Chantal drew a pen and tablet out of her briefcase. "Tell me why you've brought a palimony suit against Margaret."

Noting Chantal's brisk and efficient manner, Reid asked, "Going to sell the story?"

"To somebody," she answered ambiguously.

He leaned toward her and confided, "In that case, I'd be delighted to tell you why I brought this suit. The reasons are unmistakable. At the beginning of our relationship, Ms. Guarneri indicated she wasn't interested in marriage, and I agreed for obvious reasons." His demeanor flipped from one of sorrow to efficiency. "Am I going too fast for you?"

"Not at all," Chantal assured him.

Flipping back to sorrow, he glanced wistfully at Margaret. "As the relationship progressed, I wanted more, yet Ms. Guarneri continued to insist on an uninstitutionalized union."

"Uninstitutionalized?" Margaret exploded.

"I've insisted that until we married, we'd keep our relationship pure—"

"Good God." Shaking her head, Margaret sank her face into her palm.

"—but she's been putting pressure on me, and I don't know how long I can hold out. You see, I love her and I want her to be happy. I've finally realized she wasn't interested in making an honest man out of me—"Reid's lower lip drooped with disappointment—"and so I've brought this lawsuit. Ms. Guarneri has been living with me without benefit of matrimony while enjoying my body. I'd say she owes me support."

"Owes you support? Owes you support?" So angry she could scarcely draw breath, Margaret glanced about her in appeal. Pierre stood with his arms crossed on his chest, grinning like a hyena. Chantal wore an expression of indulgent amusement. Margaret looked behind her. In the hallway, Mr. Jim sat in his wheelchair, and Amy leaned on his arm. Abigail stood with her arm around the bandaged Nagumbi. Simon, the upstairs maid, the gardener, the chauffeur, and the cleaning crew all stood behind. "Can you believe . . ." Her voice died to a whisper. Everyone, *everyone* was smirking.

Facing Reid, she saw a wounded countenance. As they made eye contact, his face crumpled while he fought a spasm of wicked laughter, but his composure won. He returned to the sad and betrayed appearance of a basset hound.

She was angry. She was furious, yet underneath it all was a vast and surreptitious merriment. She'd told Abigail he was a jerk; if anything, she'd understated the issue.

What kind of man was Reid? Using her own sense of humor to create the kind of situation she couldn't back out of. Placing her in front of her family and friends to play a practical joke on her—a joke with its underlying serious message. Had he done it to get her attention?

He had succeeded.

Projecting her voice, she asked, "How am I supposed to support a man who makes more in a month than I make in five years?"

He sighed and confided, "I'm willing to live on your income just to be close to you."

With precise movement, Margaret laid down the flowers and slid out of her formal black coat—and stomped on it. "I don't have an income."

"Why, darling." He laid one hand flat on his chest and gasped with ostentatious astonishment. "You mean you'd quit your job just to avoid paying me my rightful support?"

"No." She stripped off her tie and vest and kicked off her shoes. "I'd quit my job just so I can give you your rightful deserts."

He eyed her bare foot warily and stepped back. "What rightful deserts?"

She picked up the flowers. "I was coming to propose."

"Uh-oh." His face was a funny mixture of horror and ruefulness.

"I was going to go down on my knees. I was going to use the flowers to persuade you to accept my offer."

Guessing, he said, "You've changed your mind."

"Oh, I'll use the flowers, all right." She pulled them back and whacked him across the chest with them. She followed him as he dodged and parried, protecting himself with uplaised arms. "You're an unprincipled—" whack!—"rude"—whack!—"manipulative"—whack! She paused, out of adjectives.

"Unscrupulous?" he suggested.

"Unscrupulous scoundrel." Whack, whack!

"I was just trying to get—"

"Murdered?"

"Fair treatment," he protested.

Petals flew as she gave him one final whack and burst into laughter. "You'll do anything to get your own way."

He bared all his teeth in that barracuda smile and caught the mangled bouquet in his fist. He tugged it, and she stumbled into his arms. "That's why you adore me."

"Adore you," she scoffed, wrapping her arms behind his head and tugging it toward her lips. "You're seeking to bind me."

"Yes; what's your point?" he said calmly, and laughed when she gaped at his honesty.

"Well, I'll bind you, too," she replied with determination. "You'll be tied on such a short leash—"

"As long as you're on the other end of the rope. Now ask me," he commanded. "Ask me loud enough for everyone to hear, and I might give you what you want."

"You know I'll be caving in for no better reason than that you're the man of my dreams."

"What kind of dreams?" He already knew the answer.

"My erotic dreams. You're a jerk."

"I know," he soothed. "Now ask me."

"Who'd want to marry you?"

"You do. Now ask me."

She smoothed the hair on the nape of his neck and discovered a sudden shyness. Her eyes dropped, but he bent his knees and followed her gaze and smiled at her with such sweet understanding that the words bubbled up from her soul. "Will you marry me?"

"At the first opportunity."

He let her bring his mouth to hers and he let her kiss him while Chantal's camera shutter clicked, forever preserving the proof that Reid Donovan loved his lady in black.

SHARE THE FUN . . .
SHARE YOUR NEW-FOUND TREASURE!!

You don't want to let your new books out of your sight?
That's okay. Your friends can get their own. Order below.

No. 128 LADY IN BLACK by Christina Dodd
The cool facade Margaret worked at so hard, melted under Reid's touch.

No. 66 BACK OF BEYOND by Shirley Faye
Dani and Jesse are forced to face their true feelings for each other.

No. 67 CRYSTAL CLEAR by Cay David
Max could be the end of all Chrystal's dreams . . . or just the beginning!

No. 68 PROMISE OF PARADISE by Karen Lawton Barrett
Gabriel is surprised to find that Eden's beauty is not just skin deep.

No. 69 OCEAN OF DREAMS by Patricia Hagan
Is Jenny just another shipboard romance to Officer Kirk Moen?

No. 70 SUNDAY KIND OF LOVE by Lois Faye Dyer
Trace literally sweeps beautiful, ebony-haired Lily off her feet.

No. 71 ISLAND SECRETS by Darcy Rice
Chad has the power to take away Tucker's hard-earned independence.

No. 72 COMING HOME by Janis Reams Hudson
Clint always loved Lacey. Now Fate has given them another chance.

No. 73 KING'S RANSOM by Sharon Sala
Jesse was always like King's little sister. When did it all change?

No. 74 A MAN WORTH LOVING by Karen Rose Smith
Nate's middle name is 'freedom' . . . that is, until Shara comes along.

No. 75 RAINBOWS & LOVE SONGS by Catherine Sellers
Dan has more than one problem. One of them is named Kacy!

No. 76 ALWAYS ANNIE by Patty Copeland
Annie is down-to-earth and real . . . and Ted's never met anyone like her.

No. 77 FLIGHT OF THE SWAN by Lacey Dancer
Rich had decided to swear off romance for good until Christiana.

No. 78 TO LOVE A COWBOY by Laura Phillips
Dee is the dark-haired beauty that sends Nick reeling back to the past.

No. 79 SASSY LADY by Becky Barker
No matter how hard he tries, Curt can't seem to get away from Maggie.

No. 80 CRITIC'S CHOICE by Kathleen Yapp
Marlis can't do one thing right in front of her handsome houseguest.

No. 81 TUNE IN TOMORROW by Laura Michaels
Deke happily gave up life in the fast lane. Can Liz do the same?

No. 82 CALL BACK OUR YESTERDAYS by Phyllis Houseman
Michael comes to terms with his past with Laura by his side.

No. 83 ECHOES by Nancy Morse
Cathy comes home and finds love even better the second time around.

No. 84 FAIR WINDS by Helen Carras
Fate blows Eve into Vic's life and he finds he can't let her go.

No. 85 ONE SNOWY NIGHT by Ellen Moore
Randy catches Scarlett fever and he finds there's no cure.

No. 86 MAVERICK'S LADY by Linda Jenkins
Bentley considered herself worldly but she was not prepared for Reid.

No. 87 ALL THROUGH THE HOUSE by Janice Bartlett
Abigail is just doing her job but Nate blocks her every move.

No. 88 MORE THAN A MEMORY by Lois Faye Dyer
Cole and Melanie both still burn from the heat of that long ago summer.

Meteor Publishing Corporation
Dept. 293, P. O. Box 41820, Philadelphia, PA 19101-9828

Please send the books I've indicated below. Check or money order (U.S. Dollars only)—no cash, stamps or C.O.D.s (PA residents, add 6% sales tax). I am enclosing $2.95 plus 75¢ handling fee for *each* book ordered.

Total Amount Enclosed: $_____.

_____ No. 128	_____ No. 71	_____ No. 77	_____ No. 83
_____ No. 66	_____ No. 72	_____ No. 78	_____ No. 84
_____ No. 67	_____ No. 73	_____ No. 79	_____ No. 85
_____ No. 68	_____ No. 74	_____ No. 80	_____ No. 86
_____ No. 69	_____ No. 75	_____ No. 81	_____ No. 87
_____ No. 70	_____ No. 76	_____ No. 82	_____ No. 88

Please Print:
Name _____
Address _____ Apt. No. _____
City/State _____ Zip _____

Allow four to six weeks for delivery. Quantities limited.